MEET ME IN MUMBAI

sabina khan

Published in the UK by Scholastic, 2022
Euston House, 24 Eversholt Street, London, NW1 1DB
Scholastic Ireland, 89E Lagan Road, Dublin Industrial Estate,
Glasnevin, Dublin, D11 HP5F

First published in the US by Scholastic Inc, 2022

Text © Sabina Khan, 2022
Cover art © Muhammed Sajid, 2022

ISBN 978 0702 31943 3

A CIP catalogue record for this book is available from the British Library.

Printed by CPI Group (UK) Ltd, Croydon, CR0 4YY
Paper made from wood grown in sustainable forests and other controlled sources.

1 3 5 7 9 10 8 6 4 2

www.scholastic.co.uk

Book design by Maeve Norton

To all those who love with abandon,
and to the three bright stars
of my own love story

part one

AYESHA

December 2000, Bloomington, IL

CHAPTER ONE

I stare at the stick, willing the second line not to appear. But my powers of persuasion must have dulled because it shows up, a pretty baby pink, which is ironic considering there's nothing pretty about this. An avalanche of thoughts threatens to bury me. Suresh hasn't responded to any of my emails or messages. I don't even have his home number in India.

It's starting to dawn on me that I might be alone in this.

There's a loud knock on the bathroom door, and I almost drop the stick. "Ayesha, are you done? You're going to be late for school." Salma Aunty sounds anxious, which is nothing new. The woman could win a gold medal if there's ever an Olympic event on how to worry yourself into an early grave. But she's sweet, and I hate it when she worries about me.

"Coming, Aunty." I quickly wrap the pregnancy test stick in a wad of toilet paper and shove it into the pocket of my Dora the Explorer robe, a gift from my cousin Reshma, who's only a couple of years older than me and headed back to college just before I arrived in Bloomington, Illinois. Apparently, she thinks I'm seven, not seventeen.

I open the door to find Salma Aunty smoothing the duvet on my bed. Then she turns around and begins to straighten the things on my desk. She picks up a few sketches that I've left on top of my notebooks and puts them together in a neat little pile.

"You don't have to do that, Aunty," I say in protest, mostly because I don't like her touching my stuff, but partly also because I promised my mom that I would be super polite and always keep my room neat and tidy, so as not to bring shame upon my family back in India.

Salma Aunty is my mom's cousin. She settled here in Bloomington-Normal about twenty years ago when her husband got a job teaching physics at Illinois State University. She graciously offered to let me live with them during my senior year of high school so I could apply to college from within the US. It's a bit complicated because my parents moved back to India soon after I was born here. So, I have a US passport but an Indian accent and brown skin, which is what drew Suresh and me together in the first place. There aren't a lot of brown people in our school, and it's nice to have someone else who misses eating pav bhaji and ragda patties at Elco Market as much as I do.

"Come down and have breakfast before it gets cold," Salma Aunty says. "I made Bombay toast. It's your favorite, na?"

"Yes, thank you, Aunty," I say, giving her arm a quick squeeze before disappearing into the walk-in closet to get changed.

The thick slices of fried bread soaked in egg with onion, green chilies, and cilantro are still hot and crispy as I slide into a chair at the breakfast table. Normally I would inhale at least three slices, but today all it does is make the bile rise up to my throat. I've been feeling this way for a couple of days now, starting right after I realized I'd missed my period. When I woke up that morning, I just knew.

I didn't really need a test to confirm, but I bought one anyway. And now I would kill for a cup of coffee, which I'm pretty sure is bad in my condition. *Condition. Is that what this is?* I meet a cute boy who feels like home, we hang out, talk a lot, and I end up getting pregnant? It's like we've known each other for a long time, but in reality, it's only been three months. Though here, far away from my parents and my little sisters, even a week feels like an eternity.

I have no idea what I'm going to do.

CHAPTER TWO

I met Suresh about three months ago, a month after I arrived from India, when Natasha, my new best friend, dragged me to my first American party. Salma Aunty believed I was sleeping over at Natasha's because of a late-night group project. Mike Taylor, who sat behind me in English, was throwing the party at his house while his parents were out of town, and he had a cool older brother who supplied beer and an alibi in case their parents called.

I didn't really want to be there, but Natasha insisted that I needed to experience a "real high school party." She deserted me as soon as we arrived to go make out with Brian.

The basement was pretty crowded, but I managed to find an empty spot on the green couch in the corner. A few people I vaguely recognized from school attempted to dance to Britney Spears's "Oops! . . . I Did It Again," but they mostly ended up shuffling awkwardly on the spot. I pulled out my little sketchpad and pencil and attempted to capture the scene in front of me. By the time I was done, I realized I'd drawn the faces of my friends from back home. I contemplated how

Natasha and I were going to get back to her house, because I didn't really plan on getting into a car with her after watching her chug beer from a hose. I did not understand the appeal of parties like these.

At home in Mumbai, if I was going to lie to my parents and sneak out, it would be to go to Juhu Beach and walk under the stars with my friends. We would get little plates of bhelpuri and drink fresh coconut water. Some of my friends smoked cigarettes, but none of us really drank alcohol. Later we'd stand around our cars listening to music blaring on someone's stereo. That felt natural to me. But this basement scene felt strangely artificial.

I watched my classmates having drink after drink and getting more and more "frisky," as my dad would say. It was as if they needed the alcohol to enjoy each other's company. I got up to grab a soda and was trying to decide what I wanted when someone held a red Solo cup out to me. I looked up to see a boy, about half a foot taller than me, smiling down. He was kind of cute, with thick curly hair and a dimple on his right cheek, his skin a slightly darker shade of brown than mine.

"Don't worry, it's just a cold drink," he said.

Here in Bloomington, other than Salma Aunty and Hafeez Uncle, I hadn't heard anyone use the words *cold drink* for soda.

When I still didn't take the cup, the mystery boy set it down and reached over the table behind us. He pulled out a can of Sprite and handed it to me.

I tucked my sketchpad and pencil back in my purse and took the can from him with a smile.

"Thanks."

"I'm Suresh."

5

I pulled the tab and took a long swig.

"Ayesha." I didn't recall seeing him around the hallways at school . . . and I was pretty sure I would have remembered him if I had. Judging by his accent, he didn't sound like an ABCD—an American-Born Confused Desi. In fact, he sounded like a Mumbaiite. As far as I knew, there wasn't anyone else at my high school who was from India, which made me really excited to meet someone who was. But I didn't want to give him the wrong impression, so I played it cool and basically ignored him while casually taking sips from the can he'd just given me.

"So how long have you been here?" he finally asked.

"I just got here half an hour ago." It was hard to hear over the music, so I moved a tiny bit closer.

"I meant, how long have you been here in Bloomington?" he said.

"Oh, about a month," I said. "What about you?"

"I came here in August of last year," he said. "I take it you don't go to school in Normal. I mean, I'm pretty sure I would've remembered if I'd met you before."

"No, I go to Bloomington High. How do you know Mike?"

"I don't really," he said. "I came with my friend Rick. You're from Mumbai too, right?"

"What gave it away?" I asked with a grin. "My tapori accent?"

He smiled back, a really wide smile, showing off very white, straight teeth.

"Obviously. And can I just say how great it is to meet someone else who even knows what that is? I don't know a single person here from Mumbai."

I knew exactly what he meant. We Mumbaiites had a unique

way of speaking; our vernacular was heavily influenced by dialogues from Bollywood movies. Or maybe it was the other way around; I couldn't be sure. It was hard for me to explain, but the sound of my mother tongue here in Bloomington, half a world away from home, touched me in a way nothing else could.

"So where do you live? In Mumbai, I mean," he asked.

"Chembur. You?"

"Bandra. Did your whole family move here?"

"No, just me. I live with my aunty."

"Same," he said. "I mean no aunty, just me," he added hurriedly. "And my dad's college buddy. That's who I stay with."

His nervousness made me smile . . . and I was glad that I wasn't the only one.

He cleared his throat. "It's a bit loud down here. Want to find somewhere quieter to talk?"

I nodded, not giving it a second thought. Anything to get out of this space, which was becoming more and more suffocating by the minute.

We walked up the stairs and out of the house into the starlit night. The patio was empty except for one couple making out on a chair in the corner, but they were too oblivious to notice us. I sat on the steps and took a long deep breath of the night air. It smelled like lavender and faintly of pot, but it was way better than downstairs. Suresh leaned against the wooden post and smiled down at me.

"So, is this everything you thought it would be?" he asked.

"This party?" I raised an eyebrow at him. "Or America in general?"

"Both, I guess." He plonked himself down beside me, and I got a faint whiff of his aftershave. Something woodsy and fresh, unlike Hafeez Uncle's Old Spice, which forced me to breathe through only one nostril whenever he was around.

Suresh's shoulder brushed against mine, just a glance, but it was enough to make me very aware of him.

"Well, I wouldn't say *everything*," I replied. "I think it's so weird how people ask what's up and then, when I start to tell them, they don't really seem to care."

Suresh grinned at me. "I know exactly what you mean. When I first got here, I was so surprised that everyone wanted to find out how I was doing. And then I realized, it's just something they say."

I nodded. "You know, I used to think that I was so familiar with all this just because I watched *Dawson's Creek* and *Friends* back home, but honestly, it's been really hard."

I had no idea why I was talking so much to a guy I'd just met a few minutes ago. It had to be a combination of seeing someone from back home and the loneliness I'd been trying to keep at bay for weeks now. Either way, it was embarrassing. But when I looked up, he was smiling.

"I get it," he said. "I've been here for a while now, and it's still hard sometimes."

"Do you miss your family?" I leaned back against the wooden post and took a sip of my soda.

He nodded. "Yeah, we're really close. And Dad's not been doing well lately. He has heart issues."

"I'm sorry," I said. "I hate being so far away. Every time my phone rings in the middle of the night, I panic."

"My mom can never remember the time difference," he said with a laugh. "And that's not even taking into account—what do they call it? Daylight savings time?"

I shook my head. "What's up with that anyway? I swear only

Americans would try to manipulate time just to make themselves feel better."

"Last year I missed a test because I forgot about it," Suresh said. "Luckily, my teacher let me take it after school."

We didn't say anything for a while, just listening to the muted sounds of music coming from inside.

"Do you ever feel like you're on *National Geographic*?" I said when the silence became too much.

Suresh let out a loud laugh, startling the couple making out in the corner behind us. They looked up to glare at us briefly and then went back to what I could only describe as an attempt to inhale each other's faces.

"Are you kidding?" Suresh said. "I've only been asked a million times whether we ride to school on elephants."

"I can do you one better," I said. "My social studies teacher asked me how it feels to finally be liberated from the burqa."

"No, she didn't." Suresh narrowed his eyes. "You can't be serious."

"Oh, but I am. It was right after our unit lecture on world religions, which lasted a whole half hour."

He shook his head slowly. "That's so stupid. What did you say?"

"I didn't know *what* to say. I mean, where would I even begin?"

We sat in silence again for the next few minutes, lost in our own thoughts. There was something about his presence that comforted me. It didn't make sense, but I felt like I knew him even though we'd just met. The cadence of his speech, the way he used his hands and face when he talked, all felt like home. I'd been pretending to myself that I wasn't completely alone in a sea of strangers for hours every day, longing to be around desi people my age who could understand what I was going through. But I knew I had to be cautious. I had a history of getting too attached too quickly, and I couldn't afford to make that mistake again.

CHAPTER THREE

The chill in the air made me shiver, and I got to my feet.

"I should go and find Natasha," I said. I was a bit worried about how I was going to be able to spend the night at her house if she wasn't even okay to drive. I couldn't exactly go home at this hour without making Salma Aunty majorly suspicious.

"I'll come with you." Suresh jumped to his feet, and soon we were weaving through the crowd in the basement. I found Natasha all tangled up with Brian on the pile of coats that had accumulated on a futon in the corner. I did not want to unwittingly see anything I wasn't supposed to, so I closed my eyes and tugged on Natasha's sleeve.

"What?" Natasha lifted her head from Brian's and looked at me with sleepy eyes.

"Umm, can we go home now?" I asked, trying to figure out if Brian was awake or not. His eyes were half open, but they weren't moving, so I couldn't be sure. I *was* very sure that I wanted to get out of there, though.

Natasha unwrapped herself from Brian and stood, swaying slightly. This did not look good.

"I can drive you both home if you like," Suresh said.

"Who's that?" Natasha mumbled sleepily.

"Suresh, meet Natasha. Natasha, this is Suresh," I said perfunctorily. "I think it would be best if he drove us home, right?"

Natasha threw a disdainful look at Brian and nodded. Soon she was safely ensconced in the back seat of Suresh's car while I slid into the front passenger side. We exchanged phone numbers when we got to Natasha's house, and he promised to come back in the morning to drive us to get her car.

We snuck inside and tiptoed to her room, careful not to wake her parents. I was about to doze off when Natasha turned to me.

"He's really cute, isn't he?" she asked. "Do you think you'll see him again?"

"Maybe," I said. "I just met him, Natasha."

"Ayesha, c'mon, you know what I mean," she said, nudging me under the covers with her foot.

"He's okay, I guess," I said as nonchalantly as I could. "He was pretty nice."

"*Nice* . . . Sure, let's go with that," Natasha said. "I saw how he was looking at you."

"He was driving, so I'm pretty sure he was looking at the road," I said. "Speaking of which, he's coming by in a few hours to drive us back to Mike's to get your car, so I think we should go to sleep now."

"Yes, ma'am," Natasha said. I could hear her smiling in the dark. "Sweet dreams."

• • •

I woke up to the sound of a very loud bird chirping outside the window, and it took me a few minutes to remember where I was. As the memories of last night washed over me, I looked over at Natasha still fast asleep, one leg sticking out from under the covers. A quick glance at my phone reminded me that Suresh was going to be here soon. I gently shook Natasha awake and went to get ready.

By the time I went downstairs, Suresh was already pulling up, and soon we had retrieved Natasha's car. Since Natasha had to go to work, Suresh offered to drive me home. He wasn't at all surprised when I asked him to let me out a couple of houses down. It was Saturday, and the last thing I wanted was for Hafeez Uncle or Salma Aunty to see me coming home in a strange boy's car.

"Did you finish your project?" Salma Aunty asked as soon as I walked in.

"Yes, we did," I said. "But I still have some other homework left to do."

"Of course, beta. Go ahead and I'll call you when lunch is ready," she said. "I made suji ka halwa for dessert."

I went upstairs feeling awfully guilty for lying. My aunt and uncle were sweet, but their idea of fun was going to dinner parties with the other South Asian families here in Bloomington and its twin city, Normal. Pickings were slim to say the least, and what I'd seen so far was not appealing. I didn't come halfway across the world to be surrounded by yet another gaggle of desi aunties with nothing better to do than gossip and lord their offspring's accomplishments over everyone else. Not that I wasn't homesick for the comforts of being around my own people, but the friends and family I missed were nothing like the stuck-up professors and their snooty kids who treated me with pity for some reason. As if they couldn't understand why any parents would send their young daughter so far away all by herself to finish high school. The fact that I was born in the US and that my parents had moved back to India when I was only four didn't sit well with them. It was as if they judged people who had decided that life here was not for them and had decided to move back to India. It made them question why I was here now. And I wasn't about to defend my parents' decision to send me here to finish high school so that I would have more opportunities. It was a selfless act by two loving people who always put my future ahead of their desire to keep their daughter close to home. I was keenly aware that this was a huge sacrifice for them, not only financially but also emotionally, and I wasn't going to let a bunch of strangers make me feel bad about it.

Plus, it wasn't like I went out to get drunk or have wild sex, but as far as Salma Aunty was concerned, that was exactly what happened at high school parties with white kids and no parents around. So, if the only way for me to have any fun at all was to lie to her, then that's how it had to be. I already had a reputation for being a rule follower back home. I'd be dammed if I let that haunt me here as well. The one good thing about living so far from home was that there wasn't an army of aunties running around town, ready to pop up at the most inopportune moments. I'd had several run-ins with the aunty brigade back home, and the speed with which they spread misinformation rivaled any fake news media outlet in the country.

I haven't done anything wrong, I reminded myself.

As long as I could say that, I figured I was okay.

CHAPTER FOUR

I spent the rest of the weekend eating the obligatory desi meals my aunt prepared in my honor. Somehow, she had convinced herself that I missed desi food, which I did. But to be honest, I would have preferred a cheeseburger and fries most days because Ammi's cooking had spoiled me for anyone else's Indian food. But to be polite, I ate Salma Aunty's oily egg curry and overly spiced meat kormas. Between that and their obsession with watching taped episodes of *Maury Povich* and *Oprah*, my weekend threatened to slip away. Thankfully, my part-time jobs at the local Baskin-Robbins and the public library gave me an excuse to leave the house.

I'd just started my Sunday shift at Baskin-Robbins when I saw Suresh standing in line behind a family of four. He caught my eye and smiled. My stomach did a weird thing even as I smiled back. It was funny how I'd just met him, but now suddenly he was here, especially since I'd never seen him in here before. Was that odd? Or just a coincidence? I mean, this was an ice-cream place and lots of people came here even though the weather had turned quite cold already. He was standing in front of me now, and I was suddenly very conscious of my bright-blue-and-pink work uniform with the pink-and-blue visor on my head.

"What can I get you?" I asked as professionally as I could.

His eyebrows lifted almost imperceptibly at my tone as he perused the selection behind the counter.

"Can I please get two scoops of rocky road?" he said.

"Sure, did you want that in a cup or a cone?" The scoop slipped a little in my suddenly sweaty hands.

"A waffle cone, please."

I pushed the first scoop as far down the cone as I could and added another big scoop.

"Here you go." I reached over the counter to hand him the cone. He took it with one hand while fishing out money from his jean pocket with his other.

"It's on me," I said quickly. "For keeping me company at the party the other night."

He hesitated for a second. Then he shrugged and shot me another disarmingly brilliant smile.

"When do you get off?" he asked.

"At six."

"Do you wanna grab some food after?"

Was he asking me out on a date? Or just a hangout? I was so confused, and I really wished that Natasha was here to help me.

"Why not? Meet you at the food court?"

"I'll grab us a table," he said before turning around and walking out of the store.

The rest of my shift went by very fast, with a steady influx of customers and my mind occupied with thoughts of Suresh. I dissected everything from the short exchange I'd had with him. I was lonely—there was no denying that fact. And because I was lonely, maybe Suresh was more appealing to me here than he would have been if we'd been back in Mumbai. My mind whirled with these thoughts as I finished up and walked over to the food court to meet him.

I spotted him by the water fountain and smiled in spite of my misgivings. Once again, a warm feeling washed over me at the sight of his face so familiar in its brownness, the way he carried himself reminding me of my life back home, and I decided that I would stop listening to that voice in my head that was forever cautioning me and getting in the way of anything fun. I was just grabbing a slice of pizza with this guy, not meeting his family.

I caught his eye and waved even as I hurried over to him.

"How was the rest of your shift? Anything exciting happen?" he asked.

"There was this one aunty who came in with her kids," I said. "And she started asking me where I was from and told me I should join the Indian Association and go to their events."

"And what did you say?" he asked with a grin.

"What do you think? Of course I said yes. Her ice cream was making a mess on the floor."

"Okay, promise me I can come with if you go to any desi functions," he said, a glint in his eyes.

"Why, have you been? How bad is it?"

"Hmm, let's see. Imagine you're at your dad's colleague's brother-in-law's neighbor's daughter's wedding and you don't know a single person there," he said. "And then imagine all the aunties trying to set you up with their neighbor's uncle's son. Sounds like fun, no?"

"Well, I guess it can't hurt to go once and check it out?" I said. "I mean, it's not like I haven't been in that exact situation a thousand times back home."

"Yes, but you must have had some buffers then, right?" he said, leaning back in his chair.

"That's true. My parents were pretty good at shutting stuff down really fast. Who wants their daughter to get married at seventeen these days?"

"But seriously, if you do end up going, don't forget about me," he said as he stood and pushed his chair back. "I'm starving. Let's get some food."

"I think I'm feeling pizza," I said, grabbing my purse.

"Please, it's my treat," he said quickly. "I'm in the mood for pizza too."

I shook my head. "No, it's okay. I can get my own. But thank you."

"You can get it next time," he said.

There was that smile again, and the dimple appeared, so I couldn't refuse. Plus, I liked the idea of a next time.

"Okay, in that case I'd like a slice of veggie pizza, please."

He nodded before heading to the pizza counter. I sat back down and watched the crowds walking about. Everywhere I looked I saw groups of people, families, friends—and for the first time in a long time, I didn't feel the loneliness that usually filled me. I missed being part of a group, people who already knew me, to whom I was not an exotic stranger with tales from faraway lands that made their eyes go big with wonder. I just wanted to be part of something. I wanted to belong. And today, after a long time, being here with Suresh, waiting for him while he got us pizza just like I used to with my friends back home, I felt less alone.

CHAPTER FIVE

"Do you want to come over and watch *Mohabbatein* at my place?" Suresh asked when he came to the library right after my shift a few days later. We'd started hanging out together more and more, especially since Natasha was obsessed with Brian these days.

"What about your dad's friend?" I asked. I'd been hearing about this movie for months. It starred my three favorite actors: Aishwarya Rai, Shah Rukh Khan, and Amitabh Bachchan. It couldn't get more perfect than that. But Hafeez Uncle was not a fan of Bollywood and Salma Aunty secretly watched really old movies when he was at work, so I badly needed a current Bollywood fix.

"He's cool, trust me," Suresh said. "He's always telling me to bring friends over."

"Okay, sure, that sounds great," I said. "I've been dying to watch it. Where'd you get a copy?"

"Uncle Paul goes to Chicago a lot for work, so he picked it up there on Devon Avenue."

"Oh, is he desi?" I asked.

"Yeah—he and my dad went to college together at Northwestern. So when he heard I was coming here for high school, he offered to let me live with him."

"That's nice. Were you born here too?"

He nodded. "I was. Dad was in grad school, and then, after a few years of working here, he got a really great offer back in Mumbai. Mom was homesick too, so they moved back when I was two."

"It was the same for my parents," I said. "My grandparents weren't doing well, so my mom thought it would be better to live near them. I was four when we moved back."

I shivered a little because it was already freezing in Bloomington and, even though Suresh had the car running with the heater on, I was still cold. I put my gloves on and stuck my hands in the pockets of my winter coat.

"It's weird, isn't it?" Suresh asked.

"What is?"

"How people go through so much just to come here and then in the end they're not even happy, so they go back."

I nodded slowly. "I've heard my parents talking about what their lives would be like if they'd stayed."

He looked at me thoughtfully. "Do you ever think about what your life would've been like?"

"I used to a lot. But if we'd stayed, I wouldn't be as close to my grandparents and all my cousins the way I am now. And I can't imagine what it would have been like growing up so far from everyone."

"That's exactly how I feel." His face lit up. "My dadaji used to watch cartoons with me on the weekends. *Spider-Man* on Saturdays and *Scooby-Doo* on Sundays. And we'd eat parathay and dum aloo."

"That sounds so sweet," I said softly, trying to picture him as a little boy, same curly hair and dimple. He must have been adorable.

"What about you? Do you miss your family?"

"So much," I said with a deep sigh. "Especially my two sisters."

"How old are they?"

"Hena is ten, and Uzma is thirteen." A wistful smile plays on my face. "I'm afraid I'm going to miss so much of their lives while I'm here."

"They must miss you too."

"They've taken over my role as assistant gardener to my dad," I said. "He grows these amazing roses on our rooftop. Mostly hybrids, so they come out in these gorgeous colors, like blood red with pink swirls and bright pink ones with white streaks. My favorites ones were black with splashes of yellow. They were just so beautiful. I used to help him plant them in these huge containers, and then we'd go up there every evening to water them. And we'd just talk about stuff. I miss that more than anything."

His hand found mine, and he held it gently.

"I'm so glad you came to Mike's party," he said.

I felt suddenly shy and looked down at our fingers interlaced with each other's.

"Me too." I raised my eyes to look at him. "I used to be so homesick until I met you."

"We have to stop hanging out like this in my car, though," he said with a smile. "You look like you're going to turn into a Popsicle."

I smiled back at him, then closed my eyes and inhaled deeply. Being here with him, like this, was a balm for the loneliness that still engulfed me sometimes. And even though we'd only just met, I knew in my gut this was something special. I just hoped that he felt it too.

CHAPTER SIX

That Saturday, I stood in front of Suresh's place. I rang the doorbell and waited nervously outside the door. A few seconds later, it opened, and a man who looked to be around my dad's age was smiling at me.

"Come in, come in. You must be Ayesha." He took my jacket, and I handed him the bucket of ice cream I'd brought.

"Thank you for letting me come over to watch the movie," I said, following him into the living room.

"Arre, of course, I'm glad you could make it," he said. "Suresh has been talking about you nonstop."

"Thanks a lot, Uncle Paul." I turned to see Suresh grinning at us, and my heart skipped a little beat. His damp hair lay in curls on his forehead, and he was wearing a cream-colored kurta with jeans. The scent of sandalwood incense was in the air, and if it wasn't snowing so heavily outside, I might have thought I was back home in Mumbai.

Uncle Paul slapped Suresh on the back playfully.

"Well, I have to get going, but you kids have fun. Not too much fun, though." The last bit was directed at Suresh with a wink. "I don't want to get in trouble with your mom and dad."

And with that he left. My cheeks were on fire, and even Suresh looked a little embarrassed. I found it hard to look at him directly.

"Can I get you something to drink?" he asked, breaking the awkward tension. "Some chai maybe?"

My eyes lit up. "Chai? I'll have some if you are."

"I haven't had any today yet, so I'm dying for a cup."

I grinned at him. "Okay. Full disclosure, though: I won't be able to help you make it."

"Seriously? You don't know how to make chai?"

"Why do I have to know how to make chai? Because I'm a girl?"

He threw me a look of disbelief. "No, because you like drinking chai."

"Okay, fine, that's true," I said with a shrug. "I've just been too lazy, and so now you get the honor of teaching me."

"If you insist," he replied, sighing dramatically.

"Can you grab the mugs?" he asked when we stood in the kitchen. "They're up in that cabinet to your left."

I went to take them out but realized they were too high for me to reach.

"Umm, I'm sorry, but I'm not a giant," I said, turning to him.

He walked over with an indulgent smile, and when he reached up, his arm brushed against mine. I felt a tingle run up and down my spine. I stood as still as I could so he wouldn't realize the effect he was having on me. He pulled down two Illinois State University mugs and handed them to me. I couldn't help wondering if he'd felt anything too.

"Okay, so first things first, you put the water to boil." He poured water into a small saucepan and set it on one of the front burners.

"Okay, gotcha. Boil water first."

He opened a drawer and pulled out a few spice jars and a small mortar and pestle.

"Crush a couple of cardamom pods, cloves, a few peppercorns, and some star anise"—he looked up at me—"ginger for you, or no?"

I shook my head. "No ginger for me, please."

"Okay, you throw all that in with the tea and a cinnamon stick, and let it come to a boil," he said.

We watched the mixture as it began to bubble. Suresh turned off the stove.

"You have to let it steep for a few minutes before you add milk." He looked at me and smiled. "You know there's going to be a quiz after, right?"

"I'm taking copious notes in my head. Aren't you supposed to heat the milk before you add it in?"

"Yes, you do. Someone's getting an A on their quiz. Can you grab the strainer from that drawer over there?" he asked. Then he flashed me a grin. "It's not too high for you, is it?"

"Haha, you're not as funny as you look, you know," I grumbled as I pulled out the strainer and handed it to him.

"And now you just pour it through the strainer . . . and there you go," he said, handing me a steaming mug.

I added a little milk and sugar, blowing gently on it before taking a sip.

"Oh my god, this is so good," I said. "My aunt and uncle are coffee people, so I haven't had a decent cup of chai in ages."

Suresh disappeared into the pantry and came out with a

packet of Parle-G biscuits. I let out a little squeal, which elicited a huge grin from him.

"I know, right?"

"Where do you get all this?" I asked. "The only Asian store I've found here had like six inches of shelf space for desi stuff. Most of it looked like really old packets of National spices."

"Devon Avenue," he said. "Uncle Paul and I go every few weeks and stock up on stuff. You should come with us next time."

"Yes, please. Salma Aunty doesn't really like to drive too far from home and Hafeez Uncle works really late, so they don't really get out much."

For the next little while, we enjoyed our chai and cookies in silence. There was no need to talk when our mouths were filled with sugary deliciousness.

"So how come you're wearing a kurta today?" I asked.

"Uncle Paul took me to the temple this morning," he said, brushing some crumbs off his jeans. "It's my grandmother's death anniversary, so Mom asked me to do a little puja."

"I'm sorry, I didn't know," I said, suddenly feeling really awkward for being here on a day that must be pretty sad for him.

"No, no, it was a long time ago," he said quickly. "But we do a puja at home every year. Since I can't be there, I usually go to the temple here."

"I've never been inside one," I confessed.

"You can come with me next time. I mean, if you want to."

"That'd be cool." As a Muslim, I haven't really had much occasion to go into a temple. My parents are pretty religious, but they have many friends from other faiths, as is fairly common in a city like Mumbai. And even though I too have many

26

Hindu friends back home, I've never really shared in any of their religious events.

"Shall we watch the movie?" Suresh said after we'd polished off a whole packet of cookies and finished our chai.

"Yes, let's do it," I said, carrying the empty mugs and plates to the sink.

I walked over to the couch and sat in one corner of it, and to my surprise, Suresh sank down next to me. Like really close. Even though we'd hung out in his car a couple of times since the party, we'd never been alone in a house this way. My hands were suddenly clammy. I wiped them on my jeans and tried not to let my nervousness show.

He pressed play, and for the next few minutes, I was kind of tense, my insides all knotted up, but outwardly I was the picture of calm, pretending to be engrossed by the opening credits of the movie. I deserved an Oscar.

It was excruciating sitting like this, his leg touching mine, but just barely, and one of his hands casually thrown over the back of the couch. Finally, I couldn't stand it any longer, and I almost sprained my eyeballs trying to look at him unobtrusively. He appeared to be mesmerized by Aishwarya Rai and Shah Rukh Khan, and rightfully so. I knew I should probably do the same, but I couldn't help it. I was too nervous to relax, wondering what he was thinking. Since this wasn't the only piece of furniture in the room, clearly, he had no reason to sit like this, practically glued to me. So, was he going to make a move or not? Did I want him to make a move? The answer was a resounding *yes*. But maybe he was afraid of how I would react. Maybe I needed to give him some sort of a signal that I would be completely fine if, say, he decided to turn toward me and gently cup my face in his hands. And it wouldn't be terrible if he slowly lowered his lips to mine and kissed me. All of this would be perfectly acceptable. But how could I convey this to him without appearing utterly desperate?

I took a deep breath and ever so slightly moved my hand closer to his. It was a move imperceptible to all except maybe a puma or a housecat. But since neither was present at the moment, I was pretty sure Suresh hadn't noticed that I was inching my hand closer and closer to his leg. Then I waited. Nothing. He made no attempt to touch my hand even though I clearly made it so easy for him. Maybe I needed to angle myself better so that he wouldn't have to make all the moves. I was an independent woman after all, and this was the year 2000. If I wanted to be kissed by a guy I really liked, I shouldn't feel weird about it.

But what if I'd read the situation completely wrong? I looked down at my hand and almost pulled it back. But I stopped myself just in time. I was sweating more and more by the minute. At this rate even if anything did happen, I'd probably slide right out of his arms.

I tried to read his expression once again and felt a strain in my neck. After this evening was over, I would be in urgent need of muscle relaxants.

"Are you okay?" he asked abruptly, and I almost jumped out of my skin. "You look uncomfortable."

"No, no, I'm good," I said hastily, using the moment to create a little distance between us. Clearly, he was someone who didn't have any concept of personal space. Obviously, he just thought this was a typical movie night with a friend, and here I was concocting all sorts of romantic scenarios in my head. Maybe it was better to lay off the drama of Bollywood movies for now.

He tossed me one of the throw pillows, and I took it, mortified that I'd almost made a complete and utter fool of myself. Phew, that was close. We watched the rest of the movie in companionable silence, and after it was over, we went into the kitchen to eat some of the chutney sandwiches Uncle Paul had left for us in the fridge.

"These are so good," I said after I'd inhaled my second one.

"I'll be sure to pass along your compliments to the chef," Suresh said with a smile. "It's usually just me and Uncle Paul raving over whatever desi food we decide to make."

"Wait, are you saying you actually help him?"

"What are you trying to say?" he said, glowering at me but with a twinkle in his eye. "I'm not a princess like you who doesn't even know how to make a cup of chai."

"Hey, I shared that with you in confidence," I said, taking our plates to the sink. "You can't throw that in my face."

I turned around with my hands on my hips, and suddenly he was right there. I froze, but my insides turned to mush. His face was inches away from mine, and a breath hitched in my throat. I leaned back against the sink with my feet rooted to the ground. He gazed at me with an intensity as if he knew exactly what I was thinking.

"I'll make you chai whenever you want," he said softly. He raised his hand and gently touched my cheek. I leaned into him and then his lips were on mine and somehow my arms were around him and he was pulling me in even closer. I raised myself on the tips of my toes, my hands cupping his face, and then, for the next little while, I was lost in his arms.

CHAPTER SEVEN

The next couple of weeks went by in a haze of stolen kisses behind the bushes on the side of my aunt's house when I knew they were watching TV and secret rendezvous at Uncle Paul's house when he was away. Luckily, he went on a lot of business trips and we got a lot of alone time together. Mostly we watched Hindi movies and made out. A lot. It was like we couldn't get enough of each other, and I spent every moment that we weren't together thinking about him. I spent more time in class sketching pictures of him and me together than I did taking notes. I was distracted to the point that my teacher called me in after school one day to ask me what was going on.

"Ayesha, I wanted to talk to you about your last test," Mrs. Watkins said. "I was surprised you didn't do better. I thought you had a good handle on the trig equations."

My stomach dropped. I'd already applied to Northwestern, my dream school, and this was not a good time for my grades to drop. But I knew exactly why they had. Lately, with all the time I'd been spending with Suresh, I hadn't been putting in a lot of hours studying like I usually did.

"I'm sorry," I said. "I'm going to make sure I do better on the next one."

"Well, this one was only a chapter test, but remember the unit test is coming up before Thanksgiving break and that one counts for twenty-five percent of your grade."

She put her folders away in the drawer and stood. "Don't forget I'm giving everyone the option to drop their lowest mark at the end of the semester, so hopefully this one will be it for you. If you really want to go to Urbana-Champaign or Northwestern, you'll have to keep your grades up."

I nodded. "I will. And I promise I'll be ready for the unit test."

As I waited for the bus in the freezing cold, I chided myself for being so stupid. How did I not see this coming? During the last few weeks, my brain had been like a sieve. I was too preoccupied with Suresh, and it had to stop. If I couldn't pull up my math grade quickly, I would hate myself. By the time I got home, I knew I'd have to talk to Suresh about this.

"It's just one test, Ayesha," he said when I called and told him what happened. "I'm sure you'll do better next time."

"You don't understand," I said, panic making my voice higher than I intended. "The whole reason my parents let me come here was so I could get into a good college. I can't screw up now."

"Okay, okay, please don't panic," he said. "What can I do to help?"

"I think we need to cool it for a bit," I said. "At least until Thanksgiving."

"Wait . . . are you saying I'm not going to see you until then?" he said. "That's, like, three weeks away."

"I know it sucks, but I think I really need to focus on school."

"What if we just see each other once a week?" he said. "And we'll just study together, I promise."

I got a little tingly thinking about the last time we said we'd study together. Let's just say there were books and worksheets present, but no one was touching *them*.

"I think we both know that's not going to happen," I said softly. I knew he was remembering the same afternoon last week.

He groaned on the other end. "Okay, I guess you're right," he said. "But promise me you'll spend Thanksgiving weekend with me. Uncle Paul's going out of town to visit a relative, and we'll have the whole house to ourselves."

A thrill shot through me at the thought of having an entire uninterrupted weekend with him. No schoolwork to worry about, just him and me, cuddled up in front of the fireplace. It sounded heavenly.

"I don't know if I can convince Salma Aunty to let me go," I said. I couldn't resist toying with him.

"I think if I tell you what I have planned, you'll come up with something good," he said, his voice soft and low, sending delicious shivers down my spine.

"Are you sure? Because I don't think Salma Aunty will like your plans at all."

"Haha, you're hilarious," he said, but I could hear the smile in his voice.

"I promise I'll make it up to you," I said, already longing to be in his arms. But I had to stay strong because my future literally depended on it. Not to say what my parents would think if they found out how badly I'd done on my test. They checked in regularly, and it wasn't like I could lie about it because Salma Aunty saw all my report cards.

"I'm going to hold you to that," Suresh said before we hung up.

It took me a while to get started on my homework, but eventually I did, and surprisingly after a couple of hours, I'd done more math problems than I'd completed all last week. It felt good to get caught up, and I promised myself that I would stick to this and not let anything distract me until Thanksgiving. But then I started thinking about how Thanksgiving weekend with Suresh was going to be so amazing and spent the next twenty minutes daydreaming.

The phone rang, and it was Natasha asking to come over. A little later, we were sitting at the dining table, an array of snacks laid out around us as we tackled reviewing for our physics test.

"I don't get friction at all," Natasha said. "I mean, how am I supposed to know all the different forces acting on an object if it makes no sense?"

"I'll help you with that if you can solve this one problem that's been driving me nuts," I said, pointing at a question that I'd been working on for an hour now.

We were still working when Salma Aunty and Hafeez Uncle walked in carrying several bags of groceries.

"Ah, working hard, I see," Hafeez Uncle said. "Or hardly working?" He chuckled at his own joke, putting the bags on the kitchen island.

I jumped up to help Salma Aunty with hers.

"Hello, Natasha, it's nice to see you here for a change," she said. "It seems that Ayesha spends a lot of time at your place. I hope your parents aren't getting tired of seeing her there all the time."

Natasha shot me a look before replying, "No, not at all, Mrs. Rashid."

She winked at me when Salma Aunty stuck her head in the fridge to make room for the milk carton. "In fact, we were hoping that she could spend Thanksgiving with us," she said.

I could have kissed her. Earlier I told her about my plan for the long weekend, and she just gave me the perfect alibi.

Salma Aunty's head popped back out. "I'll have to talk to your parents about that first," she said.

I froze, but Natasha recovered with remarkable speed.

"Actually, it's their twentieth anniversary at the end of November," she said. "My brother and I have been planning a surprise for them. I could really use Ayesha's help with all the arrangements. It would just be for that weekend."

I could see that Salma Aunty was racking her brain to come up with a reason to say no, but I had to admit, Natasha's idea was genius.

"That's so sweet of you and your brother to do that for your parents," Salma Aunty said. "Of course Ayesha can spend the weekend with you."

"Yes, and please wish your parents a very happy anniversary," Hafeez Uncle added.

I thanked my lucky stars that they weren't friends with Natasha's parents because that would have made things très awkward.

CHAPTER EIGHT

"Natasha, you're a genius," I said as soon as we were in my room. I threw my arms around her. "Seriously, you're the best."

"Hey, I've only been saying this forever," she said, giving me a tight squeeze. "Besides, why should I get to have all the fun over Thanksgiving break?" she added with a sly grin.

"Why? What are you planning?" I said, conveniently ignoring the worksheets glaring accusingly at me from my bed. "C'mon, tell me everything."

"Well, my parents are actually going away for their anniversary and my brother's going with his friend's family . . . so guess who's going to have the house all to herself?" She did a little dance around my room.

"Aren't your parents worried about you being all by yourself?" I couldn't imagine my parents leaving me to fend for myself with everyone gone.

"Nah, they know I can take care of things. Besides, I'm almost eighteen, and starting next fall I'll be living alone anyway."

"Lucky you," I said wistfully. "Depending on where I end up going to college, I bet you my parents will find some relative I can stay with. I'll never get to live on my own."

"Isn't that up to you, though? I mean you could always talk to your parents and convince them that you're old enough and responsible enough to be on your own."

I sighed. "They know that, but it's more that they worry what people will say if their daughter's living all by herself in a foreign country."

"That must be hard. Always having to worry what other people will say."

"It's not just that, though. If I'm on my own, they'll never stop worrying if I'm okay, you know? Like what happens if I fall sick or get into an accident or something?"

"I guess I kind of get that," she said. "But at some point, you'll have to learn to figure stuff out on your own, right?"

"I know. But as far as my parents are concerned, they'll always want to look out for me and make sure I'm safe. It's just how they are."

We spent the next hour finishing up our worksheets while I thought about what Natasha had said. It was true that sometimes I resented how overprotective my parents could be. But at the same time, I loved them for how much they always looked out for me and how they usually knew what was best for me. And even though they did care a lot about what people might say, they never let it get in the way of anything important, like me coming to finish high school here in the US, despite all the negativity and warnings from their relatives.

A few of my cousins weren't so lucky. Their parents were a lot more traditional, and their chief concern was arranging a good marriage for their daughters. Sending them out of the country for education was out of the question. Not that I thought there was anything wrong with staying in India as long as they were given a choice, but I considered myself very fortunate that my parents didn't base all their decisions on what people may say. But they were still traditional enough that they would never approve of my relationship with Suresh. First and foremost, he was Hindu, and while they had many Hindu friends and acquaintances, their daughter being involved with one was an entirely different matter. It was a strange philosophy, one I didn't understand at all. As long as the boundaries stopped at friendship, it was all well and good. But there was no way they would accept anything more than that.

Whatever it was that Suresh and I were doing, it would have to remain a carefully guarded secret, at least for now. Trying to imagine their reaction to Suresh, if they ever found out, made me realize that I was already long past that imaginary line I'd promised myself I wouldn't cross. I was falling for Suresh, which was why I was playing out different scenarios in my mind.

So much for being cautious and taking it slow.

CHAPTER NINE

I couldn't wait to tell Suresh that I was good for Thanksgiving weekend, and I got my chance a couple of days later when we decided to meet up in a public place for a quick meal after my shift at Baskin-Robbins. Our pact to not see each other had lasted less than a week. But at least it wouldn't end up being a whole make-out session because Hafeez Uncle was giving me a ride home. Now that it was getting dark so much earlier, he and Salma Aunty didn't want me taking the bus or walking home after work.

"Did you figure out what to tell your aunt and uncle?" Suresh asked as we sat in the food court. I hadn't told him anything yet because I wanted it to be a surprise.

I was having a bowl of tomato soup, and I took a steaming spoonful, leaning back as it warmed me from inside.

"Natasha asked them if I could help her with her parents' surprise anniversary party over Thanksgiving weekend." I dipped my buttered roll into the soup and took a bite.

"That Natasha is a genius," he said, reaching across the

table to take my hand. "I've missed you so much." He held my gaze, and I looked around nervously.

"It's only been a few days," I said, extricating my hand from his.

"So you're saying you didn't miss me," he said, trying to look sad but failing miserably. The twinkle in his eye gave him away.

"I didn't say that." I took another bite of my roll. "I'm just saying if you can't wait a few days, how are you going to last until Thanksgiving?"

"What do you mean?" he said. "I thought you were all caught up at school."

"Yes, I am, but I have a bunch of tests and assignments coming up before the long weekend, so I have to really buckle down and study."

"But that's still ten days away." He sounded petulant, and sadly I found even that cute. I was in so much trouble.

"Yes, well, hopefully they'll go by really fast. I found someone to cover all my shifts to focus on studying, so I really have no excuse to get out of the house that much."

"This is so unfair," he said. "What am I supposed to do until then?"

"Miss me, obviously," I said with a smile.

"Okay, fine," he said with a big sigh. "I guess I don't have a choice. At least I'll get to spend the whole long weekend with you. Thank goodness your aunt and uncle are letting you go."

"I feel really bad lying to them. But with school closed, they'll ask too many questions every time I step out of the house."

"I know what you mean," Suresh says. "My parents are pretty cool, but all the questions drive me nuts." He took a bite of his burger.

"Seriously?" I said, my tone a little sharper than I intended. "I mean, how bad could it be for you?"

He narrowed his eyes. "What's that supposed to mean?"

"It means you're probably the golden boy in your family and I'm sure you get a lot more freedom than I ever do."

"You're right about the golden-boy part. I'm an only child, and my parents are hyperfocused on my every move. It's harder than you think."

I reached over and grabbed a couple of fries off his plate.

"I didn't know you were an only child. So, you're spoiled." I grinned at him. "That actually explains a lot."

He threw a fry at me, but I caught it and popped it into my mouth.

"What's it like for you, being the oldest daughter and all that?" he asked.

"It's a lot." I push my bowl away from me with a sigh. "I'm supposed to set a good example for Hena and Uzma, which means I'm not allowed to screw up. Ever."

"That's gotta be tough," he said, smiling gently.

"It is, sometimes. I love them all, but there are times I just want to scream and let loose, you know? But I can't, because what will people say?"

"Ah, yes, the people. Always on the lookout for one of us to trip up," Suresh said, his tone slightly bitter.

I glanced at my watch. "Hey, I have to go. My uncle's picking me up, and I don't want him to come in here looking for me."

He grabbed my hand again. "I'll really miss you, you know." The way he looked at me made me want to wrap my arms around him and forget everything else.

"I'll miss you too." I squeezed his hands. "I can't wait for Thanksgiving."

"That's all I've been thinking about," he said. "Promise me you'll think about me every time you watch *Gilmore Girls* until then?"

"Only if you promise you won't watch any *Buffy* episodes without me."

"You can't do that to me," he said, all worked up suddenly. "I need to know what happens to her mother."

"I know," I said. "But just tape it and we'll watch it together."

He sighed. "Okay, fine, but only because I love you." As soon as the words were out of his mouth, his eyes widened. I couldn't decide who was more surprised, him or me. A smile began to play on my lips . . . but then I spotted Hafeez Uncle by the food court entrance and froze.

"Oh shit, my uncle's here," I said in a panicked whisper. "I have to go."

Suresh looked stunned as he watched me run off. Just before heading out the door, I turned to look at him. He was still standing there, a funny expression on his face.

I wanted to go back. It was like I was pushing against gravity to go with my uncle.

Thanksgiving, I reminded myself.

CHAPTER TEN

By the time we got home, I was still not over what Suresh had said to me. Especially since I never got to say anything back. All through dinner, his words echoed in my head, and I found it difficult to follow the conversation Salma Aunty and Hafeez Uncle were having about their daughter, Reshma.

"Is Reshma Apa coming home for Thanksgiving break?" I asked as I helped myself to another roti. Salma Aunty's shami kebabs were really good today, and I'd already eaten two.

"She was going to, but then at the last minute she decided to go to a friend's family cabin," Hafeez Uncle said. "She said they were going to ski."

"When did Reshma learn how to ski?" Salma Aunty asked. "She should have come home. We haven't seen her for almost four months."

"Let her have some fun, na, Salma," Hafeez Uncle said. "It's not as if we celebrate Thanksgiving."

"Hanh, that's true," Salma Aunty agreed. "But I miss her too much."

"Maybe you two can visit her in New York after she gets

back," I suggested. My cousin was attending Columbia University, and her parents were very proud of her. I hoped that I would also get into a school like that. I was more of a math and science person, but I also liked languages and literature, so I was still all over the place as far as narrowing down a career path was concerned.

Upstairs in my room I tried to concentrate on the chapter about RNA replication our biology teacher had assigned. But of course, I kept going over and over what Suresh had said instead. No one had ever really said those exact words to me before. I mean, there had been a brief thing with Ismail Bakhtiar in grade ten, but we'd never actually said those words to each other. Plus, that whole thing had mostly consisted of secret phone calls on those rare occasions that I actually managed to get to the phone before Ammi or Abbu, and a whole lot of one of us letting the other's phone ring two times before hanging up as a signal that we wanted to talk to each other. We would have been good as spies but weren't so much in the relationship area.

This thing with Suresh, this was different. There was an undeniable connection, something electric that drew me to him right from the beginning. When I wasn't with him, all I could think about was the next time we'd be together. And when we were together, I forgot about the rest of the world. That had to be love, right? He felt like a part of me already, as if we'd been in each other's lives much longer than just a couple of months. And we were so comfortable with each other, so I knew it wasn't just physical. The way we bonded over desi food and movies, and our relationships with our families and the way I could talk to him about anything made me feel like we were meant to be together. It all had to mean that there was something truly special between us. And how could I deny the way he made me feel whether he was standing right in front of me or on the phone? It wasn't just about how my entire body tingled when I was near him; it was more the way we fit with each other, like we were made for each other. And clearly, he felt the same way. I could tell by the look on his face today that he hadn't planned to tell me how he felt but since it came out involuntarily, it had to mean something. I picked up my phone and called him.

"Hey, you," he said. "I was hoping you'd call."

A warmth spread all through my body at the sound of his voice. "I wanted to call as soon as I got home, but I couldn't get away."

"So, about what I said . . ."

"I love you too," I blurted out before I lost my nerve.

He didn't say anything for a while, but I could hear him breathing softly, and that was enough.

"I was so worried that I scared you off," he finally said.

"Well, you didn't."

"I've been wanting to tell you for a while now. But I just couldn't get up the nerve to say it."

"I must be scarier than I think," I said, wanting desperately to be in his arms right now.

"Can you sneak out?"

"Now?" I was already standing to go and check on Salma Aunty and Hafeez Uncle. I tiptoed halfway down the stairs and saw them watching TV. It was Friday night, and I knew they watched *CSI* religiously, so when it started in about fifteen minutes, they'd be glued to the TV.

"Can you come out, in, like, twenty minutes?" Suresh said.

I scampered back up the stairs to my room.

"Okay, yes, I'll meet you by the rosebushes," I whispered. "But you have to be really quiet. My neighbor's dog likes to bark at anything that moves."

"Okay, see you in a bit."

As soon as I hung up, I went into warp-speed mode. I jumped in the shower, using my favorite rose body wash, and was out in a record ten minutes. Then I spent the next few minutes changing in and out of several outfits trying to find the perfect one for a secret, hiding-behind-a-rosebush rendezvous. After I'd pulled on my favorite black flared jeans and decided on a burgundy top, I applied some black eyeliner, mascara, and pink lip gloss. Then I put on a pair of silver hoop earrings and some fuzzy socks before sneaking down the stairs as quietly as I could. I threw a glance toward the living room, where Salma Aunty and Hafeez Uncle had their eyes glued to the television screen. I quickly put on my winter coat and stuck my feet into a pair of sherpa-lined boots before slipping out the door as quietly as I could. I tiptoed through the snow toward Salma Aunty's carefully tended rosebushes. I didn't see Suresh anywhere, so I stuck my hands in the pockets of my jacket, regretting that I had neglected to grab my gloves. It was freezing outside, and I could see my breath in front of me. Suddenly I felt a pair of arms around my waist, and I turned, ready to let out a bloodcurdling scream. Before I could, Suresh's warm lips were on mine, and my arms wound themselves around his neck. When we came up for air, I narrowed my eyes at him.

"You scared me half to death," I said, a little out of breath from our kiss.

He grinned at me. "Why, were you expecting someone else?" He bent to kiss me again. "Did you really mean it?" he said, gently dropping kisses all along the side of my neck until I was weak in the knees. It was a good thing he was holding me up because I seemed to be melting into his arms.

I didn't get a chance to reply. My neighbor's dog appeared and began to bark loudly enough to wake the whole street.

"Shit, I have to go back in," I said, extricating myself from him.

"Wait," Suresh said, pulling me close. "Tell me again that you love me," he whispered in my ear.

"I love you," I whispered. "But unless you want to explain to my uncle why you're lurking in the shadows, I should really go."

"I'll tell him I came to meet the girl of my dreams," he said with a sexy smile.

"I'll say I've never seen you before in my life," I said with a grin before running off. Luckily, the dog had found something more interesting to do, and I snuck back into the house unnoticed.

• • •

Before bed, I called Natasha and told her about our little secret encounter.

"It sounds like something out of a historical romance," she said, her voice several pitches higher than usual. "Secret meeting in the dark of night, the fear of being caught. It's so romantic."

"Try terrifying," I said. "When that dog started barking, I was sure my uncle would come out and check. Good thing *CSI* was on. Nothing can tear them away from that."

"Brian and I never do anything like this," Natasha said with a sigh. "He just honks from his car when he comes to pick me up. He's never come all the way from Normal just to sneak a quick kiss."

"Trust me, I wish Suresh could pick me up from home like a normal person. My aunt and uncle would have a fit and ship me right back to Mumbai."

"Well, I guess you'll have to sneak around a little longer, then," she said. "At least until you go off to college. Has he told you where he's planning to go?"

"We haven't really talked about that," I said. "To be honest, we don't do a lot of talking when we're together." My cheeks flushed at the thought of our heated kisses.

"Hey, there's no need to rub it in, little missy," Natasha chided. "I get it, you're hot for each other."

"But you're right, we should probably talk about stuff," I said. "Especially since he told me he loves me," I added casually.

"Way to bury the lede, Ayesha," she said. "Are you serious?"

"Yes, I'm serious. It was kind of funny because I had to run off as soon as he said it and then I didn't get a chance to call him until after dinner."

"So? Did you say it back?"

"Yes, of course I did."

"Hmm, now it all makes sense," Natasha said, as if she'd solved the world's biggest mystery. "No wonder he came to your place in such a hurry. Well played."

"I can't wait for Thanksgiving. It's just going to be me and him, all alone for the whole weekend."

"I can't wait either," she said. "Brian said he's planned the whole weekend for just the two of us."

"See, he *is* romantic," I said. "You'll have a great time."

"Now we just have to get through our bio test and turn in our term papers for English lit."

"Ugh, I haven't even started on that," I said with a groan.

"Well, then you better get on with it. I'm almost done with mine. I think I can hand it in next week."

"Show-off!" I said just before hanging up.

I knew I had to focus on my schoolwork.

I also knew that was going to be nearly impossible.

CHAPTER ELEVEN

The next few days went by in a flurry of papers, tests, and reading, but finally it was getting closer to Thanksgiving, and I could barely contain my excitement. Just a few days until I could be with Suresh. We hadn't seen each other for over a week, and even though we talked on the phone every night, it just wasn't the same. But it did make the thought of the upcoming weekend that much more thrilling. As I sat in class, I could barely concentrate on the teacher droning on about what we could look forward to after the long weekend. In my mind I was already sitting in front of a crackling fire, cuddled up with Suresh.

I went to meet up with Natasha in the hallway after biology class. Right away I could tell that she'd been crying because her eyes were puffy and her nose was red. I ran up to her immediately.

"What's wrong?" I asked, putting an arm around her shoulder as we walked down the hall to the washrooms.

"Brian and I just broke up," she said, her voice shaky.

"What? I thought things were going great between you two. What happened?"

Natasha stopped in her tracks and looked tremulously at me.

"He's been cheating on me," she said, her face wet with tears. "The whole school knows by now. He's been seeing Ashley behind my back. And, as usual, I was the last one to find out."

"I'm so sorry, Natasha," I said as she dissolved in more tears. I pulled her into the girls' room and hugged her until she was out of tears. The bell rang, but I ignored it. There were more important things in life than logarithms.

I handed her some tissues, and after she composed herself, we slipped out the back door and walked over to the bleachers. It was deserted at this time, and I was freezing because I hadn't thought to grab my coat. But she was telling me all about Brian and trashy Ashley while I wondered why I'd never seen them together.

"Who told you about it?" I handed her another tissue and waited while she blew her nose loudly.

"It was Ashley B.," she said through her tears.

"Wait . . . Ashley told you she's been cheating with Brian?"

"No," Natasha wailed. "Ashley B. told me that Ashley T. has been screwing around with him."

"Have you talked to Brian about this?" I tucked a few strands of her hair behind her ears. "You know Ashley is a bit of a gossip, right?"

"Wait." Natasha looked up. "Ashley B. or Ashley T.?"

I could feel a slight headache coming on. "I'm just saying that maybe you shouldn't just take Ashley B. at her word."

"You think she was messing with me?" She narrowed her eyes. "You know what, I bet you're right. BriBri would never do that to me."

"Okay, then. I think you should go and talk to BriBr—Brian first before you do anything else."

She wiped her nose on her sleeve even though I was literally holding an entire pack of Kleenex.

"Will you come with me?" She looked at me with watery eyes, and I couldn't say no.

"Yes, of course I'll come with you. He has a free period now, doesn't he?"

Natasha looked at her watch and nodded.

"Okay, I'll help you find him and then I'll go to the rest of math class. I don't think Mrs. Watkins is particularly impressed with me these days."

"I'm so sorry I'm making you miss class," Natasha said.

"Don't even worry about it." I gave her shoulder a squeeze. "You'd do the same for me."

We walked back into the school, stopping at the vending machines because Natasha needed a drink. Then we went looking for Brian and found him near the lockers. When he saw us approach, he got a strange look on his face. Before I could do anything to stop her, Natasha rushed over to him and threw her drink in Brian's face. He looked at her in utter disbelief, but she didn't give him a chance to speak, instead ripping off her necklace and throwing it to the ground at his feet. I figured it must have been a gift from him, given how forcefully she yanked it off. Brian was still speechless, and just when he finally opened his mouth to speak, Natasha turned on her heels, grabbed me by the elbow, and dragged me away.

"Natasha, I thought you were going to talk to him first," I said, slightly out of breath from trying to keep up with her long strides.

"There's nothing to talk about," Natasha says, her eyes blazing. "That little shit went behind my back, and he did it with someone I've hated since kindergarten."

"I didn't realize you've known her for so long," I said.

"That's not even the point. Brian knows how much I hate her. She always wants what I have. In third grade, she stole my best friend, Cassidy, from me."

This sounded more like a long-standing feud than anything and also a lot more complicated than just Brian cheating on Natasha.

"Shouldn't we make sure it's true, though?" I asked. "I mean, what if Ashley B. is just trying to make trouble between you two?"

For a moment, it felt like Natasha was actually considering what I was saying, but then I saw the look on her face, and I knew she wasn't ready.

"Look, Ayesha, I know you're trying to help, but you just don't understand. Ashley and I have always kind of competed for everything since we were little. But this time she's gone too far."

"No, I get what you mean, Natasha. I'm just saying—"

"I'm sorry . . . I just need to be alone for a bit," she said. "You understand, right?"

"Of course I do. Whatever you need," I said quickly. "But promise you'll call me later?"

She nodded before walking away, and I felt completely useless. I tried to get through the rest of the day, but all I could think about was how much Natasha was hurting. Then something struck me. If she and Brian were broken up, then she'd be all alone for Thanksgiving. I couldn't let that happen, so as soon as I got home, I called Suresh.

He picked up right away. "Hey, you. I was just thinking about you." He sounded so happy to hear from me that my heart sank.

"Hey, listen, I have to tell you something."

"What's wrong? Is everything all right? Did your aunt and uncle find out?" I could hear the alarm in his voice.

"It's Natasha," I said. "She and Brian broke up."

"Oh no, that's too bad," Suresh said. "What happened? The last time I saw them, they were all over each other."

"That's what I thought too," I said. "So, remember how I told you that she and Brian were going to spend the long weekend together?"

"Yes, I remember." His voice had grown quiet.

"Well, now she's going to be all alone, because her parents are going to be away and . . ."

"Of course, she can totally hang out with us if she wants," Suresh said. "We can do a whole Thanksgiving meal for her and have a movie night or something. That'll cheer her up, I'm sure."

"That sounds really great, but I was thinking that maybe I should just stay with her. Especially at night, you know, so she has someone to talk to."

He said nothing, and I could feel his disappointment from the other end of the line.

"So, what you're saying is that our whole weekend is canceled?"

"I can still come by for a bit, but you understand, right? This is going to be a really hard weekend for Natasha and she's always been there for me. Please try to understand."

He let out a long sigh. "I get it, but I was just really looking forward to spending time with you. I haven't seen you for almost ten days."

"I'll make it up to you. There's always Christmas." I felt awful, but I knew I'd feel worse if I left Natasha alone.

"Hey, look, I'm getting another call," he said abruptly. "I'll try to call you later." And with that, he hung up. I sat on the edge of my bed, not sure what to do. I felt awful canceling our special weekend plans, but what kind of a friend would I be if I wasn't there for Natasha at a time like this? She'd been the first friend I'd made when I'd arrived in Bloomington. Suresh was overreacting a little, in my opinion. I mean, if it had been his friend, I would have totally understood. I'd have been disappointed, but I would have understood. I wouldn't have gotten mad and hung up on him. If he wanted to be like that, I was perfectly okay with it. Natasha and I would have an amazing weekend without cheating or sulking boyfriends.

Who needed them anyway?

CHAPTER TWELVE

I finally got hold of Natasha after calling her and leaving, like, ten voice mails. She sounded like she'd been crying for hours, nothing like her usual self.

"Hey, Natasha, how would you like to spend the long weekend with me?" I asked.

"What about your plans with Suresh? You were so excited about that."

"We can do that over Christmas—it's no biggie." I tried to sound nonchalant.

"Are you sure?" she asked. "I don't want you to miss out on that for me."

"C'mon, as if you wouldn't do the exact same for me."

"What about Suresh?"

"He'll get over it," I said. "Besides, he's not my best friend— you are."

"Okay, then—yes, I'd love that," she said, sounding a lot more cheerful. That made my heart happy.

We spent the next half hour discussing all the fun things we'd do, and I was sort of relieved that I wouldn't have to sneak around and lie to my aunt and uncle.

After hanging up, my thoughts kept going back to Suresh. I got that he was disappointed, just like I was, but why did he have to be such a baby? Ending our phone call so abruptly was rude. Whatever. Natasha and I were going to have a blast, and she was going to forget all about Brian.

• • •

Two days before Thanksgiving, Natasha caught me just as I was heading to the library to check out a few books for the English lit paper that I was barely going to finish on time.

"You'll never guess what happened!" she said, her eyes bright with excitement.

"What? Hurry up and tell me," I demanded.

"You were right," she said. "Ashley B. made the whole thing up."

"No way! Are you serious?"

"Yes. And my poor BriBri. He kept trying to tell me it wasn't true, and I was too mad at him to listen."

"Hmm," I said, thoughtfully tapping my finger on my chin. "I wonder if there was someone else who was trying to tell you the same thing."

"Yes, I should have listened to you," Natasha said, throwing her arms around me and squeezing me tight.

"I'm so happy for you, Nats." I hugged her back. "Come with me to the library. I just have to grab some books."

"Can't. Gotta go. Brian's waiting for me. I have to make it up to him," she said with a wink.

"Ew, I really don't want to know what that means," I said. "Have fun."

"You too. Now you can have your *special* weekend," she said, making smoochie faces while several students stared at her as they passed by.

I shooed her away before she drew any more attention. As I went through the rest of my school day, I couldn't help wondering if Suresh would be excited by this new development or if he was still hurt. We hadn't talked since I'd told him, so I had no way of knowing where his head was at.

I couldn't wait to get home and tell Suresh that we were back on for Thanksgiving. But when I got there, Salma Aunty was busy in the kitchen preparing food for a dinner party I'd completely forgotten about. She had invited a few of their desi friends and asked me to help out. By the time we were done, it was time to shower and get ready.

I hadn't worn a shalwar kameez since I'd arrived in Bloomington, so I enjoyed the silky feel of the lavender-and-silver churidar kurta set that Ammi had sewn for me before I left Mumbai. I added some silver jhumka earrings and six thin silver bangles on each wrist before going downstairs to greet the guests.

The first to arrive were Mr. and Mrs. Rahman, a younger couple whom Salma Aunty had met at a function organized by the local Indian Association. The husband, Arif, was an associate professor at Illinois State University in Normal, and the wife, Sharmin, was an accountant and also very pregnant. They seemed quite nice and a little out of place when the rest of the guests came. There were two other couples, a little older than my aunt and uncle, so for most of the evening, I ended up talking to Arif and Sharmin about my plans after high school and how I was adjusting to life in the US. They were probably only ten years older than me, so I had a far better time than I'd anticipated. They seemed quite interesting, and I found out that they'd both grown up in Chicago and had met in college. The conversation gave me a glimpse of what my life could be like over the next few years. I could actually picture myself with Suresh, ten years later, with college behind us and a baby on the way. I knew it was way too premature, but that was typical of me, daydreaming about stuff like that. It made me feel warm and fuzzy inside, and by the time the dinner was over and everyone had left, I was exhausted, but not so much that I wasn't dying to talk to Suresh.

"Hey," he said. "What's up?"

Did he sound a little cold, or was I imagining it?

"Nothing much," I said, trying very hard to sound casual. "Except I have some really good news."

"Oh yeah?"

Definitely cold.

"So, Brian and Natasha got back together," I said. "It was all a big misunderstanding."

"That's nice," he said. "I'm happy for them."

Clearly, he was not going to make this easy for me.

"So, you know what that means, right?"

"No, what does it mean?"

Now he was just pissing me off.

"You know what? Never mind," I said. "Good night."

I hung up and flung the phone across the bed.

It rang almost immediately. I didn't answer right away but picked it up just before it went to voice mail.

"What?"

"I'm sorry," he said softly. "I was really mad that you canceled our weekend."

"Well, I didn't want to, but I couldn't leave Natasha all alone. I thought you'd understand."

"I do," he said. "And I love you for being such a great friend, but I'm sorry, I was looking forward to being with you. Can we please stop fighting now?"

I let out a big sigh. "Okay, fine. I don't want to fight either. Do you still want me to come over on the weekend, or have you made other plans already?"

I swore if he said he'd made other plans I would go over there right now to kick his ass.

"Well, I met this chacha and chachi at the grocery store and they said weren't doing anything for Thanksgiving, so I invited them and—"

"Have I ever told you how much you suck?" I turned onto my back and pulled the covers over me.

"What? I was just being a nice guy and opening my home to an elderly couple who seemed really lonely." I could hear him smiling, and I wished he was here right now, next to me in bed, so that I could wrap my arms around him and squeeze really tight. But instead, I hugged my giant pillow as I drifted off with Suresh's voice lulling me to sleep.

CHAPTER THIRTEEN

It was finally Thursday morning, and I was all packed and ready to go on my fake hangout with Natasha and my very real dream weekend with Suresh. I could barely contain my excitement. I'd packed my favorite pair of soft pj's, my fuzzy socks, and a few comfy T-shirts. And, of course, my sketch pad and pencils. The plan was to cuddle together in front of the fireplace, order pizza, and have a Bollywood movie marathon. Obviously, we couldn't go out together because someone might see us, and I couldn't risk my aunt and uncle finding out what I was really up to. Besides, Suresh and I just really wanted to be together without having to worry about curfews and Uncle Paul coming back home and all the other things that prevented us from hanging out for any long periods of time. Suresh said he'd stocked up on desi snacks and Bollywood DVDs the last time he'd gone to Chicago with Uncle Paul and there was a pretty decent collection of board games at his place, so it was going to be the best weekend.

I wanted to wear something special when I went there, so I picked out a soft cotton kurta, burgundy with tiny black flowers embroidered all over the bodice. I pulled on my black flared jeans and added black-and-silver earrings to complete the outfit. I was thrilled with how my hair had turned out today, smoother than usual but with a few tendrils curling in just the right places. I applied a little pink lipstick, and then I was ready. I grabbed my bag and headed downstairs to say goodbye to Salma Aunty.

"You're all ready to go?" she asked when I walked into the kitchen. She was sitting at the table, grading some tests.

"Do you have a lot of these left?" I asked. Salma Aunty had recently started working as a math instructor at the local community college.

"I'm hoping to finish them this weekend," she said. "Have a good time with Natasha."

"Thank you, Aunty," I said. "I'll be back Sunday evening."

"Okay, I think I'll make haleem this weekend," she said. "I'll save some for you."

I gave her a hug and a quick peck on the cheek before heading out.

I walked down the street to where Suresh was waiting in his car and hopped in.

"Any trouble getting out of the house?" he said, taking my hands and rubbing them with his to warm them up.

"No, not really," I said. "I just feel so guilty for lying to them."

"We're not doing anything wrong, Ayesha," he said. "We just want to be together, and if they can't understand that, then what other choice do you have?"

I let out a deep sigh. "I know, I want to be with you too, but it's just hard."

"How about we forget all that and enjoy the time we have," he said.

I nodded and turned to him with a big smile on my face. "Yes, let's do that."

"So what would you like to do first when we get home? Movie or dance party?"

I grinned at him. "A dance party? With just the two of us?"

"If you want, we can try to pick up some people along the way." He grinned back at me.

"I'm game for a dance party, but just let me warn you—back home my nickname was Footloose." I sat back with a smug look on my face.

"Footloose, you say," he said with a crooked smile and an exaggerated American accent. "Well, then you'll be happy to know that my nickname back home is Kevin Bacon."

I laughed out loud, and it felt so good to be with him that it was worth all the lies and subterfuge.

It turned out he wasn't kidding. He was a really good dancer, but so was I, and so for the next couple of hours we danced to '70s and '80s Bollywood dance songs and I'd never been happier. We collapsed in a heap on the couch after the *Qurbani* soundtrack and just stayed like that for a while, content to listen to each other's heartbeats. But then a slow number came on, and he got up and pulled me to my feet. He put his arms around me, and we swayed to the gentle rhythm of "Hum Tumhe Chahte Hain Aise," which is, in my opinion, the most romantic song from the movie. I closed my eyes and let the music transport me to a magical place where there was nothing else but the love we felt for each other.

I don't remember how long we danced like this, but I opened my eyes when I felt his finger under my chin, lifting my face. He lowered his mouth to mine and kissed me softly. It was the sweetest, gentlest kiss, filled with such tenderness and promise.

We ordered a large veggie pizza and watched *Qurbani* since we'd just danced to most of the soundtrack. It was an old movie from 1980, but even though I'd watched it at least twenty times since I was fifteen, I loved it a little bit more each time. Luckily for me, Suresh did too, and we finished the entire pizza as we watched it, pausing frequently to argue over plot points. But then we'd start kissing and forgot what we were arguing about. We came up for air after a while and finished watching the movie. Wrapped in his arms like this, the fire crackling and snow falling outside, I felt as if I was in some magical place, and I never wanted this to end.

"Do you think we would have met if I hadn't gone to Mike's party that night?" I asked him.

He looked at me thoughtfully for a moment.

"I don't know," he said. "I like to think that we were meant to be together, so we would have met some other way."

"Maybe at the ice-cream place?" I looked up at him, and he bent to kiss my forehead.

"Maybe. Or maybe at some desi function."

"Can you imagine if some aunty introduced us?" I said with a grin. "I would have automatically rejected you."

He put on a hurt expression. "How can you say that?" he said, wiping an imaginary tear from his eye. "I'll have you know that I'm considered quite the catch in the aunty circles of Bloomington-Normal."

"Yeah, right," I sneered. "I am allergic to aunty referrals. No one cool needs an aunty to meet girls."

"Excuse me?" he said, his eyebrows raised. "I do not need help to meet girls. I'm actually really good at meeting them on my own."

"Sure, if you say so. But if you hadn't met me that night, I'm pretty sure you'd be sitting here all by your lonesome self, crying like a baby."

I jumped up and out of his arms just in time to avoid his wiggling fingers as he threatened to tickle me. He jumped over the back of the couch in a single leap and chased me around the room while I squealed. At the last minute, I decided to make a break for the stairs, but he grabbed me around the waist just when I changed directions and we both collapsed on the carpet, breathless with laughter. I'd barely caught my breath when he brought his face closer.

"Take back what you said," he whispered, his mouth tantalizingly close to mine, our lips almost touching . . . but not quite. I trembled in anticipation.

"What if I don't?" I whispered back, just before his mouth closed on mine and we melted into each other's arms.

This time his kisses weren't so gentle, his touch becoming more and more urgent.

The passion between us grew until we couldn't hold back anymore.

CHAPTER FOURTEEN

When I woke the next morning, I basked in the warmth of his arms for as long as I could, watching the way his chest rose and fell rhythmically, his eyelashes impossibly long as he slept peacefully. He looked like he was smiling in his sleep, and I hoped he felt the same way I did. I don't think either of us had planned for things to go as far as they had, but what happened between us was so beautiful and natural and right. Like it was meant to be. I banished any intruding worries as Suresh stirred and opened his eyes.

"Hey, you," he said. His hand found mine, and he interlaced his fingers through mine.

"Hey yourself." I rested my head in the crook of his arms, loving the way it felt just to lie here with him.

"Hungry?" He lifted his head to look at me and then kissed me softly.

"Starving."

"Do you want some Bombay toast?"

My stomach growled loudly, and I sat up quickly.

"Umm, I guess so," I said with an embarrassed laugh.

Downstairs in the kitchen, Suresh chopped some onions, green chilies, and cilantro while I whisked a few eggs in a bowl and added some milk. We worked together like clockwork. He got some butter sizzling in the pan, and I dipped several slices of bread in the egg mixture. He cooked, flipped, and browned the bread slices in the pan as I got two mugs out of the cabinet and made us coffee.

Soon we were sitting at the table munching on crispy Bombay toast and deciding what we'd do that day.

"You know, while I was watching you sleep, I realized you've never really told me a lot about your family," I said.

He shrugged. "What do you want to know?" he said between bites.

"What're they like?"

He took a sip of his coffee. "Hmm, I guess I'm closest to Mom. She's super protective of me, but that's because I'm an only child and she thinks everyone is out to get me."

"And your dad?" My coffee had grown cold, so I just swirled it around.

"Dad's always been all about work and his business, so I never saw him much as a kid," he said. "He was away a lot . . . I guess I never grew really close to him."

"Do you think he'll want you to take over the business when you're done with college?"

"That's always been the plan. I'm applying to Wharton. That's where Dad went too."

"So your future's all set out for you, huh?" I said. "Does that ever bother you?"

He looked at me in surprise. "No, not at all. Why would it bother me?"

"I don't know. What if you wanted something different?"

"Like what?" He looked genuinely confused. "My dad took over from his father, and I'm going to take over from him. It's tradition. There's no one else, so if I don't do it, who will?"

"That's true." I played with the edge of the tablecloth. "I guess it would be hard for me if I didn't have choices."

"Like what? What do you want to do after college?"

"I've always wanted to travel around the world and live in different places. I've been thinking, maybe I'll go study international relations and join the Foreign Service."

"That sounds so exciting," Suresh said, getting up and carrying our plates to the sink. "One of my older cousins is a diplomat, and she moves to a different country every four years or so. She says she loves really being able to immerse herself in a different culture."

"Yes, that's exactly what I've always wanted to do. I mean, there's a lot I still want to see here over the next few years, but there are so many other places I want to explore."

We finished washing and drying our dishes and cleaned up the mess we made on the kitchen counter.

"Do you mind if I jump in the shower real quick?" he said. "Or did you want to go first?"

"No, you go ahead. I can wait."

"I promise I won't be long," he said, giving me a quick peck on the lips.

We walked up to his room together, and I hung out there while he went to shower.

I looked around, really seeing it for the first time, since I'd been otherwise distracted the previous night. The walls were painted a generic off-white and were pretty bare. But on his bedside stand was a framed family photo. I picked it up to get a closer look. His mother was seated while Suresh and his dad stood on either side of her. There was something very imposing about her, the smile not quite reaching her eyes, while Suresh and his dad had identical wide smiles, their eyes crinkling at the corners. It looked like it was taken in their living room, and from the impressive furniture and the massive double staircase behind them, it looked like they were a wealthy family. I wondered what they would say if they knew about me. Would Suresh tell them? After what we'd done, I couldn't help but wonder if he would.

The way I'd been raised, I always assumed that I would only have sex with the man I was going to marry. While I never judged the few friends back home who'd already had sex, I could never get my mother's teachings out of my head when it came to my own choices. I wasn't a prude, but it was just the way I'd always felt about this kind of intimacy.

For a brief moment, the warning thoughts I'd banished earlier returned, but then Suresh came back into the room and I quickly forgot all about them.

I went to take a shower and changed into fresh clothes. When I came out, he was sitting at his computer, typing something. As soon as he heard me come in, he stood and walked over to put his arms around me.

"What should we do now?" he asked, dropping a kiss on my neck.

"We could go for a drive," I suggested.

We drove around the streets of Normal for a while, but then we decided to go down to Miller Park in Bloomington. It was a winter wonderland, the water in the lily pond reflecting the snow on the trees. It was beautiful and serene as we stepped out into the cold day and held each other tight. I didn't know

why, but I had a desperate urge to hold on to this moment forever. Maybe it was because of our conversation earlier or
because deep down I knew it wasn't something that could last
forever.

I just wanted us to stay like that, with nothing in the world
coming between us.

CHAPTER FIFTEEN

"Suresh, is everything okay?" I asked as I walked into his room a couple weeks later. He was hunched over his computer, his face serious.

"It's my dad," he said. "He's not doing so well. Mom just emailed."

"I'm so sorry," I said quickly.

He looked devastated. "I don't think she would've told me if it wasn't serious. He has some heart issues, but it's always been kept under control."

"What're you gonna do? Do you think you should fly back home?"

"I think I should," he said. "I mean, if nothing else, at least it'll make Mom feel better if we're all together."

Since he was an only child, I could only imagine how much it would mean to his mom to have him there.

"Is there anything I can do to help?" I asked.

I wanted to be supportive, but I'd be lying if I said there wasn't a tiny part of me that was a little apprehensive at the thought of him leaving. What if he didn't come back? I hated myself immediately for even thinking that at a time like this. Of course he'd come back. After everything we'd shared, he wouldn't just abandon me. I believed him when he told me how he felt about me because I could see it in his eyes.

"I'm just glad you're here with me," he said, turning in his chair to put his arms around me. He buried his head in my stomach, and I stroked his hair gently.

"It's going to be fine," I reassured him. "Once you're there, I'm sure your dad will feel better too."

"I hope so. I'm going to call Uncle Paul so he can book a flight for me."

"I can help you pack if you like," I offered.

He stood and kissed the top of my head. "That would be great."

It didn't take long to grab a few shirts, jeans, and some other items, so we were done packing by the time Uncle Paul called to say he'd booked Suresh on a flight the day after next. I made turkey-cheese-and-tomato sandwiches for the two of us and we sat down to eat, but I could tell that Suresh's mind was somewhere else. I didn't blame him at all. If it had been me, I was sure I would have been a complete wreck. He seemed to be holding it together pretty well, even though I was sure he was more worried than he was telling me.

"When will you call your mom?" I said.

He checked his watch. "Probably around eight or so tonight. But I should email my teachers and let them know."

He went off to his room while I plopped on the couch and turned on the TV. Luckily Uncle Paul was cool with our relationship, mostly because he didn't know the extent of it. I'd been spending so much time here that Suresh had started recording episodes of *Charmed* for me. I turned one on now, but my head was too full of thoughts tumbling around, and when Suresh came back and joined me on the couch, we just snuggled together and watched. Once again, I had a feeling this might be the last time we were together like this for a while and I wanted to savor every second for as long as I could.

● ● ●

A day and a half later, we were at Uptown Station dropping off Suresh. Uncle Paul wasn't able to drive him to O'Hare because of work, so Suresh was taking a charter bus there to catch his flight to Mumbai.

Uncle Paul stepped away to take a phone call while Suresh and I said goodbye.

"It's going to be fine," I said, putting my arms around him and holding him tight. In this moment, I didn't even care if anyone saw us and reported back to Salma Aunty and Hafeez Uncle.

"I'll miss you so much," he said. "I'll call as soon as I get there, I promise."

"I'll miss you too." My eyes started to well up, but I didn't want him to see me cry, so I blinked back the tears.

"Hey," he said softly, cupping my face in his hands. "I'll be back before you know it."

"I'm fine," I said. "Don't worry about me. Just go be with your dad."

He nodded. "It'll be good to see my parents again," he said. "It's been a while."

"I'll talk to you soon, okay?" I gave him a quick peck on the cheek, too self-conscious to do anything else with Uncle Paul standing just a few feet away.

"I love you," he said as Uncle Paul walked toward us. They said their goodbyes too, and then Uncle Paul dropped me off at home. Thankfully, Salma Aunty and Hafeez Uncle were both out, and no one would question why a strange Indian man was dropping me off in the middle of the day.

School was closed for winter break, and since I had the whole house to myself, I could at least cry as loudly as I wanted and eat chocolates in front of the TV. I already missed Suresh so much I didn't know how I was going to make it until he came back. Natasha was vacationing in Mexico with her family, so I didn't have anyone to turn to. When Salma Aunty and Hafeez Uncle came home, I pretended to have a headache because I really didn't have it in me to sit through dinner and act as though everything was all right. Instead, I tossed and turned for hours before finally crying myself to sleep.

CHAPTER SIXTEEN

I was late.

Suresh had left for India a week and a half ago, and I'd been so busy missing him, I hadn't realized that my period was four days late. Normally that wouldn't have surprised me, but this seemed different. I felt different. Suresh had called as soon as he'd reached home to tell me that it would be hard getting hold of him for the next little while. His dad had taken a turn for the worse, and there was a lot going on with the business that he would have to help out with. His mom was in bad shape emotionally, and he needed to be there for her.

"I love you. You know that, right?" he'd said the last time I talked to him. He spoke in a low voice, so I assumed that he wasn't alone. "I'll text you with my new cell number when I switch out my SIM card."

"I'm sorry about your dad," I'd said. I could hear voices in the background. "I love you too." There was static on the line, and then the call was disconnected. I wasn't sure he'd even heard my last words.

Now I was sitting on my bed, an incessant pounding in my

head as I considered the implications. Could I really be pregnant? We'd always been very careful the few times we'd had sex, so how . . . ? I knew how, but I didn't want it to be true. I didn't know why, but something told me this wasn't just my period being erratic as usual, and now I couldn't get hold of Suresh to tell him. I decided to email him, hoping that he'd check his inbox and call me right away. I finally fell into an uneasy sleep plagued by dark thoughts about Suresh.

When I woke up feeling sick, I knew with certainty that it was true.

The next day, I popped into the pharmacy on my way home and bought a pregnancy test. I came home and checked my email as soon as I got to my room. There was an email from Suresh. His dad's condition had worsened, and he had a lot to deal with, but he would try to call as soon as he could. I quickly emailed him back telling him how sorry I was about his father and not to worry about me. There was no way I could tell him anything now, but by the next morning, I knew I couldn't wait any longer. I had to take the test. If nothing else, at least I'd know for sure.

I'd have to face reality.

CHAPTER SEVENTEEN

January 2001

I stand in front of the walk-in clinic, my stomach just one big knot, contemplating whether I should go in or stay in my bubble of delusion just a little bit longer. Natasha squeezes my hand, and I turn to her.

"I don't know if I can do this," I say, the lump in my throat making it hard to speak.

"It's going to be all right," Natasha replies. I know she's being supportive, but nothing about this is going to be all right. But I'm not ready to face that irrevocable truth yet.

"Can we get some ice cream first?"

Natasha nods. "Of course. Let's go to the food court. Wanna split a banana split?"

Her attempt at levity reminds me that I'm grateful for her friendship. I smile weakly at her as we walk across the mall to the Dairy Queen on the other side.

A few minutes later, we're digging in, my worries temporarily frozen by the sweet coldness. But they push their way through soon enough as the nausea makes me run to the nearest washroom. When I come out of the stall, Natasha is standing right outside. She's abandoned our barely eaten ice cream, which is good because right now even the thought of it is making me feel sick again. We walk back to the clinic in silence. There's no more avoiding the inevitable. I have to face my dilemma head-on. A small part of me wishes that the doctor will say my pregnancy test is negative and that store-bought test kits are known to be inaccurate. I hold on to this thought as I make my way inside and sign in. I got cash from the ATM because I can't have my aunt and uncle knowing why I'm here.

Natasha holds my hand while we wait. My throat is raw from throwing up and having to pretend that I'm fine at home. It's been a week since I took the test at home. A week of crying and praying and beating myself up for being so stupid. When did I become the poster child for bad decisions? Why did I trust Suresh to be careful enough for the both of us? We used condoms, but I also wasn't paying attention to them after we were done, so if something had gone wrong, how would I have known? I wish desperately that I'd listened to the nagging voice in the back of my head the whole time Suresh and I were together, the one saying, *Be careful.* I'd *been* very careful . . . except for the times when I was so free of worry that I simply forgot.

"Ayesha Hameed?" The door that leads to the inner office opens, and a young woman in scrubs scans the waiting room. I get up and wordlessly follow her down the hall to an exam room.

"Can you confirm your name and date of birth, please?" she asks. Her name tag says *Jessica.* She's brunette, short, and has the kind of warm smile that would normally put me completely at ease. But not today. Today I'm barely suppressing the urge to scream, and I have to force myself to answer her.

"Ayesha Hameed, January 3, 1983."

"And your family doctor?"

I don't answer immediately, and she looks up from her form.

"I don't have one."

"Insurance?" she asks.

I can't look her in the eye. "I'll be paying cash."

She scribbles something on her form before looking up at me again.

"And what are we seeing you for today?"

"I'd like to get a pregnancy test, please."

She looks up at me, and I can't tell if she's surprised or disappointed or concerned. I don't know why it matters.

"It won't be long now," she says with a gentle smile. "The doctor should be with you soon."

After she leaves the room, I lean back in the chair and press the back of my head against the wall. I close my eyes, and my mother's face flashes before me.

"What did you do, beta?" she says, her eyes filled with disappointment. "How could you shame us like this?"

I open my eyes and her face disappears, but her voice echoes in my ears. My head throbs, and I fight the urge to get up and run out of here, away from the consequences of my actions, from the knowledge that they will devastate my loved ones. I don't know how I will ever face them again. I don't know if they will ever want me to.

The doctor comes in and asks me about my last period, a bunch of questions about my health in general, any family history of diseases, and I rattle my answers off one by one. I have a huge family back home in India and I surprise myself with how much information I've gathered from years of gossip over chai and at numerous gatherings. It's not something I ever thought I needed to know while I was here alone. Of course, I imagined myself pregnant one day, but it was always with Ammi by my side, beaming with pride and joy at the prospect of becoming a nani, ushering me into motherhood. It was never supposed to be like this.

I pee into the small container I'm handed and then return to the exam room to await the result. My palms are sweaty, and the knot in my stomach has grown into the size of what feels like a bowling ball. I think about Suresh and what he must be doing right now. Does he even think about me anymore? Or were the past couple of months just a casual fling? How could someone pretend to be so sincere and genuine? Was I that bad a judge of character?

The doctor comes back in and confirms what I already know: I'm nine weeks pregnant, which means it happened on that Thanksgiving weekend. The doctor asks if I have any questions. I do, but none that he can answer. He leaves, and the nurse returns with some pamphlets about places and options for me. I take them and walk back out to where Natasha's waiting.

"What did the doctor say?" Her concern for me has wiped away her usually cheerful demeanor. I feel guilty and responsible.

"I'm nine weeks pregnant," I say softly.

"But you said you guys only did it a few times," she whispers. "And you said he used a condom."

I don't know what to tell her. I've become a statistic, a case study on why there are warnings on condom boxes. I have an irresistible urge to laugh, but that would be melodramatic, and I don't have the energy for that.

It's like I've become someone else. I used to be someone who trusted her instincts, who was head over heels in love with a boy who made her feel whole again. But how can I be like that now? I don't want to go back to my aunt and uncle's place because I don't think I can pretend that everything's normal. I have a lot of decisions to make.

"Do you mind dropping me off at the park?" I ask Natasha.

"Of course," she says. "Is there anything I can do? I can call in sick for my shift and stay with you."

I can tell that she's really worried about me, and I love her for it, which makes it all that much harder to say no.

"Thanks, Natasha, but I think I have to figure this one out on my own. I just need to sort it out in my head." I put my arms around her and squeeze tightly.

"Whatever you need," she says, returning my hug. "But promise you'll call if you want to talk or anything?"

"I promise," I say. "And, Natasha . . . thanks for being here."

She smiles at me as we start to walk out to the parking lot. I really don't know how I could ever get through this without her. But I also know there's only so much of the burden I can pass along.

• • •

I have a huge knot in my stomach as the phone rings thousands of miles away on the other side of the world. It's early evening for Suresh according to my calculations, and my heart is beating loudly in my chest as I wait for him to pick up. Part of me hopes that he'll come back as soon as he hears, to be by my side, but there's another more practical side of me that knows it's a lot more complicated than that.

"Hello?" The sound of his voice brings tears of relief to my eyes. It's as if we're connecting after a very long time even though it's only been a few weeks. Distance has a funny way of warping time.

"Suresh," I say, my voice hoarse with emotion and the effort to keep from crying. "I'm so happy you picked up."

"I'm so sorry I haven't called you back. It's been just—"

"No, it's okay, I understand. It must be so hard for you right now." I'm trying to work up the nerve to tell him the news, feeling guilty to burden him further at such a bad time.

"It's been rough," he says. "Dad's gotten worse and Mom has completely fallen apart and the business . . . it's just a lot to deal with."

"Suresh . . . there's something I have to tell you," I say.

"What is it?" he says, his voice full of concern. "Are you okay?"

"Kind of," I say hesitantly. "Look, I'm just going to say it, and we'll figure this out together."

"Okay, I'm freaking out a little here," he says. "What's going on?"

"I'm pregnant."

Suddenly it's like a weight has been lifted off me. Just telling him reminds me that I'm not alone in this. We'll figure it out together. It's going to be all right.

"Oh my god," he says after an unbearable silence. "Are you sure?"

"Pretty sure," I say. "I went to a clinic and got a test."

"When did it happen?" He sounds shaken, and I wish he was standing in front of me right now. "We were always so careful."

"Well, it happened," I say.

"Thanksgiving weekend?"

"Yup."

We don't say anything for a while. I understand his silence because I've had a little longer to get used to the news than he has. Of course he needs a little time to let it sink in.

"Suresh." A voice calls him in the background. It's a woman's voice, and I assume it's his mother. "Suresh!" It sounds more urgent now.

"Ayesha, I'm so sorry," he says. "I have to go deal with this. But I promise I'll call as soon as I can. I love you."

"Okay . . . well, take care. I love you too." I don't know what else to say. We have a lot to talk about, but this is a very stressful time for him, so I try to stay calm even though on the inside I'm feeling anything but.

I wonder what he's thinking. I'm sure it must have come as a shock, but I'm hoping that once he's come to terms with it, we'll be able to figure out what the next steps are going to be.

There are a lot of things to consider. First and foremost, I don't want him to feel like he has to propose to me or something, but at the same time, I want him to want it. If he does, I'll be able to tell my parents. Not that this will make things any easier, but at least I can tell them. If we got married quickly, then there's no reason for them to even know that I got pregnant before. But when I do the calculations in my head, I realize that it's going to be a stretch to convince anyone of that. But babies are born early all the time, and maybe there is a way.

● ● ●

For the next few hours, I walk around in a daze as I imagine what things will be like if he comes back and we get married. I start to get used to the idea even though there's a little voice in the back of my head that keeps trying to remind me to keep my head on straight. I try my best to ignore that voice, and for the most part, I succeed.

The phone rings.

"Hey, you," I say, a little out of breath after running out from the bathroom. If it's afternoon for me, it must be early in the morning for him.

"Hey," he says, and from his tone, I fear that my bubble is about to burst.

"How is everything over there?" I ask.

"It's . . . Listen, we need to talk. I've been thinking about what you said."

"Good. Me too."

"You know how much I love you, but . . . with everything going on, I just don't know . . ." His voice trails off.

"What do you mean?"

He doesn't answer me right away, but I can hear him breathing and suddenly I remember the first time we spent the night together and the way it felt to wake up in his arms, listening to him breathe.

"I think you should have an abortion," he says. "I don't know what else there is to do."

I don't say anything because I can't form the words that I want to scream.

"Ayesha?" His voice is so full of concern, and I know this is hard for him to say. But it's even harder for me to hear, and right now I hate him for making me feel this way.

"Ayesha, I wish there was another way," he says. "But we're too young. We're not ready for this. At all. You need to go to university and have the future you've been working so hard for. And with everything going on over here, I don't even know if I can come back this semester. I can't leave my parents like this, and my dad's business . . . everything's a mess, and I have to help them take care of things. I can't tell you how much I hate this. I want to be there with you. But my dad—I don't think he's going to make it, Ayesha. And I can't leave my mother when that's hanging over us."

His words are like cold, hard stones pelting me with pain and disappointment. I feel as if I'm not even in my own body anymore. It's like I'm watching myself hearing his words and a vise is closing around my heart as what he's saying sinks in. Really sinks in. He has to be there for his family, and clearly in his heart I'm not that. When had I convinced myself that we were family? Was it when I fell in love with him or when I gave all of myself to him for the first time? Or was it when I knew that there was a life growing inside me that was a symbol of our love for each other? I can't tell anymore because somehow all those moments have fused into one big reminder of how stupid I was, thinking that dreams actually come true and that, when you love someone, they'll always be there for you.

"Ayesha?" he says. "Say something."

"I'm here," I say, almost in a whisper.

"So, you understand, right?"

"Sure. I understand," I say. "I'll take care of things, don't worry. I have to go now."

I hang up and run to the bathroom to throw up.

CHAPTER EIGHTEEN

The reality of my situation is starting to take over, and it's not pretty. I have to accept the fact that I'm all alone in this. Suresh calls a few times over the next few hours, and then a few more times over the next few days, but I don't want to talk to him. I just don't see the point since he's made it perfectly clear that he's not interested and that he might not even be coming back. So, if I'm on my own, I'll do this my way. It'll be my decision and mine alone.

I walk to the bus stop after my shift at work and wait in the blistering cold to catch the bus back to Bloomington. By the time I get home, Salma Aunty and Hafeez Uncle are in the kitchen getting dinner ready.

"Where have you been, Ayesha?" Salma Aunty says. "I tried calling a few times, and I was starting to get worried."

"I'm sorry, Aunty. I was just working."

"Did something happen there? You look upset."

"No, I'm fine." The lies come easily now, and although I still feel a little guilty every time, I can't exactly tell her the truth. I mean, what would I even say? I'm sorry, I just found out I'm pregnant, but my boyfriend doesn't want me to have the baby and now I don't know what to do?

Instead, I begin peeling the potatoes and Hafeez Uncle turns on the TV, so our attention is drawn to the screen, where two family members are screaming at each other and the host is trying not to lose control.

As I finish with the potatoes and get started on the carrots, I can't help thinking about where my life is going to go from here. What am I supposed to do? I have five months to go before I graduate, a little over seven months before this baby is born. Eventually I'm going to start showing, and then everyone here and back at home will know. I cannot let that happen. I'll have to make a decision soon.

After dinner, I go up to my room and pull out the brochure the nurse at the clinic gave me.

It's from Planned Parenthood, and it tells me I have many options: parenting, adoption, abortion. There isn't one on what to do if your family can't find out that you're pregnant because it would destroy them. It talks about all the people and places you can turn to for support during this time. But none of that applies to me. I have to figure this out on my own.

Natasha has been diligently calling me every night to check up on me before bed, even though we see each other at school every day. I'm grateful because she's the only person I can trust with the truth. Tonight she offers to come with me if I want to make an appointment at Planned Parenthood. That seems to be my best option right now, and I feel a little bit better knowing that I won't be alone. I decide to call them in the morning so that I can at least begin to make a plan.

● ● ●

The stark lighting of the Planned Parenthood center does nothing to ease my nerves. Natasha sits with me as I wait for Carol Shephard, the counselor with whom I have an appointment. She comes out to walk us into her office. Ms. Shephard looks like she's in her forties, with dark-rimmed glasses on a round face. She has kind eyes, and I feel a little more at ease.

"So, Ayesha, why don't you tell me about your situation in detail, and we can go from there." She gives me an encouraging smile. "You can call me Carol. And remember, whatever you tell me here is completely confidential."

I take a deep breath and sit up a little straighter.

"Thank you, Carol." I hesitate and turn to look at Natasha. She smiles, glad to be here with me.

"So, I'm about nine weeks pregnant. My family can't find out, and the father is no longer in the picture. What are my options?"

There it is. My current life in a nutshell. It seems so simple to blurt it all out, but it's so much more complicated. For right now, though, this is all the information that's relevant.

"Well, Ayesha, I think you've come to the right place," Carol says. "I want to tell you, first of all, that we're only here to provide you with options. We will not push you in any direction, and we can't make the decision for you."

"I understand," I say.

She tells me about the same options that were in the brochure: I can raise the baby myself, place it for adoption, or have an abortion.

"Do you have any questions?" she asks after explaining the options.

"When will I start showing?" My biggest concern is time. I need to figure out something before other people begin to suspect.

"Well, typically between sixteen to twenty weeks, but it can vary. Your ob-gyn should be able to give you a more accurate answer after an examination."

I breathe a small sigh of relief. This means I have a little time.

Natasha clears her throat. "Does she have to get permission from her parents to proceed?"

I throw her a grateful smile.

"Actually, since you're already eighteen, you don't," Carol replies.

I don't even want to think about what would have happened if my birthday wasn't in January. I guess I should consider myself lucky.

Carol tells me more about each option and asks me if I have any questions. I know I should have plenty, but my mind right now feels blank, wiped out.

Carol hands me some other brochures and says, "I'm sure you'll have more questions after you've had some time to think about everything."

"Thank you." There doesn't seem to be anything else left to say for now, so we leave and go to Natasha's house.

Once we get there, we head straight for her bedroom. She brings me some ginger ale and crackers, and we spread the brochures all over her bed. I think back to my conversation with Suresh and pick up the one about abortion, but I'm overwhelmed by panic. The nausea isn't helping, and I lie back on Natasha's bed with a huge sigh.

"This is all a lot to take in, isn't it?" Natasha says. "Why don't we go through all of them together and make a pros and cons list?"

I sit up. "I don't even know where to begin," I say, skimming a pamphlet about childbirth. "Oh my god, Natasha, look at this."

Natasha takes it from me. "Ew, that looks really painful."

I feel like throwing up again, but I'm too tired to get up.

"How am I supposed to do this by myself?" I say. "I always thought my mom would be with me when the time came."

"I'll be there with you," Natasha says softly. "I'll help you however I can."

I lean against her, and she strokes my hair gently. This is not how I ever pictured going through this part of my life. I don't know if I have it in me to go through with this alone, without my mother, my family to support me.

"It's too hard, Natasha," I say. "I don't think I can do this."

"Well, let's look at some more of these," Natasha says, picking up a couple of the pamphlets.

"No, I just can't. I mean, where am I even going to live for the next seven months? And what about after the baby comes? How am I supposed to pay for all this?" My heart is beating really fast, and I feel dizzy.

Natasha gently touches my forehead and then my cheeks. "Ayesha, you don't look so good," she says, getting off the bed. "Here, why don't you lie down for a bit. I'm going to go get my mom."

She starts to walk away, but I grab her by the arm.

"No, please, don't tell your mom," I say. "She'll tell my aunt, and I can't let that happen."

"I'll tell her not to," Natasha insists. "I'm just really scared. What if something happens to you? You look really pale."

I pull her back onto the bed. "Nothing's going to happen— this is all just too much. Please. Don't tell your mom. If my aunt finds out, then that's it."

"I'm not sure about this," Natasha says, still hovering.

"I think I have to get an abortion," I blurt out.

Natasha sinks slowly onto her bed. "Are you sure?"

"I'm not sure of anything right now. But I know I can't care for this baby. I can't go through this without a place to stay, or any money, and somehow without anyone back home finding out."

"What about adoption?" Natasha asks.

"I thought about that too," I reply. "But where will I stay until the baby's born? And how will I hide it from everyone?"

"Maybe you should talk to the Planned Parenthood lady again before you decide anything for sure."

"I'm going to," I say. "I'll call her first thing tomorrow. For now, I think I need to go home and rest."

"I'll drop you off." Natasha gathers all the pamphlets and shoves them into her desk drawer. "Can't risk your aunt seeing these on you."

"Thanks, Nats." I give her hand a squeeze, and we leave the room. As we step out into the cold, snowy afternoon, I can't help wondering if my life will ever be the same again.

CHAPTER NINETEEN

I call Suresh on his cell phone again when I get home. The last few times, I let it ring about twenty times before hanging up. I'm not really hopeful that there will be an answer this time either—after his calls to me stopped, I decided to call him but got the same result. Still, I have to try. I'm about to hang up when he answers.

"Suresh? Oh, thank god you picked up," I say, letting out a huge breath of relief. But there's only silence on the other end. "Suresh? It's me."

"Who is this?" It's a woman's voice, stern and cold. I panic and hang up. It has to be his mother. Maybe he left his phone lying around and she saw the call. I'll have to wait and try again later.

I remember the family photo in Suresh's room. The voice matched the stern countenance of the woman in that picture. We never talked about whether he had told his family about me, but I highly doubt that he did.

● ● ●

The next morning, I wake up with resolve. I've made my

decision. I'd planned to call Carol at Planned Parenthood today to discuss adoption, but the more I thought about it while I tossed and turned in bed last night, the more I realized that it was too complicated and risky. I have no idea where I'll live and how I'll continue to go to school here while I'm waiting to give birth without my family finding out. It's safer to get an abortion. I have to put all this behind me and move on with my life. This is the only way. I'm going to try to talk to Suresh one more time to see if he's had a change of heart, and then I'm going ahead with my plan.

The same voice answers again.

"Who are you? Why are you calling this number?" she asks before I have a chance to hang up. I'm tempted to say something, but panic wins again and I disconnect the call.

• • •

A week later, I walk into BroMenn Women's Center at eight in the morning with Natasha by my side. I'm clutching her hand as tightly as I can, fighting the urge to turn around and run away, as far as I can. But I know this is the right thing to do. There's really no other option. I can't go through a pregnancy all alone, and I can't tell anyone. I can't even think of what would happen if my family ever found out. I'm doing the sensible thing. I tried to call Suresh a few more times and sent more emails, but ultimately, I had to face the facts. He isn't coming, and I have to do what is best for me and my future.

We sit in the waiting room until my name is called.

"Ayesha, I'm going to take you to see a counselor," the nurse says. "And when you're done, just come back out and wait here."

I walk in through a set of glass doors and into an office to the right. *Dr. Katherine Wagner* the sign announces. She's sitting behind her desk but stands up when I walk into the room and comes around, pointing to a couple of chairs.

"Hello, Ayesha, I'm Dr. Wagner. How are you feeling today?"

I nod. "I'm okay, I guess."

"I understand this must be quite difficult for you," Dr. Wagner says. "I just thought we could talk for a little bit and make sure you don't have any questions."

I don't know what to say, so I don't say anything.

"Do you have anyone with you, someone to take you home? You're going to need some TLC after the procedure," she says with a gentle smile. "You should have been given some information on that."

"I have my friend," I say quietly. "She's waiting for me outside."

Dr. Wagner nods. "I'm glad you're not alone. Is there anything you'd like to talk about?"

I shake my head.

"I just want to make sure that you've thought this through and that you're sure about your decision." She smiles at me and there's a kindness in her eyes and I can't help wondering how many times she's had to say this.

"I don't really have a choice," I say.

"And you've come to this decision completely by yourself?"

"Yes."

"Do you have any questions about how you might feel afterward?"

"I think I'll be all right," I say. I don't have any idea about how I'll feel, but I can't bring myself to talk to a complete stranger about my feelings right now.

"I just want to make sure that you're prepared and that you have someone to talk to," Dr. Wagner says. She hands me a card. "This has my direct number. You can call me anytime, day or night, if you need to talk."

"Thank you," I say. I look down at my hands in my lap. I feel disconnected from my body, and it's a strange sensation. It's like this is all happening to someone else.

"You can go and wait outside now, and someone will be by shortly to take you to see the doctor." Dr. Wagner smiles warmly at me as she ushers me out of the room.

I don't have to wait long before the same nurse comes back for me. She walks me into a room with an examining table, some medical equipment, and a single chair. I change out of my clothes into a paper gown and lie down on the table. My hands are sweaty, and my mouth is dry. Suresh's face flashes in front of my eyes, and my heart begins to race. What if he didn't get all my messages? Or maybe he just got them and is flying back to be with me. Will he regret suggesting that I get an abortion? Later on, will he still think we were too young to handle a baby? I stare at the door, willing it to be flung open and to see Suresh standing there, rushing to hold me in his arms and take me away from here. Far away.

Something doesn't feel right. It's not just this whole situation; it's much more than that. I believe that a woman should have total control over her body and that hasn't changed, so I know it's not the idea of having an abortion that feels wrong. I just can't shake the feeling that this is not the right decision for me. What if I'm making a huge mistake? There's no coming back from this once I go through with it. What if this future baby is meant to be in my life? Maybe I'm stronger than I'm giving myself credit for.

I sit up, my entire body trembling, my eyes full of tears. I can't do this. I know nothing has changed, but I just can't do this. There has to be another way. Maybe I don't need Suresh. Or anybody. A very small part of me thinks that maybe he'll come back and everything will work out. But that's not what I'm going to focus on. Right now, I have to listen to my heart, and my heart is telling me not to go through with this.

I put my clothes back on and leave the room. Natasha is sitting in the same spot where I left her. She stands as soon as she sees me.

"Ayesha, what happened? Are you okay?" Her dark eyes are full of concern, and she puts her arms around me. I fall into them, my body racked with sobs.

Some of the other people in the waiting room turn to look at us but quickly look away. I don't imagine this is something unusual.

"I can't do it," I say, stepping back to look at her. "Can we go home, please?"

"Yes, of course," she says quickly. "Just wait here, and I'll bring the car around."

"No, I'm fine. I'm coming with you." I need to get out of here, out into the fresh air and sunlight. I step out and take a deep breath. The trembling subsides, and we walk in silence to Natasha's car.

"Can we just stand here for a bit?" I need to clear my head and sitting in the car makes me nauseous.

"Of course," she says. "Are you sure you're okay?"

"I think so," I say, taking another deep breath of air.

"Do you want to talk about what happened in there?"

"Honestly, I'm not sure. One minute, I was lying there waiting for the doctor to come in, and the next thing, I had this strong urge to get out of there."

"What do you mean?"

"It just felt wrong. Like I'd be doing something really wrong if I stayed there any longer."

"Like morally wrong?" Natasha looks a little surprised.

In all our conversations about pregnancy, I've always been very clear that I absolutely support a woman's right to choose. "That's not it at all," I say. "I just mean it doesn't feel like the right thing to do for *me*. Not that getting an abortion is wrong if that's what a woman chooses to do. I could *never* think that."

"Okay, I'm sorry," she says. "I guess I'm just a little confused about everything. But do you know what you're going to do now?"

"I have no idea." I look at her and smile for the first time in days. "Are you sure you're still along for this ride?"

She smiles back and loops her arm in mine. "Always. Can we please get some food now? I'm starving."

CHAPTER TWENTY

I feel lighter somehow, spending the whole day with Natasha and just eating whatever we want. When we get tired, we pop into a movie theater and watch *Save the Last Dance*. Luckily, Salma Aunty and Hafeez Uncle are in Chicago for an event and won't be back until much later so we can stay out as long as we want. But around ten o'clock, I'm exhausted, and Natasha drives me home. I trudge up the stairs and barely manage to brush my teeth and change into pajamas before dropping into bed. I fall asleep immediately.

Unfortunately, the next morning, reality smacks me squarely in the face as I realize that I still have a situation that needs to be dealt with. If I'm going to keep this baby, I need to figure out finances, a place to stay, and how I'm going to stop this from ever reaching my parents. And what will happen after I give birth? Am I going to hide myself and my child for the rest of my life? How am I going to explain this to my family? Yesterday, walking out of that clinic had felt like an act of courage, but now I'm beginning to wonder if it really was. Maybe I'm simply suffering from delusions. This isn't miraculously just going to work out. It's not a Bollywood movie; it's my life. My very real, messed-up life. I still think not having the abortion is the right move for me. The question is: Am I meant to be a parent right now? Or is it best for the baby for me to find the right people to be the best parents? My heart is telling me that I want to raise this baby myself, to be the best mother I can be. But my head tells me that this is not possible. I haven't even graduated high school, I have no support system, at least none that I can turn to, so how can I begin to care for a baby? How will I manage college, work, and a baby all by myself? In my gut, I know the answer.

The next day, I'm back in Carol Shephard's office, tears rolling down my face.

"Ayesha, it's going to be okay," she says, holding out a box of tissues. "You still have other options."

"I don't know what to do," I say. "When I was on that table at the clinic, I just knew I couldn't go through with it. But now I don't think I can handle all this by myself."

Carol looks at me thoughtfully for a minute. "Would you consider adoption?"

"I've thought about it. But I can't live with my relatives and go to school here while I'm pregnant. How would it even work?" I ask.

"Well, first of all, you would work with an adoption agency that would help you with every step. We can help you find one if that's the path you want to take. They have counselors who have experience with situations such as yours. They will guide you in drawing up an adoption plan that is best for you and your baby. You would consider prospective parents," she says, "and then once you've narrowed down your choices, you can meet them and talk about all your concerns, if you wish.

Or if you don't want to ever directly meet them, the agency can give you all the information you need to make a decision."

"What about the cost? I don't know if I can afford to pay without making my family suspicious."

"There's no cost," Carol assures me. "In fact, often the prospective parent will cover the cost of prenatal care."

"But how do I even know if it's the right choice? Last week, I thought getting an abortion was the right thing to do. But then I just couldn't go through with it."

Carol comes around her desk to sit on the chair beside mine.

"This is a tough decision for anyone." She smiles gently at me. "It's not a bad thing to be unsure. That way you know you'll consider everything carefully. You have to think about how you'll feel knowing someone else will be raising your child. It's not going to be easy, and you have to be sure it's the right thing for you. You just take your time and not let anyone pressure you."

That's easier said than done. I don't really have too much time on my hands. I thank her and leave. I spend the next few days thinking about everything, about my choices and how much I'll really be able to handle. This isn't something I can share with Natasha or anyone else. It has to be my decision alone. After going around in endless circles in my head, I call Carol and tell her what I've decided.

I will have the baby and then place it for adoption with a couple that will cherish my baby and provide a loving home. Somehow, I'll have to find the strength in me to do that. Even if it might be the hardest thing I've ever done. But there's still the matter of where I'll stay and how I'll keep it a secret from everyone who loves me.

• • •

A couple of weeks later, I've spoken with a counselor at an adoption agency and apprised them of my situation. Luckily, since I'm eighteen, there's been no issue of permission from a guardian or anything like that. But because this is a time-sensitive matter, they said they would find some prospective parents as soon as possible. They would try to match me up with a couple who'd be willing to take on all the expenses associated with my pregnancy as well as help me with my living situation. If that actually happens, then I can come up with some story for Salma Aunty and Hafeez Uncle to explain why I'll be moving. Even though I'm a little afraid to get my hopes up, this is the first time in weeks that I think there might be a way out of this dark hole I've dug myself into. If I can just stay safe and healthy throughout the pregnancy and find the baby a good home, then I will find a way to go on. At least that's what I'm telling myself. It's all I can do for now.

I call Natasha to have our nightly talk. Now that I've made my decision, I want to tell her. She's been my rock through this whole ordeal, and she'll probably never know what she means to me.

"Hey, Ayesha. Is everything all right?" she asks as soon as she picks up.

"Yes, everything's fine," I say. "I've made a big decision."

"Do you want to come over to my place?"

"I'd love to." I don't really want to talk about all this with my aunt and uncle just downstairs.

"Okay, I'll be right there to pick you up," Natasha says.

I head down to the living room. Salma Aunty is grading tests again. I ask, "Is it okay if I go over to Natasha's house for a bit?"

"Sure, just let us know if you'll be home for dinner," she

answers before turning her attention back to the stack of papers in front of her. "Your uncle can pick you up on his way back. He's working late today."

"Okay, thank you," I say, putting on my coat. "I'll call you later."

Natasha's pulling up just as I open the door to step out into the frigid afternoon.

A few minutes later, we're on her bed with mugs of hot chocolate warming our hands.

"I've decided to place the baby for adoption."

If Natasha is shocked at my announcement, she does a really good job at hiding it.

"And how do you feel about that?" Natasha says.

"I don't know," I say slowly. "It's kind of weird. I know it's the right thing to do, but at the same time I'm really sad, you know?"

"Of course you're sad," she says. "But if you feel that it's the right thing to do, then it's the right thing to do." This is why I love Natasha so much. She always knows how to make me feel good about myself. I put my arms around her, and suddenly I'm sobbing all over her shirt.

"It's going to be okay," she says gently, stroking my hair. She grabs a box of tissues from her nightstand and hands me a bunch.

"Do you really think I'm making the right decision?" I ask.

"Honestly, I would be really worried if you decided to keep it and raise it yourself. I mean, don't get me wrong, I'll support you no matter what you decide, but it would be really tough for you and the baby. I think you're doing the right thing here."

"I really don't know what I'd do without you, Nats," I say,

before dissolving into tears again. "You've been so great to me."

"You're my best friend, Ayesha," she says. "I'm always going to be there for you."

"I wish there was something I could do for you," I say. "Lately it feels like it's always *The Ayesha Hameed Show*."

"Remember in November when Brian and I broke up?"

I nod. All that seems like it happened a lifetime ago.

"Well, if you hadn't pushed me to talk to Brian and really listen to him, we probably wouldn't be together now."

I take a deep, shaky breath. "Was that just three months ago?"

"It was. I know, it feels like forever."

"What did I do wrong, Nats?" My eyes well up. "Why hasn't he called? He said he loved me."

Natasha holds me in her arms as I cry until there are no more tears left.

"You didn't do anything wrong, Ayesha," she says. "He's the one who messed up."

"I don't ever want to speak to him again," I say, sitting up and wiping my face with the bunched-up tissues in my hand. "Even if he shows up, I don't want to see him."

Natasha doesn't say anything, instead pulling me closer into a tight hug.

"I'm so sorry, Ayesha," she says. "You don't deserve any of this."

We sit like this for a while, and then I know I have to shake this off, so I stand and put on a brave face.

"Who needs him anyway? We've got this, right, Nats?" I force a smile and my throat still feels tight, but I'm determined to make this work even though my heart is breaking into a thousand little pieces.

CHAPTER TWENTY-ONE

A week later, I'm on my way to meet Sarah Carlson, the counselor at the Adoption Center of Illinois with whom I've been chatting over the phone. Today I'm going in so she can give me some profiles of prospective families to look at. It's a sunny afternoon although the air is so cold it's hard to breathe without feeling that my lungs will freeze over. I get off the bus and walk over to the entrance of the adoption agency. There are a few people outside going about their normal lives, and it's so strange to watch them because I suddenly want nothing more than for mine to be just that. Normal. What's strange about it is that only a short time ago I was back home in Mumbai, wishing desperately that something exciting would happen, something enviable, something that would make me feel alive. That version of me doesn't exist anymore, or at least that's what it feels like. As if the Ayesha who had been so thrilled at the prospect of going to school here in the US and meeting exciting people and falling in love has just disappeared. So here I stand, at this juncture in my life where the next decision I make will change everything, not just for me, but also for my unborn child. Suddenly my legs are heavy, and I have to use all the strength I have just to put one foot in front of the other until I'm at the door. The doors swoosh apart, and it's a good thing because I'm not sure I have it in me to even open them. Then I'm standing in front of the reception and someone asks for Sarah Carlson and I realize it's my voice coming out of my mouth, but it sounds distant, as if someone far away is speaking.

A few minutes later, Sarah walks toward me and motions for me to take a seat in one of the chairs in her office. My focus returns, and I sit facing her across a table. I feel nothing, and it's scaring me. I notice that she's wearing a brooch, and it reminds me of one that Ammi always wears with her favorite green-and-black silk sari. The brooch is gold with pearls. As a little girl, I used to ask her to put it on me whenever I played dress-up. Suddenly it's as if my mother is in the chair right next to me, speaking to me in her soothing voice.

"You're doing the right thing, beta," she says, smiling at me, her beautiful brown eyes full of love. She takes my hand and squeezes it, and a warmth flows through me until I can feel again.

"Ayesha, I have some profiles here that I think you should look at," Sarah says, pointing to a stack on the table in the corner. "Feel free to take them home and go over them. And call me if you have any questions."

● ● ●

Later that day, Natasha and I are poring over scrapbooks and albums prepared by families looking to adopt. It's a strange feeling, going through the pages full of photographs and blurbs about their personal lives. One of these could be the family my baby will call its own. It makes me scrutinize every detail and read between the lines as I try to decide my baby's fate. What if I choose wrong and my child is unhappy? Will I even know? And if I do, what will I be able to do if I have no rights left? Sarah has told me to take my time and not rush to make a decision. But time is not a luxury I have and yet I cannot bring myself to pick.

• • •

A few days later, I call Sarah to tell her that I still haven't made a decision. She wants me to come in to look at more profiles.

"There's a couple who's going to be in town from Texas, and I think you might want to meet them in person while they're here," she says when I get to her office.

"Who are they?"

She hands me a folder.

"Here's some information about them. I should tell you that they're a lesbian couple, and since they cannot get legally married, only one of them can adopt your baby for now. But they have been together for seven years, and in my opinion, you should treat them just as you would any legally married couple."

I take the folder from her wordlessly and open it. The first thing I see is a picture of two white women, arms around each other, smiling into the camera. Until I came to Bloomington, I don't think I'd ever met a lesbian before. At least not any I knew about. In fact, I don't think any of my friends or family back home are friends with any lesbian or gay people. But I've heard the gossip and the whispered conversations and I've always wondered what it is about a person loving someone that bothers people so much. They would probably have the same problem with me, a Muslim girl, being in love with Suresh, a Hindu boy. I turn my attention back to the folder in my hands. I try to picture my baby with these two women, but my mind is a blank. I know I should be relieved that two complete strangers are hoping to become my baby's parents. The baby that I can't raise myself because my own family wouldn't understand. And the strange thing is that part of me is relieved that this couple isn't brown. Because now I won't have to worry about what they'll think of an eighteen-year-old Indian girl who got knocked up and doesn't have anywhere to go. Back home, they would wonder what kind of people my parents are, raising a girl who ended up pregnant the moment she was away from her family. They look kind, the women in the picture. They're smiling, their eyes crinkled at the corners, one short-haired, the other with longer curls. Their eyes seem full of affection, and suddenly a weight is lifted off my heart. They will love my baby, I know it. I hope they will. Hope. It's the best I can do.

I read more about them and discover that they're Melissa Jensen, a pediatrician, and Samantha Fuller, a high school science teacher. They go by Mel and Sam, and they've made a scrapbook full of photos and fun little details about themselves. I learn that they love swimming and line dancing and that they're huge animal lovers. They love to travel and have been all around the world. India and Egypt are on their bucket list.

The thing that touches me most is a little note on the last page. It says that they've tried for some time now to have a baby on their own. But ultimately they realized they have so much love to give that they want to give it to a baby they adopt. They say that family is made up of the people you choose to let into your hearts and lives. As I read their words, tears roll down my face. I know I've found my baby's family.

"They sound really nice." I dab at my eyes as I hand back the folder. "I'd love to meet them next week."

"I should warn you, though, Ayesha, adoption for them might be a lot more complicated. I don't want you to get your hopes up in case it doesn't work out."

My heart sinks. "Exactly how complicated do you mean?"

She lets out a deep sigh. "Unfortunately, we've found that sometimes in Illinois it can be more difficult for adoptions to be approved for gay and lesbian couples."

"That doesn't seem fair," I say. "If they want to give someone's baby a home and a family, why shouldn't they be able to?"

"It's not fair and I would even go so far as to say it's completely wrong, but this is how things are at the moment. I just wanted to make sure you're clear on everything."

I clutch the folder to my chest as I walk out of the building. Despite Sarah's cautioning, I can't help feeling lighter than I have in weeks.

• • •

Sarah calls a few days later and says the meeting's set up for Sunday afternoon at four. That's three days away. She reminds me not to make any commitment until I've talked it over with her, no matter how much I like them. She's seen too many arrangements go south because of hasty promises. I want to ask Sarah what would happen if they decide that they don't like *me*. But in the end, I don't say anything to her. I've been preoccupied with too many negative thoughts recently, and I want to get to know them with a clear mind.

I'm meeting them and Sarah at a Denny's that's just a short bus ride away. As soon as I put down the phone, a wave of nausea overwhelms me. I have to sit. It's a good thing that Salma Aunty and Hafeez Uncle are out. I wish I could ask them for a cell phone so I can make my calls in private, but I don't think they've left the last millennium yet because Hafeez Uncle still carries around the brick he's been using for the last five years. Salma Aunty would ask why I need one when all I do is go to school and the library. It's a really good thing for me that she isn't particularly observant, otherwise she might wonder why I've suddenly started wearing extremely loose clothes. I'm pretty sure she thinks that she's been a good influence on me. I know that according to her all my clothes are too tight and revealing although I dress more conservatively here than I did in Mumbai, which might sound ridiculous but is very true.

I'm distracted for the rest of the week, partly because I have morning sickness, a term I've come to loathe since I'm sick all day long. I have to be discreet because no one at the school can know. I'm losing weight, and I'm pretty sure I hear Chantal and Brittany whispering about eating disorders when I run into a stall while they're reapplying their lipsticks. I don't say anything to correct them. Better that than pregnant. If even a hint of it gets to my aunt and uncle, I'm completely screwed.

On Sunday morning, I stay in my room under the pretense of cramming for a test, so when I come down in the afternoon and announce that I'm going to meet some friends for a milkshake, Salma Aunty nods approvingly.

"Yes, beta, go and get some fresh air," she says, looking at me with concern. "Ayesha, I'm not liking these dark circles under your eyes. Are you sure you're feeling all right?"

"It's nothing," I say quickly. "I've just been staying up late to study. And you know how bad my migraines are."

I've been throwing up so much lately, I've had to make up all sorts of lies. They also gave me a perfect excuse to stay in my room.

I bundle up before stepping outside. Snow still covers the trees and fences. The streets and sidewalks have been cleared, so it's an easy ride to Denny's. One of the things I love most about the snow is the way it covers everything in a pristine blanket. Every morning I step outside and it's as if the whole world is new. A blank slate. It's a short walk from the bus stop, but still, by the time I get to Denny's my nose is frozen and I can't feel my cheeks anymore. A few minutes later, I'm sitting in a booth next to Sarah and across from Mel and Sam. The two of them seem even nicer face-to-face, and suddenly all the trepidation that has filled me for the last few days dissipates.

"So, tell us a little bit about yourself," Mel says. "Sarah's told us a little bit about you, but we'd love to hear it from you if you don't mind."

"Yes, I'm really here to answer any questions you have, but otherwise pretend I'm just a fly on the wall," Sarah says.

"Of course, that's fine," I say. I tell them everything, and it's a lot easier than I'd anticipated. There's something about them that's calming, and I find them incredibly easy to talk to.

"That sounds really rough, and I'm sorry it's been so hard," Sam says. "Is there anything you'd like to know about us?"

"Sarah told me how difficult it is for couples like you to adopt. Do you think that it will work?" I ask.

"There's no way to know just yet," Mel said. "I'm the one who'll be petitioning for the adoption since we can't get married." She looks over at Sam. "But we both want a baby so much that we're willing to jump through any hoops we have to."

Sam nods in agreement. "And we want to be as open and honest with you as we can. This is such an important decision."

I take a sip of my chocolate milkshake as I try to gather my thoughts. I have so many questions. Where do I even begin?

"I want to be completely honest with you too," I begin. "What happens if I decide to give my baby to you, but I change my mind later? I don't want to disappoint you or hurt you, but what if I can't do it in the end?"

Mel and Sam look at each other before turning back to me.

"Look," Mel says. "We know how incredibly hard this must be for you. This is your baby, your life. But we do need to have some kind of assurance that you at least intend to let us raise the baby. Unfortunately, we've been through this before."

"Of course. I completely understand," I assure them. "I would never make a commitment like this if I wasn't serious. It's just that I want to be completely honest with you right from the start."

"That's really what we wanted and needed to hear," Mel says.

"Listen, we know things can change," Sam adds. "And we know there can't be any sort of a contract until after you've delivered, but for now all we want is your word and you've given us that."

"Do you have other questions for Mel and Sam?" Sarah asks.

I don't know how to raise the next question I have to ask. I know I need to get away from Bloomington to some place where no one knows me while I wait for the baby to come. I still have one more semester to finish before I can graduate . . . but I can't possibly stay here when I start to show. If I can stay with Mel and Sam until the baby's born, no one will have to know anything. But at the same time, I understand that's a huge ask.

"I saw in your file that you live in Texas," I say finally. "I have to get out of here, and I'll need a place to stay until I have this baby. My family can't find out about this."

"You can stay with us," Sam says without even the slightest hesitation. "We'll take care of all your expenses and you can finish high school there."

For the next hour, they tell me about their lives in Houston. It sounds like they have a busy social life with lots of close friends, many of them teachers and doctors, as well as family members. My baby will be surrounded by loved ones and will have a good upbringing and a great education with these two accomplished women. It's a lot more than I can ever do if I raise this baby by myself. The more time I spend listening to them, the more this feels like it's the best decision. But I'm going to have to find a way to push down the sadness that's in my heart casting a shadow over everything. This isn't just about me anymore.

Sarah, Sam, and Mel also mention open adoption, and how we can figure out how much I'd want to be in my baby's life, whether it's visits or just getting updates from them from time to time. I can control whether they tell the baby anything about me or whether they keep my identity a secret forever. Sarah says I don't have to decide any of this now, and I'm glad she says that, because I really have no idea what I'll want to do.

As I look at Mel and Sam across the table, I wonder what brought them together and what kind of parents they'll be. Will they be strict but loving like my own parents?

"Look, I know this is a little unorthodox, but we have to fly back out tonight and we certainly don't want to pressure you," Sam said.

Mel smiles warmly, her eyes pleading. "What Sam's trying to say is . . . could you tell us if you're considering us at all? We just don't want to go back without knowing if we at least have a chance."

"Ayesha," Sarah says, "you don't have to answer if you don't want to."

But something tells me that I won't get an opportunity like this again. And I really do like them both a lot. They seem to be very kind and caring people, and even though Sarah has told me not to rush into anything and that this was just an initial meeting, I can't help feeling that they are the ones who are meant to be my baby's family.

I finish my milkshake, not quite sure what to say and

overwhelmed by all the emotions coursing through me. Tears start to flow down my face, and I bow my head, embarrassed, as I fish in my pockets for a tissue.

Mel and Sam both look at me in alarm. "We're so sorry if we've upset you," Mel says, handing me a pack of Kleenex. "Please take all the time you want. We can wait until you're absolutely sure."

I shake my head. "It's not that," I say through my tears. "I've just been so afraid, and you're being so nice to me. And I've been crying all the time lately." I take a shuddery breath, trying to compose myself. People at the tables around us are sneaking looks, and I'm mortified.

"It's okay," Sam says gently. "This is a really difficult thing you're going through, and we just want to make sure you'll be able to take care of yourself and your baby."

I nod, finally able to stop crying. "I think you'll both be great."

"There's no need to give any kind of final answer now," Sarah says. "You and I have a meeting tomorrow. Let's continue the conversation then."

"It's a good idea to sleep on it," Mel says. "And I promise if you change your mind, we'll understand completely."

"Thank you," I say, my eyes filling with tears again. "For the milkshake and everything."

We all walk out together, and they watch me as I step into the wintry evening. There's still a little light out, and a short while later, I'm under the covers in my bed. I've successfully evaded Salma Aunty's attempts to get me to eat the mutton stew she's made. The smell of it made me gag as soon as I entered the house, and I barely made it to the bathroom in time. But no one is upstairs to hear me retch, and now I'm pretending to be too tired to go downstairs.

CHAPTER TWENTY-TWO

The next day after school, I meet Sarah in her office at the adoption agency.

"So how do you feel the meeting went yesterday?" she asks as soon as we're seated.

"I still think they're the ones," I say.

Sarah looks at me carefully. "Ayesha, are you sure about this?"

"I am," I say.

"Well, that's the first step," Sarah tells me. "There's a process for these things. There are a lot of formalities, and several steps to go through. I'm fine with starting those steps, but I really want you to be sure. Mel and Sam seem great, but you haven't met any other potential parents yet. I don't want you to make a hasty decision that you might regret later."

"I don't have a lot of time," I say. "I need to move somewhere else before my aunt and uncle find out. And Sam and Mel said I could live with them in Texas until the baby comes. And they'll pay for everything, and I can finish school. They even said they'd understand if I change my mind in the end."

Sarah sits back with a sigh. "I understand how appealing this all sounds to you right now, but, Ayesha, what if *they* back out? What if they think about it and decide that it's too much?"

"But they were so nice, and I really don't think they would say something like that if they didn't mean it." My eyes well up and I feel sick to my stomach. What if she's right?

"Look, I'm not saying they will. I just want you to be a little more cautious. Since you're eighteen, you're in the driver's seat . . . but I'm also very aware that you are still in high school and a long way from home, so I want to be extra careful on your behalf. I will have to talk some more to them, as well as to a lawyer. This is a highly unusual arrangement, and I want to make sure you're protected. Until then, please don't talk to them without checking with me first." Although her tone is stern, her smile is warm as she escorts me out.

Natasha and I meet up at the library after I leave the adoption agency. I tell her everything that's happened in the last two days.

"They sound really nice," Natasha says after we've found a quiet corner table in the back. "So, you'll really move to Texas?"

"I have to," I say. "I'm going to start showing soon. Plus I want to enroll as soon as possible so I can finish spring semester. Otherwise, I won't graduate on time."

"I can't believe we're not going to go to the same prom," she says wistfully. Then she turns to me, her face turning red. "I'm so sorry, I can't believe I just said that. I'm such an idiot."

"No, it's okay, I get it. There are so many things I'm going to miss out on. I'll have to graduate with a bunch of complete strangers."

"But we'll stay in touch," Natasha says. "We can email each other and talk on the phone, and maybe I can go down there to visit sometime."

I squeeze her hand. "That would be so great."

We have to work on our math homework, but it's hard to focus with everything that's going on. After a couple of hours, I give up and ask her to drive me home.

"Ayesha, beta, good, you're home," Salma Aunty calls out from the kitchen as soon as I step inside. "Do you want to watch *Oprah* with me? It's just starting. I made pakoray. Do you want a cup of chai?"

"Salma Aunty, I'll get the chai," I say, walking into the kitchen. "Why don't you go and sit down? I'll bring the tray."

Now that I've decided to move away, I suddenly realize that I don't have a lot of time left with my aunt and uncle. Once I leave, I won't exactly be able to visit with them during the rest of my pregnancy, and I realize that I'll miss them. They're my only family in this country, and now I won't even have them. At least I can enjoy the little time I have left with them. As I carry the tray into the living room, I feel a sense of peace settling over me. But I know the hardest part is still coming, and I have to steel myself against the pain.

CHAPTER TWENTY-THREE

"Have you spoken to your parents about this?" Hafeez Uncle asks over dinner. I've just told them about my plans to leave for Texas, and so far, it's going better than I'd anticipated.

"No, but I'm calling them later tonight," I say. With the almost twelve-hour time difference, it'll be morning for Ammi and Abbu and I can catch them before they start their day.

"So, this program," Salma Aunty says as she adds some spicy eggplant to the khichdi on my plate. "Are you sure it will help you get into a good college?"

"Yes, my counselor said it's a very good program," I reply. I try to be as vague as possible. The less I have to lie, the better. I'm already taking a huge risk telling them that joining this program in Houston was an opportunity I can't pass up. Now I just have to pray that they won't decide to surprise me with a trip while I'm down there.

"If your parents are fine with it, then of course we are too," Hafeez Uncle says.

We finish the rest of the meal with general chitchat, so I'm relieved. But later that night, as I'm calling home, a nervousness settles over me.

"Ayesha, beta, it's so good to hear your voice," Ammi says. "Shahid, come quickly, it's Ayesha," she calls out to Abbu. Soon they're both on the call, interrupting each other as we catch up.

"Ammi, Abbu, there's something I wanted to tell you," I begin hesitantly when there's a break in the conversation.

"What is it, beta?" Abbu says. "Is everything all right?"

The concern in his voice almost breaks my resolve, and I want nothing more than to confess everything and ask them to forgive me. But that's not an option, so I take a deep breath and continue.

"There's a really good program I got into for my last semester," I say. "It's a university prep course, and it only takes the top students from around the country."

"Masha Allah, beta, that's wonderful," Ammi gushes. "It will be helpful for you when you start at Northwestern, no?"

"This is great news, Ayesha," Abbu chimes in. "We're so proud of you."

A huge lump forms in my throat. I don't know if I can do this anymore. How can I lie to them like this when all they're doing is being so loving and supportive? They don't deserve this. But if I tell them the truth, all I'll do is break their hearts.

"The program is in Texas," I say. "I'll be staying with a host family, so it's going to be completely safe. I also got a full scholarship, so you won't have to pay a thing. Isn't that amazing?"

There's silence on the other end, and I can see my plan falling apart. If they say no, I'll have to figure out another way to disappear for the duration of my pregnancy. Panic rises in me, but then I hear Ammi's voice.

"Beta, if this is something you want to do, then go ahead," she says. "But please send us all the details of the family you'll be staying with, and remember to be careful at all times."

I let out huge sigh of relief. "I will, Ammi."

They ask a few more questions, but nothing I can't skirt around easily and then we hang up. It's getting late, and I get ready for bed. But I can't sleep because my guilt is eating me up inside. Once again, I consider the repercussions of coming clean to my parents. Maybe I'm being too hasty in assuming they wouldn't understand. They've always had my best interest at heart. Surely, they could find a way for me to keep my baby. But what about my sisters? When people back home find out—and they will—everyone is going to look at my family differently. We'll become pariahs in Mumbai society.

It's not as if these things don't happen back home. But not to people like us, respectable Muslim families with daughters. I can already hear the comments about how my parents should never have sent me here all by myself. Ours will become a cautionary tale for keeping daughters close to home until they're married. It's the twenty-first century and maybe it will sound ridiculous to a lot of people here, but back home none of my fears are unfounded. It's not as if my parents will disown me or refuse to accept my baby, but it will cost them. And I can't do this to them.

I can face my own cowardice, but I can't face their disappointment.

CHAPTER TWENTY-FOUR

The girls laugh as I waddle past them to go to my locker. My lower back is killing me, and I can't see my feet anymore. These girls are lucky I don't hit them over the head with my bag. Almost six months into my pregnancy, with a baby pressing into my bladder and dancing around at night while I try to sleep, and I'm still pulling one of the three top grades in calculus, while they're standing around making fun of me. That's right, being pregnant is no excuse to not study and do my homework. I may be a lot of things, but I am not a slacker when it comes to school. I haven't forgotten how quickly my grades dropped when I first started to see Suresh. I'm not going to let anything get in the way this time, no matter how much my back hurts and how tired I am all the time. Tutoring students from my school is also helping since it reinforces concepts for me as I explain them to others.

Luckily, Mel and Sam have said I can tutor students in their living room in the afternoons because I need all the money I can get. They've already done too much for me; I can't let them pay for my sour gummy and ginger ale addiction too. They pay for all the new clothes and shoes I've had to buy as I get bigger and bigger with each passing week. My ob-gyn, Dr. Vasquez, asked me the other day whether I was having twins, and I almost had a heart attack. But it turns out he has a warped sense of humor, which in my current state I do not appreciate as much as I should.

Back at Mel and Sam's place, I make myself a bowl of popcorn and settle on the couch trying to get as comfortable as I can. *Gilmore Girls* is on and no one else is at home yet, so for an hour, my eyes are glued to the screen. I try not to think about how Suresh and I watched the first episode together what seems like a lifetime ago. I remember he needed a little convincing to watch it at first, but I can be persuasive when I really want something. By the time we were on the third episode, he was as hooked as I was. Just before leaving for India, he made me promise I would record every episode I watched so we could see them again together when he got back. But promises are like soap bubbles. Some last a little longer, but most pop almost as soon as they're made.

Mel and Sam have been good to me. Here in their home in Houston, I have my own room with a TV, and I don't have to share a bathroom with anyone, which is a good thing given how often I have to pee these days. Salma Aunty and my parents still think I'm in a special university preparatory program here, and when they call, I give them just enough information so that I'm not lying outright. I'm thankful for the distance because hearing the concern and love in their voice is killing me. It takes everything in me not to blurt out the truth. But I can't place this burden on them. It's mine and mine alone to bear. And my baby's, even though she never asked for it. I know I'm having a girl. I can picture her face clearly when I close my eyes, and she's already burrowed herself into my heart. At night when I can't sleep because she's kicking around inside, I imagine what she'll be like as an infant, then a toddler, and even when she's my age. What will she think about me? Will she hate me, or will she be curious about me? I stare at the ceiling while these thoughts fight each other in my head. Sometimes I wish I could run away to a place where no one knows me and where I can keep my baby. Other times I cry myself to sleep wishing that Suresh would come back from India and find me. I dream of us going back home together. We tell our parents, and even though they're upset at first, they come around and there's a big wedding, and everything is fine. Then I wake up in the morning, my eyes puffy from crying and my heart bruised. But my resolve is stronger. I will no longer wait for Suresh or anyone to save me. I will do what's best for me and for my baby. And I will do it my way.

CHAPTER TWENTY-FIVE

Graduation is almost upon us. Everything is strange, like I'm living someone else's life. Most days I have no desire or strength to get out of bed. I'm getting ready to move out of Mel and Sam's place before the baby comes in August, because I know it'll kill me to see them coming home with my baby. I know I won't be able to put myself through that. Besides, my current bedroom is going to be the baby's nursery, so I made arrangements with a family that hosts international students.

It's hard to get excited about graduation when just a few months ago Natasha and I were talking about it with such hope. We still talk often, but it's not the same. She'll always be my best friend, but her life is so different from mine right now. She's looking forward to going to prom with Brian and shopping for her college dorm room. I'm trying to face the fact that in a couple of months I'll be leaving my baby. It's not exactly an easy segue in the conversation, and I don't want to bring her down when she's so excited. It's been difficult getting close to anyone at school here, and part of it is because I really don't want to. So I stick mostly to myself, even leaving the house for long walks whenever Mel and Sam are home. I'm happy and resentful at the same time whenever I hear them talking about the baby in hushed tones. It's getting harder and harder each day, but I try my best not to let my true feelings show when I'm around them. It's the very least I can do after everything they're doing for me.

I put my hands on my belly, which is approximately the size of a very large watermelon. A kind of calm settles over me. I read that stress isn't good for the baby, and I've been trying my best to stay positive. It's really challenging to move around even though my due date is still more than two months away. I don't even want to think about how much worse it'll get. I can't help thinking about how different everything would be if I was back at home in Mumbai. Ammi would probably fuss over me and make sure that I was eating enough fruit and veggies and that I was getting plenty of fresh air. She would also make sure I was being pampered with foot massages and back rubs. She would rub coconut oil in my hair, her hands moving gently on my scalp, taking the heat out and leaving it cool and tingly. Abbu would make sure I had all my favorite things to eat, like shrimp malai curry and bhelpuri. He would make his raita for me, because as far as I was concerned, no one made it the way he did, with just the perfect amounts of black salt, cumin, and sugar combined with the yogurt, onions, and tomatoes. And Abbu would get me mints. Ever since I was a little girl, he always made sure he had a steady supply of Polo mints on hand because I was addicted to them. It's funny how the things I miss aren't the big ones but the small, mundane acts of thoughtfulness.

As always, my ruminations end when reality comes crashing through. If Ammi and Abbu could see me now, their heads would be bowed with shame, and they would wonder what happened to the daughter they raised. Once again, I ask myself if I'm making a huge mistake, if maybe I can still tell them everything. Maybe they'll be angry and disappointed at first, but then they'll come to understand that I loved Suresh and that I wanted to be with him forever and that this baby is a symbol of our feelings for each other. But then the anger I feel toward Suresh comes barging in and I know I can never forgive him for abandoning me like this and that every time I look at my baby it will serve as a reminder that I was foolish enough to trust someone with my whole heart and my body. I don't know if I can bear that for the rest of my life. No, it's better this way. I have to make a clean break and find a way to go on with my life, knowing that my baby is with a good, loving family who will love her the way she deserves.

• • •

"Assalamu alaikum," I say when Ammi picks up the phone. It's the night before graduation, and I want to talk to my parents. I miss them desperately, and I'm sad that they won't be here to see me walk across the stage with a diploma in my hand. But I know that it's a blessing in disguise that they can't be here.

"Kaisi ho, betiya?" Ammi says. "Have you been well?"

"I'm good, Ammi," I say, wishing I could put my arms around her and hug her tight.

"Abbu's here too, so I'm putting you on speaker," Ammi says.

"Hello, beta, how are you?" Abbu's booming voice comes through, and my eyes fill with tears. I would give anything to be there with them right now, sitting on our living room couch watching TV together and sipping chai.

Instead, I'm thousands of miles away, super pregnant, and lying through my teeth to the two people I love most in this world.

"Betiya, I wish we could be there to see you graduate tomorrow," Abbu says. "But my doctor has cautioned me not to fly because of my heart condition."

"But we promise we'll be there when you graduate from college," Ammi adds.

"Abbu, are you okay? Have you been having any more problems?" I say, worried now that they may be hiding something from me.

"Nahi, nahi, beta, it's all okay," Abbu says reassuringly. "You know, na, how Dr. Hassan is? He just wants to make sure nothing happens, and it's such a long flight."

"You promise you're telling me the truth, hai na, Abbu? Ammi, tell me you're not hiding anything."

There's silence on the other end, and my heart sinks. I know there must be something wrong, and here I am completely obsessed with myself.

"Ayesha, it was nothing, just a minor attack," Ammi finally says. "Dr. Hassan says he's not in any danger at all. He just has to exercise and eat right. You know your Abbu, na? I can't get him to stop eating all this fried food."

"But now that I'm missing my betiya's important day, I've learned my lesson, I promise," Abbu says. "From now on, only daal and vegetables and long walks every morning."

My eyes tear up. "And when I come to visit, I won't even recognize my fit and fab Abbu," I say in a shaky voice. "You'll look ek dum like Jeetendra."

"Hanh, yes, he's still your abbu's favorite Bollywood star." I can tell by the way Ammi sounds that she's crying too.

"Ammi, it's going to be fine. You can all come for my college graduation in four years."

"Let's talk about happier things now, okay?" Abbu says, as usual trying to lighten the mood.

"I'm really excited about tomorrow," I say. "I wish Uzma and Hena could be here. They would love it."

"Yes, they were so disappointed when they found out we weren't going."

"I miss you all so much," I say, on the verge of more tears.

"Ayesha, you sound a little down," Abbu says. "Are you sure you're all right? You know you can tell us if anything is wrong, beta."

His words almost break me. Ever since I can remember, Abbu and I have had this sort of bond, a special connection, even stronger than the one I have with Ammi. He can always tell when something is bothering me, and he always knows how to make me feel better. But this is not a friend breakup or a hurt feeling that I can share with him. This is so much bigger. It's a betrayal of their trust. I fight the urge to tell them everything, and it takes every ounce of willpower in me to not break down and cry. But I know I have to be strong, as much for their sake as mine. I take a deep breath and give my best performance of the perfect daughter, one I hope they'll never see through.

"I'm fine, Abbu. Just a little stressed," I say. "There's so much left to do before tomorrow."

"Inshallah, it will all go well," Ammi says. "I can't wait to see the photos. Email them to us as soon as possible."

"I will, I promise," I say, knowing full well that there won't be any photos. "I have to go now, but I'll call again soon."

"Okay, beta, Allah Hafiz," they both say in unison.

"Allah Hafiz."

As soon as I hang up, I fall back against my pillow, the sobs I've held back racking my body.

• • •

I'm not sure how long I cried last night before falling into a restless sleep, but I wake up feeling horrible. I look at my face in the bathroom mirror in dismay. My eyes are puffy, my whole face looks swollen, and I have a splitting headache. There's not much I can do about it, but I still try my best. I put chilled cucumber slices on my eyelids and sit with my feet up for a little bit before I have to start getting ready. Everything takes longer now that I'm further along in my pregnancy. Heartburn and backaches have replaced the nausea I felt earlier on, and I'm grateful not to have to run to the bathroom in the middle of class anymore. But this isn't that much better because I get tired really quickly and the baby's kicking up a storm.

I put my makeup on and curl my hair before putting on the dress I got. It's made of a stretchy material and hopefully it'll be hidden under my gown for most of the day. A wave of sadness washes over me as I finish getting ready. I miss Natasha, and I wish I could go back in time, to a place where I'd never gone to Mike's party, where Suresh had never come into my life. Then I could be getting ready together with Natasha and we could all be sharing this day, which was supposed to be special but is now something I just want to be done with. I can't wait for all this to be over and to get as far away from here as I possibly can.

CHAPTER TWENTY-SIX

By the time I arrive at the venue, most of the seats have been filled by parents and family members. Students are milling about, chatting while they wait for the ceremony to start. Soon, we're asked to gather in the lobby, where we receive instructions about the order in which the events will happen. We're organized alphabetically by our last names, and as I stand there watching everyone, laughing and talking with each other, I miss Natasha so much it hurts. I imagine her back at my old school, with all the other people we know, and I wish more than anything that I could be there with her. The next hour goes by in a haze as, one by one, our names are called. Every time one of the students walks across the stage and receives their diploma, cheers erupt from various groups in the audience. When my name is finally called, it is unsurprisingly butchered, something that no longer fazes me. As I walk across the stage, I hear Mel and Sam clapping and cheering. While I'm immensely grateful for their presence, when I look out into the audience, all I long for is to see the faces of my family and my friends from Bloomington. Thankfully, Mel and Sam find me as soon as it's over and take me home so I can change into something more comfortable. They're also taking me out to a nice fancy dinner at a steakhouse, and after we come home later that night, they have another surprise for me. It's a beautiful gold necklace with a heart-shaped pendant that opens up so that I can put a small picture inside. There's something engraved in the back.

Thank you for your precious gift. Love, Mel and Sam

I turn to them with tears in my eyes, and they put their arms around me. I don't have the words to thank them for everything they've done for me. If they hadn't come into my life at just the right moment, I honestly don't know what I would have done. I'm so happy that I can do this for them, especially since living with them has only proven to me what incredible moms they're going to be.

Later on, just as I'm getting ready for bed, Natasha calls me.

"Hey, girl, so how was it?" she asks, sounding as chipper as she always does.

"It was exhausting," I say with a groan. Now that I'm finally in my pajamas, sprawled out on my bed, every part of me hurts.

"You're getting so close now," she says. "Are you sure you don't want me to come for the delivery?"

"I'd love it if you could come. But I don't want you to miss out on all the prep for college. You have so much to do before you head out, right?" Just like I got into Northwestern, Natasha got into University of Illinois Urbana-Champaign, her top choice.

"Hey, listen, none of that's as important as being with you," she says. "What kind of friend do you think I am?"

"The best kind," I say. "Honestly, Natasha, I don't know what I'd do without you."

"Okay, none of that sappy stuff now," she says, brushing off any emotional talk as usual.

"My due date is August 15," I say. "So maybe plan to be here like a week before that because I have a feeling this baby might come early."

"That's actually perfect. My brother and his girlfriend will be here around that time and I can't stand her, so this will be a great excuse to get away."

"Well, my uterus and I are happy to be of service," I say with a smile. I realize that this is the happiest I've been all day. Natasha's always had a way of cheering me up, and she gets me the same way I get her.

"I wish you'd been here for prom," she says, suddenly wistful.

"I know, me too. But can you imagine me waddling around, trying to dance? I could barely stay upright today, I'm so huge."

"I don't care how huge you are—it would've been epic."

"Yeah, it would've been." My eyes start watering again.

"I wish I'd never dragged you to that party," she says quietly.

"Natasha, you didn't force me to go or to start a relationship with him. Those were my decisions, my mistakes."

"I just . . . I wish I could understand why he didn't stand by you." I can hear her sigh deeply on the other end.

"I know," I say. "For the longest time, I kept thinking up excuses, you know. But then I just had to face the facts. He was just not as serious about us as I was."

"He just didn't seem like that type of guy."

129

"Well, I guess it turns out he was exactly that type of guy. And I was exactly the type of girl who falls for it."

"You loved him, Ayesha," Natasha says defensively. "This isn't your fault. How were you supposed to know?"

"I can't even think about all of that anymore," I tell her. "I just need to focus on getting through the rest of this pregnancy for now."

"Are you all ready for Northwestern?"

I snort loudly. "Are you kidding? I don't have anything yet, and I have no idea how I'm going to get anything done so soon after the baby comes."

"That's what I'm here for. We'll go shopping together and get you new stuff to wear. It's a lot colder there than in Houston."

"Did I tell you I'm moving out in a couple of weeks?"

"You found a place? That's great. What did Mel and Sam say about it?"

"They understand," I say. "To be honest, I think they were a bit relieved. It's not like they would ever ask me to move out as soon as the baby's born."

"They sound like super-nice people," she says.

"They're seriously the best," I say. "Which is kinda why I want to get out of their way. They'll need time to bond with the baby, and I feel like it would be so weird if I was still hanging around. Plus, my room is supposed to be turning into the nursery."

"Oof, yeah. That sounds like it would be pretty brutal. I'm guessing they've already got the paint color picked out for the walls and everything?"

"It's hard enough when they start talking about their plans for the nursery," I say. "The other day I overheard them discussing preschools and I had to get out of the house."

"Where did you go?" she says.

"Just out for a walk," I say. "Or more of a waddle, to be accurate."

"I wish I could see you now," Natasha says. "You weren't showing at all when you left."

"Now I look like a whale," I say. "Or at least I feel like one. It's so hard to sleep because I just can't get comfy."

"Only another month and a half to go," she says. I know she's trying to be supportive, but my heart sinks because in a month and a half I'm going to be giving away a part of myself and I'm still not sure how I'm going to do it.

Shortly after we hang up, I begin to drift off to sleep. But my mind is filled with thoughts about the baby. I'll never be able to share *exactly* how I feel, and how much love I'll carry for her in my heart. After tossing and turning for almost an hour, I finally get up and walk over to my desk.

I take out one of my notebooks and begin to write.

CHAPTER TWENTY-SEVEN

I sit up in bed with a start, completely disoriented, my sheets and pajama top damp with sweat. I fumble around in the dark trying to find the switch on my bedside lamp. The light makes a circle on the ceiling as I lie back on my pillow once again, my heart beating loudly in my chest.

The dream that woke me up is nothing but a fogginess in my head, and I'm not sure I want to remember it clearly. But it comes seeping back in, regardless of what I want or need, and now my head is pounding as I try to push away the images of someone prying my newborn baby from my arms. I can feel the same panic I felt in my dream, and it's so real that my body shudders involuntarily. It's left me shaken, and now I don't think I can go back to sleep.

I can't seem to shake the sense of panic and helplessness from my dream, and it stays with me throughout the day as I try to focus on the students I'm tutoring for summer school. It's already July, and I figured it was the best option to save a little money, especially since I'm done with school now, and I'm too big and uncomfortable to stand behind a counter somewhere. By the last session of the day, my back is killing me, and I'm walking slowly to my room when I hear hushed voices coming from the kitchen. Since I have to pass by there to get to the stairs, I can't help overhearing them, whether I want to or not.

"We have to decide on a name, honey," Mel is saying. "My mother wants to start embroidering the baby blanket, and you know how she gets."

"You know the one I want," Sam says. "I just feel like it's meant for her. I can't imagine calling her anything else."

"Mira," Mel says slowly. "What did you say it means again?"

"It's Arabic and comes from Amira, which means 'princess' or 'queen,'" Sam says.

"That sounds really perfect, actually."

A sob hitches in my throat as I hear them talk. *Mira*. They sound as if she's already theirs, already a part of their lives, and a panic takes hold of me. I can't let her go yet. It's too soon.

I shuffle upstairs as fast as I can and pick up the phone. Fifteen minutes later, I've packed a duffel bag with all my stuff. I wait until Mel and Sam have gone out for their afternoon errands before leaving the house.

The place I found is only a short bus ride away. Luckily, the owner said it was ready and agreed to let me move in today. I have to get out of here. I simply cannot stay here any longer while Mel and Sam plan their life with my baby. I know I should talk to them, but I just can't bring myself to look at them right now. Because if I do, I know they will see the resentment in my eyes, and they do not deserve that. But I can't bear it anymore.

I leave a note on the kitchen counter asking them to understand that I need space and time to deal with my feelings.

●●●

I've settled into my room at the new place. It belongs to a nice older couple whose kids are grown and have moved out. But they're quite distant, probably to give me space, and I like it that way. Otherwise, I'll have to constantly reassure them that I'm fine, that the crying is nothing when in fact it's as if I'm breaking in two. My heart has shattered into a thousand pieces, first because I've finally come to terms with the fact that Suresh is never coming back and second because I'm doing the exact same thing to our baby. I don't know where I belong anymore, if I even belong anywhere, and the sadness is just one big black abyss that's threatening to swallow me whole.

Mel and Sam have been calling, but I haven't been able to talk to them—only text to say I'm fine, and that I will let them know if anything happens with the baby. I don't know what to say to them because I don't know what I'm doing anymore. All I know is that I can't be around them and their constant joy about welcoming my baby into their lives. I'm a horrible person, ungrateful and selfish, but I just can't do it any longer. Their happiness is like a cloud that's threatening to smother me, and the fact that they're so kind and generous just makes everything worse.

Natasha calls me fairly often, even more worried about me now that I've moved out of Mel and Sam's. I love that she cares so much, but lately I don't know how to talk to her anymore either. This is beyond her friend skill set, and even though I love her for trying, I constantly feel like I should let her off the hook. It's getting harder and harder to keep the conversations going because I simply cannot make her understand what I'm going through. So I stop trying. I mean, how do you explain to someone that a *part* of you is going to be leaving you soon, and you're supposed to continue living your life, but you can't even breathe because this part of you has become your oxygen, vital to your survival? But you've promised to let it go and now you feel guilty for wanting to break that promise because then you'll be taking away a lifeline from someone else.

CHAPTER TWENTY-EIGHT

My water breaks right in the middle of the produce aisle at Kroger. Given how the last year has gone for me, this shouldn't surprise me one bit. I've been cramping a lot for the last few days, but at my weekly checkup, Dr. Vasquez said they were just Braxton-Hicks contractions. Apparently, even my uterus likes to mess with me.

Since I couldn't get comfortable in any position, no matter how many ways I tried to contort my very unwieldy body, I decided to walk around the grocery store. So here I am, by the mangoes and papayas, with wetness trickling down my legs and a sharp contraction leaving me bent over the fruit like I'm the most diligent food inspector in town. I pull out my phone and speed-dial Mel and Sam. They pick up at the first ring.

"Ayesha, thank god you called, we've been so worried." Sam sounds out of breath as if she's been running. "Where are—"

"It's time," I say, the pain constricting my throat. "I need to get to the hospital."

"We'll be right there," Sam says.

"Ask her where she is," Mel says in the background.

I give them my location, and ten minutes later, they're rushing through the automatic sliding doors. As Sam and Mel are helping me walk from the produce section to their car, I flag down one of the people in the green aprons and point apologetically at the puddle on the floor.

We make it to the hospital fifteen minutes later, and Mel is already running over to the car with a wheelchair and helping me into it while Sam goes to find parking.

They haven't asked me anything other than how far apart the contractions are, which is good because the pain is racking my entire body and I can't really put more than two words together right now.

Soon I'm in a hospital bed, dressed in a fresh gown, when a very friendly nurse comes by to hook me up to an IV and a fetal monitor. She times the contractions and tells me to get comfortable and that the doctor will come around to check how far my cervix is dilated. As we wait for Sam to come in, Mel helps me put my hair in a ponytail and brings me a cup of ice chips. Sam rushes in a few minutes later carrying the overnight bag they had insisted I keep ready for exactly this scenario. In my hurry to leave, I'd forgotten, and now that the earlier moment of panic has passed, I know that I have to explain myself.

When the nurse finally leaves the room, I press the button to raise the bed so that I'm in a sitting position. "Mel, Sam, can we talk?"

They both look at me, and I can see the hurt and concern in their eyes.

"I'm so sorry. I—"

"Look," Mel says. "You don't have to say anything. We get it. You needed some space, and I think that's completely normal under the circumstances."

"We just wish you hadn't shut us out," Sam says. Mel throws her a warning look, but she ignores it. "We just wanted to know if you've changed your mind."

I don't answer right away because I know I can't be totally honest with them. I have thought about it a lot since I moved out. I know it doesn't make any sense because nothing has really changed, but that day when I heard them talking about my baby's name, it made me feel something I hadn't felt before. It was as if they were taking something that should be *mine*, something only *I* had a right to, and by naming her, they were effectively erasing my relationship to my own baby. It's a completely unreasonable response on my part since our whole arrangement is based on me placing her with them. I can't explain it. But I can't deny it either.

So I take my time, and when I reply, I only say what I know they need to hear.

"No, I haven't changed my mind," I say. "It was just hard being around all of it, you know?"

"Of course, we understand," Sam says. "And that's why we said right from the beginning that we're completely open to you having a relationship with her. We never wanted to shut you out."

I don't say anything because a million thoughts are racing through my mind, and there's just too much going on right now. I can't think clearly.

"The important thing is that you're okay, and everything will be fine now," Mel says.

Another sharp pain hits, and I try to breathe through the wave as it rises to an unbearable level and then subsides slowly. I'm sweating, and I don't even realize I've been digging my nails into Mel's hand until she's turning white from the pain.

Dr. Vasquez comes in to check me. "Well, you're only three centimeters dilated, so you still have a long way to go. I'll come back to check on you in an hour."

My mouth is really dry, and Sam goes to grab me some more ice chips.

"I'm sorry I haven't called you back." The pain has subsided for now, and I know I need to explain.

"You had us worried." Mel dabs my forehead with a cool washcloth. "I know this is hard for you, but you could have told us how you were feeling."

"I just . . . You've both been so amazing." My eyes sting, and I blink back the tears. "I didn't want to say anything to make you feel bad, so I just didn't say anything."

"Help me understand, Ayesha. You know we would never try to keep you away from her. So what is it that you're feeling?"

I can tell that Mel is struggling to stay calm, and I know I have no choice but to tell her the truth.

"You both have been nothing but kind and understanding. But I don't think I can be in her life after you adopt her. It would be too hard knowing that my daughter is right there but I can't be a mother to her. I don't know if I'm strong enough for that." The tears are running freely now. There's nothing I can do to stop the hurt from spilling out of my heart.

Mel just looks at me, and I can see how much she cares. But there's really nothing she can say to change how I feel and I think she knows it. We just sit in silence, with only the occasional beeping of the monitors in the room.

● ● ●

It's been almost thirteen hours and still no baby. Nothing except my stubborn cervix that doesn't seem to want this to happen, and the contractions are getting worse.

Then when I think I can't take one more minute of this, Dr. Vasquez comes in to examine me and announces that my cervix has been considerate enough to dilate to the full ten centimeters and I can start pushing. The pain has become unbearable, and no amount of proper breathing technique is going to help.

Another wave hits, and I grab Sam's hand and squeeze. Tears are running down my face, my hair is plastered to my forehead, and all I want is for Ammi to be here to make the pain go away.

"Please," I beg. "I can't do this anymore. It hurts too much."

"You can do this, Ayesha, trust me," Sam says. "I'm right here with you."

Mel is on the other side, dabbing my forehead with a damp washcloth. I take another deep breath and push, all the while picturing Ammi and imagining the touch of her hand on my forehead. She would know exactly what to do to help me. Sobs rack my body as I steel myself for one final push. I let out a primal scream, and then a second scream fills the room as I bring my baby into the world.

What happens right after is nothing but a blur. There's a sudden burst of activity as the nurses briefly let me hold her before rushing her out of the room in a baby warmer. I'm a little dizzy and very exhausted, but when I turn to ask Mel and Sam to find out where they've taken her, I realize everyone is gone except for one nurse.

"Where did they take her?" I say, my voice sounding like it's coming from far away. I try to sit up, but she's beside me in a flash.

"Please don't try to get up," she says, gently pushing me back on the bed. "You don't want to start bleeding."

"Where's my baby? Is something wrong with her?"

"They've taken her to the NICU," she says. "They just want to make sure everything's all right."

"When can I see her?"

"I'm not sure, honey," she says. "You'll have to wait until the doctors are done checking her out. You should try and get some rest."

She takes one last look around and then leaves the room, leaving me all alone, confused, and tired, just longing to hold my baby.

CHAPTER TWENTY-NINE

She has the tiniest mouth, puckered up, her face red from screaming. It's been four hours, and the nurse has brought her to my room in a bassinet. I long to hold her in my arms so badly it's physically hurting me. My breasts ache from the milk that's coming in. The nurse showed me how to use the pump to expel it. She said that the baby's doing great and that she's getting her formula. It's easier this way, she said. It's better for her not to get used to my milk, otherwise she might not take to the formula later and it will be harder for her and for Sam and Mel.

I don't want to make anything more difficult for any of them, especially my baby. *Is she even still* my *baby?* I've already given her the most difficult thing of all to deal with: growing up without her mother. I hope she loves Sam and Mel. I hope she feels loved by them. I have. They've been kind and generous beyond any expectations. I can never repay them, I know. What I can do is bow out, as quietly as I can, without fuss or drama, so that they can start their lives as a family. I'm going to leave behind a big piece of my heart, but I know this is the right thing to do. I must cut out this piece before it becomes impossible for me to do, before I crumble and cave, before I can no longer find the strength.

As they take her away again, I turn to face the wall, my tears falling freely as I try to wash away the image of her face, looking at me as if memorizing the face of the mother she'll never have in her life. I'm broken and empty and I don't know how I can find the strength to go on without her.

• • •

Over the next couple of weeks, my life takes on a grayness. The colors seem muted and everything looks bleak. Most days I focus just on leaving my bed, getting dressed, making it to the tutoring center where I work now, and paying attention to the students because the only thing I can still control is this. The nights are a different story, staying up late and crying as I long to hold my baby and smell the top of her head. I miss the fullness of her inside my belly, the way she used to move around to the beat of the songs I played on my MP3 player.

My mind jumps between the baby and Suresh, and I wonder where he is and if he ever thinks of me. It feels like a lifetime ago that we were cuddled up in front of the fireplace together, watching movies while it snowed outside. The smell of chai makes me sick now, and I can't bear to watch the few Bollywood DVDs we got on that one trip to Devon Avenue.

I'm supposed to start at Northwestern next month. It's been my dream school for years, and now I'll get to go just like I planned. But it doesn't feel good. In fact, I don't feel anything anymore, except the abject misery and emptiness that follows me around everywhere.

Two days ago, I went for my postpartum checkup. The doctor asked me how I was feeling, and I burst into tears. He patted me gently on the head and said it was perfectly normal to have some depression after giving birth. I'd get over it soon, he reassured me. Soon cannot come fast enough.

I call my parents back at home because it's been a while and I don't want them to get worried. A sob hitches in my throat as soon as Abbu picks up.

"Ayesha, I was just telling your ammi that I haven't heard my betiya's voice in so long."

"I'm sorry, Abbu, I've been so busy preparing for college." The lies slip out too easily, and I wonder if I've changed irrevocably. Will I ever really be Abbu's betiya again?

Ammi comes on the line. "Ayesha, beta kaisi ho?"

"I'm fine, Ammi." I can hear the tears in my voice, and I know they can too.

"Kya baat hai?" Ammi asks. "What's wrong, Ayesha?"

I can't hold it back any longer and dissolve into racking sobs.

"I don't know, Ammi. Nothing feels good anymore. I miss you all so much."

Ammi starts crying softly, and I can hear Abbu comforting her. Then he picks up the phone.

"Ayesha, meri bacchi, it's all right. Please don't cry," he pleads. "Look, whatever it is, you can talk to us. Everything will be fine.

I wish more than anything that I could believe him. But I know it will never be all right and that I can never tell him. That's the part that's breaking my heart.

"I'm sorry . . . I'm just overwhelmed with everything." I try to absolve them of worry. "It's just been a lot, you know. Being so far away and just so many changes. Sometimes it gets to me."

"Beta, if you're not happy, you can come home, hai na?" Ammi says. "There's nothing we would love more than to have all our children under one roof again."

"But, Ammi, how can I, after everything you and Abbu have done to make this happen for me?"

"Arre, what have we done?" Abbu asks. "We've only done what any parents want to do. We wanted you to have all the opportunities you deserve, that's all."

"But if you're not happy, beta, then you should come home," Ammi adds. "There are great universities here, and you can live at home and let us take care of you."

"We will be proud of you no matter where you are," Abbu says, and I struggle not to start crying again. If only they knew the truth.

"Beta, why don't you think about it and then whatever you decide is up to you," Ammi says. "We just want you to be happy."

After I hang up, I lie on my back and stare at the ceiling. Talking to my parents has made me realize how badly I want to be back in the loving arms of my family. More than anything else, I believe that is how I will get over the pain of parting from my baby.

• • •

A couple days later, Natasha and I are on the phone with each other. She feels awful that she wasn't able to be here for the birth after all but promises that she'll try to come out and visit once I'm at Northwestern. Listening to her talk excitedly about her preparations feels like I'm watching a movie about other people. Nothing feels real anymore, and I wonder if it ever will. I try to force myself to feel some excitement, but the thought of being hours away from my baby girl and not being able to see her is unbearable. Mel and Sam said I can stay in the baby's life if I want to, which I do, but not on the sidelines. I want to be her mother. I am her mother. But I'm also the person who will forever be her greatest source of sadness and grief. The one who gave up on her. I will never be able to undo that. I don't know if I even have the courage. I am a coward, and it's something I'll have to live with for the rest of my life.

I want to run away and hide somewhere where no one knows me, where everything won't be a reminder of what I've done. It's so strange knowing that I've made a choice that's brought so much joy to Mel and Sam, but it's killing me a little every moment of the day. How can a single act be both good and bad? I'm so happy for them but so brokenhearted for myself. I want my baby to have a life where she will always be cherished, and I know that it's not within my power to give her that. I hate myself for what I'm doing, but I can't give in to self-pity and change my mind, because what kind of a life can I offer her? A life in which she'll never get to be close to my family, even if I somehow gathered the courage to take her back home. Of course, I know my parents will take care of us, but we'll always be a source of embarrassment and shame for them. Can I put that kind of a burden on her little shoulders?

But I cannot continue to live here and pretend that she doesn't exist. She'll always be like a piece of my heart walking around outside my body, except I won't ever be the one to protect her, to teach her or rock her to sleep. Even just thinking about it hurts. No. I have to leave. I have to go back home and erase this part of my life. It's the only way I'll survive. And so, I make up my mind. I'm not going to Northwestern. I'm going back to Mumbai to try to rebuild my life.

Hopefully, in time, my heart will stop aching and become whole again.

CHAPTER THIRTY

I'm greeted by a familiar sight as I walk through the arrivals lounge at Mumbai's bustling airport. My parents, our driver, Muqbool, and my sisters, Hena and Uzma, are all waiting for me. I see them as soon as I turn the corner of the hallway that leads to the sliding doors at the exit. I've been with them on the other side many times over the years, welcoming various relatives who have visited from abroad. There's always a sense of excitement and celebration for the stories and presents, but mostly the bonding that took place over the few days or weeks that our guests would stay. As I walk toward them with a smile on my face, I wonder how long I'll be able to keep up the charade of a daughter returning after making her parents proud. I remember the heated conversations around the dinner table when I announced that I wanted to finish high school in the US. I can't help wondering how things would have turned out for me if I had listened to them and not left. But I know that was never an option for me. Even though things ended very differently than I had planned, I still don't regret my decisions. At least that's what

I tell myself as I step into my family's embrace, feeling like a complete impostor.

"Assalamu alaikum, Ammi, Abbu," I say, throwing my arms around them. Tears fill my eyes the instant I feel the warmth of their love, their relief at having me back home, and I'm sobbing uncontrollably. I can feel the eyes of passersby as they wonder why I'm making such a spectacle of myself.

"Beta, what's wrong?" Ammi pulls back and takes my face in her hands, her eyes full of worry for me.

"Nothing," I say through my tears. "I'm just really happy to be home."

"Ayesha, betiya, everything is good now," Abbu says, beaming proudly. "You're back where you belong, and we're all together again."

My parents have bought my story about feeling so homesick that I can't bear to be so far away from them anymore. My father's connections in Mumbai have secured me a last-minute spot at a local university, and I'll be getting my bachelor's degree here instead of Northwestern.

So I nod wordlessly and bury my head in his chest. What can I even say? If I told him the truth, would he ever look at me the same way again?

I know the answer. He can never find out.

Uzma squeezes my hand, and Hena is practically jumping with excitement.

"Ayesha baji, did you bring me the new Britney Spears CD like you promised?" Hena asks.

"And what about my Sailor Moon T-shirt?" Uzma wants to know. "Did you find one?"

"Hena, Uzma, beta, can't you see your sister is exhausted from her long flight?" Ammi says, her tone stern, but her eyes twinkling. "Once we get home, we can see what she's brought for us."

Abbu shakes his head at them. "You are all the same," he says. He turns to me and whispers, "Did you find that book I've been wanting?"

I take a deep breath and smile, feeling relieved after a long time. It's good to be home.

• • •

I'm in my old bed staring up at the ceiling. The lazy turning of the ceiling fan makes my eyelids heavy. I'm jet-lagged, but I'm also still recovering from the delivery just four weeks ago. Dr. Vasquez said the lethargy was most likely postpartum depression and that I needed to give myself time. Ammi has already mentioned that maybe I picked up a cold or something on the plane. I don't argue, allowing myself to use that as an excuse. It's better than lying or telling the truth. I close my eyes, and a face appears. Huge deep brown eyes in a small but perfect face. Damp black curls matted against her forehead, the way Suresh's hair did after a shower. My eyes immediately fill with tears, and I curl into a ball and sob into my pillow. When I hear footsteps, I close my eyes tightly and pretend to be fast asleep. The edge of my mattress dips slightly as Ammi sits and puts a cool hand on my forehead. She leans closer and places a gentle kiss on my cheek. I hold my breath because I'm afraid she'll feel the wetness of my tears. But then the mattress springs back as she stands to leave. She hesitates for a moment, and then I hear the door close softly and relax. How much longer can I hide everything from her? I know I have to, no matter how difficult it is.

• • •

The next morning, Zahira Phuppi drops by for a visit. We're

just finishing up a delicious breakfast of halwa and puri, so she joins us for a cup of chai.

"Ayesha, beta, you've put on a lot of weight," she says, scanning my face. "You must have been eating too much of that unhealthy American food."

I look at the platter of deep-fried puri and halwa, which is basically made of semolina and white sugar, but I bite my tongue because I don't really want to give Zahira Phuppi any more fodder. She already blames Ammi for everything from the monsoon season to government corruption. She's Abbu's eldest sister, so no one dares to contradict her.

"How is Samina Baji?" I ask, spooning some halwa onto a plate and adding a couple of puris to it. "Is she coming home for Eid this year?"

"Yes, of course," she says, tearing off a piece of puri and using it to pick up some halwa. Despite her insistence that she wasn't going to eat, here she is, digging in. "Her sons will be coming too."

"What about Ehsan Bhai?" Ammi's already filled me in on my cousin's marital problems.

"He is too busy with work. He is the vice president of the New York branch of his company, you know," she says with a smug smile. She throws Ammi a withering look. "I always told Shahid that you all should have stayed in Chicago. He would have done very well there."

As usual, Zahira Phuppi blames her brother's return to India on my mother. As if Abbu was a child who was being controlled by my manipulative mother. My parents have the most open and honest relationship of anyone in our large family. But a lot of his older sisters didn't approve of them moving back to be closer to my grandparents. Dada and Dadi had six children and considerable wealth. Abbu was their only son, which probably made his sisters a little insecure about their inheritance. This was completely understandable, as the law always favored male children. But Abbu just wasn't the type of person who was interested in this sort of thing. He just wanted to do meaningful work and to be surrounded by family. And he's been paying for that decision for years.

● ● ●

These days I spend a great deal of time contemplating the choices I've made. I'm afraid that my parents are starting to sense that there's a much bigger reason for my abrupt return, but they haven't broached the subject with me yet. Maybe they're afraid that their speculations might be true. I try to remind myself of all the goals I used to have for my life, my career, all the things I hoped to accomplish. I've always had such high standards for myself, but I've come up really short. Somehow, somewhere, I got completely turned around, and now I need to get back on my path and try to live a life worthy of the daughter I've left behind, thousands of miles away. I don't know if she'll ever forgive me or if I'll ever see her again in this lifetime, but I know what kind of person I want her to find if she ever does come looking for me. I want to be someone she can be proud of, just as I know I will be proud of her. I want to become the person I should have been when I had her, and now I will dedicate all my efforts to becoming that very person.

● ● ●

Days later, I watch in horror as the planes fly into the twin towers. Suddenly I'm screaming for my parents and my sisters, who rush in to see what's wrong. The impacts replay on the screen as we stand there in stunned silence. By the time the first tower falls, we're all holding on to each other and crying.

It doesn't truly sink in until hours later, even after we've listened to the news on several channels and called people we know. Salma Aunty and Hafeez Uncle are sobbing on the phone from Bloomington as we talk about loved ones who live in New York.

Throughout the day, it gets worse as we begin to hear about who was behind the attacks, and it chills us to the core. As more details emerge, so do the statistics of the people who were killed. There are heartbreaking reports of last frantic messages left for loved ones by passengers on the planes and from those in the towers. We are rooted to the television, watching the harrowed faces of the news anchors as they update the world on the devastation. Images of the sites are etched into our minds as we watch rescue efforts on the ground. It doesn't matter that we didn't know the people who perished. There's a pain we feel collectively at this act of terror committed in the name of a god whom I have only known as a synonym for love and compassion my entire life. The people who perpetrated this heinous act are not Muslims; they're not even human.

In the days that follow, stories of Muslims being targeted and harassed by those who believe that a few extremists represent all Muslims are all over the news. I can't stop thinking about Mel and Sam and Mira. I've been too scared to contact them, and they don't have my Mumbai number. I thought it would be safer this way when I left Texas. But no one had anticipated this. I want desperately to find out if they're safe, if anything happened to their loved ones. It's only been two weeks since I left, and the wound in my heart is still wide open. Some days it feels like there are other versions of me out there living a happier life. Me, when I first arrived in Bloomington and started school, full of anticipation and hope. Me, when I met Suresh and our friendship grew into something much more. Me with the baby, and Suresh and I somehow making it work together. And then there's the me now, pretending to be the good daughter my parents still believe I am.

I get through each day in a trancelike state, willing my body to perform its basic functions. Get out of bed, brush my teeth, get dressed, pretend to eat the food my mother cooks for me. I know my parents are worried about me. They've noticed the change in my spirit, but they don't know why. I ask myself a million times a day if I made a huge mistake, if I should have been less of a coward, less selfish, if I should have given them more credit, if I should have at least given them the chance to accept their granddaughter.

Deep down, I know they would have, out of love for me, but it would have destroyed them inside and I don't think I would've been able to live with all that guilt. And so, I harden my heart and my resolve and close the door to that chapter of my life.

But I can't help but worry. What kind of life have I abandoned her to, where the color of her skin will always make her a target? Will her white parents know how to protect her? Will they turn her against her own kind? My heart fills with terror at the notion that my own child may one day look at me with hatred and condone the injustices happening to thousands of innocent Muslims in the country she'll call home. I bury this fear deep inside me because there is no one to turn to, no one who will understand. And I know I'll have to live with the consequences of my decisions for the rest of my life. Whatever they may be.

part two

MIRA

December 2018, Houston, TX

CHAPTER ONE

"Mom, did you sign my permission slip for the field trip?" I take a bite of my syrupy waffle while simultaneously shoving three notebooks into my already-full backpack.

"Mira, your bag looks like it's going to have a baby." Mom sticks her head out from behind the refrigerator door and grins at me.

"Stop deflecting, Mom. Did you sign it or not?" I'm only half joking because Mom is notoriously forgetful and today is the last day to hand in permission slips.

"You left it on the coffee table, Sam," my other mom calls out from the study.

"Thanks, Mel," Mom says.

"Yes, thanks, Mama, you're the best." I pretend to ignore the daggers Mom shoots at me with her eyes before returning her attention to the contents of our fridge, as if staring hard enough will miraculously produce a fully cooked dinner for tonight.

Mama comes out from the study and puts her arms around Mom from behind.

"Hey, you know Supermom has a lot on her plate these days." Mama drops a kiss on Mom's neck, and I groan.

"Gross. Can you two please get a room?"

"We did," Mama quips. "You're standing in it."

I can't help grinning at my moms. My younger sister, Nadia, who's watching us and trying to finish her math homework at the same time, sighs loudly and rolls her eyes.

"Can you guys keep it down, please? I can't figure out this stupid problem, and all this inappropriate behavior isn't helping." She's trying to sound annoyed, but I can see a smile playing on her lips.

"Okay, off with you freeloaders," Mom says with a fake swat to my behind.

"Unless you'd like to walk to school," Mama adds. "Then Mom and I can finally get some alone time." She winks suggestively at Mom.

"Eww, you two are the grossest parents ever." Nadia runs out the front door, and I'm right behind her.

"Remember, I love you and I live to embarrass you!" Mom shouts after us as I slam the front door and run to the car.

"Nadia, make sure to check in with your peer tutor before class," Mama says when we're almost by the entrance to our school. "Your fractions unit test is this week, right?"

"Yes, Mama," Nadia replies with a groan. "I hate math." She slides down in her seat and sticks out her lower lip.

"Nadia, stop being such a baby," I say. "I'll help you after school, okay? And maybe if you paid more attention when Josh is explaining instead of making googly eyes at him, you wouldn't hate math so much."

"Mama, tell Mira to stop," Nadia whines. "I don't like Josh like that at all."

"Mira, stop tormenting your sister," Mama says, grinning at me in the rearview mirror. She pulls into the drop-off bay and turns to Nadia.

"Honey, it's okay to like Josh, but just make sure you save a little bit of the googly-eyeing for after your test."

"Mama!" Nadia screeches as she opens the door. "I hate you all," she mutters, getting out of the car.

Mama and I crack up while she storms off. We love teasing her, and she makes it so easy. I hug Mama quickly and get out.

My friend Nikhil is waiting for me by the front entrance. As usual he's wearing a bow tie, dress shirt, and gray pants. I love that he doesn't give a hoot that everyone else is dressed like they rolled out of bed five minutes before coming to school. He's always dressed as if he might be called for a job interview at any moment, his thick hair perfectly coiffed. Ready for anything. Except maybe basketball. Or soccer tryouts.

"Did you forget we have choir practice early today?" he asks.

"No, I'm here, right?" I raise my eyebrows at him. He's always so stressed about time.

"Aren't you worried Ms. Hansen will get mad at you?"

"Nik, relax, we're not late." I open the double doors to the music room. "See." I point to Ms. Hansen's usual spot in front of the stage. "She's not even here yet."

"Okay, fine," Nikhil says with a sigh. "But can you please not call me Nik?"

I raise my hands defensively. "Fine, jeez, you're so cranky this morning."

"I'm not cranky. I just don't like it when people don't say my name properly."

"So, *no one* in India shortens their name?"

"Sure, maybe they do, but I don't like it. I mean, I know

you Americans have trouble with foreign names and all, but Nikhil isn't even hard to say, so what's the big deal?"

"Oh my god, fine, I'll only call you Nikhil Verma from now on. Happy?" I grin at him because, as annoying as he is, I still really like him. There aren't a whole lot of South Asians at our school, and he's my first close friend straight from India and only real friend whose brown skin matches mine. Growing up in a white family has me kind of starved to be around people who look like me. Not that I don't love my moms and Nadia to death, but it's just different with Nikhil. We met during choir earlier this year. He has a beautiful voice, the kind that makes you stop in your tracks and turn around. He was warming up and singing a Bollywood song when I walked into the music room at the beginning of senior year a few months ago. I'm not too familiar with Bollywood, but I loved the song. When I asked him what it was, his jaw fell to the floor.

"You've never heard this?" he'd asked me incredulously. "It's a classic."

"I don't really know a lot of Indian songs," I said, suddenly feeling inexplicably embarrassed.

"I'm Nikhil, by the way," he said with a little hand wave. "Nikhil Verma."

"I'm Mira. Mira Jensen."

"Hi, Mira Mira Jensen." He smiled at me.

Oh lordy, he's a dork, I thought to myself. But he was a cute dork with unruly dark hair and thick eyebrows that sat over huge brown eyes. And his glasses made him look like he should be teaching a college class or something. Not singing a classic Bollywood song I've never heard of.

"You just started going here, right?"

He nodded. "My mom's working on a project for NASA for the next couple of years. So I get to finish high school here."

"Wow, NASA, huh? Cool. Cool, cool." I groaned inwardly. *Get it together, Mira.*

"What about you?" he asked.

"I've lived here all my life. Texas born and raised. Yeehaw."

I don't know what possessed me to add that last bit, but now I was committed. This was why my best friend, Brooke, had appointed herself as my wingwoman. Clearly, I was in desperate need of one.

As it turned out, Nikhil has a boyfriend back in Mumbai, which is where he's from, so Brooke's absence didn't make any difference. But Nikhil and I are good friends, and ever since we met, he's made it a point to make fun of me for my utter cluelessness about anything Indian. But he does it in a good-natured way so I don't take offense. Plus, he's easy to talk to about the stuff I've been thinking about lately. Like how I've been wondering more and more about the Indian part of me, and since I feel kind of weird bringing it up to my parents, who adopted me right after I was born, I've been talking to Nikhil about it.

For all the teasing and joking around between us, I like to think that we're there for each other. I try to distract him when he's missing his boyfriend, and he listens to me as I try to fill the gaps in my history, longing to feel rooted in something bigger than myself.

CHAPTER TWO

"Mira, hurry up. I don't want it to get too crowded," Mama calls from downstairs. We're going dress shopping today for prom, and I'm extremely excited. Moms and I have been planning this trip for months. I've decided on purple because it goes really well with my skin tone. I know I want something with beading but nothing too ostentatious.

An hour later, we're standing outside the boutique, waiting for the doors to open. Moms hate it when the stores get too busy, so we grabbed coffee on the way and now we're fueled and ready for a full day of shopping.

"Why did we have to come so early?" Nadia grumbles, rubbing her eyes. She's never been a morning person, unlike me. She probably takes after Mama, who gave birth to her, and who also can be really, really grouchy before noon. Moms sometimes joke that I have caffeine in my veins instead of blood because I'm always the first one up in the morning, ready to start my day.

"Look, they're opening now," I say to Nadia. "And Moms said we can get sushi for lunch after."

That perks her right up, and soon we're looking through the gorgeous dresses on the display racks. I drift away from Moms and Nadia, looking to find one that speaks to me. I notice a saleslady hovering and turn to smile at her. She looks at me coolly, barely returning my smile, but I shrug it off. Clearly, she's not a morning person either.

Then I see it. The perfect dress. I look around for Moms, but they've wandered off to another display.

"Excuse me," I say to the saleslady, still hovering. "Do you have this in a size ten?"

She darts a brief glance at the dress I'm pointing to. "I think this one is out of your price range," she says. "I can show you something that might be more suitable for you."

"No, that's okay," I mumble.

"Well, all right, then," she says before walking away.

My cheeks burn as I look around. The store is starting to fill up, and I see a couple of girls from my school, looking through the racks near me. I'm mortified at the thought that they may have overheard. I don't know what to do, but I know I have to get away from here. I find Moms in another section, and I can't believe my eyes. The same saleslady is now hovering over Nadia showing her dresses and flashing her smile at Moms. Anger surges through me, but I stay calm.

"Moms, can we go, please?"

They both look at me in surprise.

"Did you not find anything you liked?" Mama says.

"We thought we'd give you a chance to look by yourself first," Mom says. "But if you want, we can help pick a few for you to try."

"Honey, sometimes you won't know if something will look good on you until you try it on," Mama says.

The saleslady looks at the four of us, clearly bewildered. Moms don't notice, and I don't want to make a scene.

"No, please. I just want to leave," I say.

My moms look at each other. "Sure, of course, we can go."

• • •

"How about we get something to eat and maybe some hot chocolate?" Mom says as we're walking down the street.

"Yes, please," Nadia replies excitedly.

"Honey, is everything all right?" Mama asks. "You look stressed."

"I'm fine. It's just a headache." The last thing I want is for my moms to march back to the store and demand an apology from that ignorant woman. If I tell them, that's exactly what they'll do, and I know those girls from my school would have a field day with that. It's easier to just lie.

Later on, as I try to focus on my chemistry homework, I'm still fuming about the dress shop incident. I must have been ten when I first noticed a store employee looking at me funny when I was in the candy section. Moms had said I could pick out a treat for myself while they were at the other end of the aisle. The way the employee spoke to me made my moms very angry, and at the time, I didn't understand why he was being so mean. But years of living in my brown skin has made me painfully aware that the world doesn't look at me the same way they look at white people. Sometimes when they meet me for the first time, there is an element of surprise, like I've purposely pulled a bait and switch on them, calling myself Mira Jensen when I am in fact brown. Lately it angers me more and more—I'm just so tired of it. Which is probably why I've been thinking more and more about my birth parents.

When I was five, Moms told me I was adopted and that they had chosen me to be their child, to be their family. And that has been enough. But no matter how much they love me and want to shield me from the uglier truths, there have been plenty of times when I've been made to feel like I'm in the wrong skin. I've always found it hard to explain this to my parents, and as I've gotten older, I've stopped trying.

It's something I'm going to have to learn to deal with, but before I can do that, I think I have to find out more about what my identity means to me.

I also decide that next time someone makes me feel bad about myself, I will not stand down and walk away.

• • •

"Maybe she thought she was being helpful," Brooke says when I tell her about the dress-shopping incident the next day. I'm still angry about it but sadly not shocked that Brooke thinks it wasn't what I know it is. In my experience, white people have a funny way of gaslighting without even realizing they're doing it. I mean, I love Brooke, but it's more than annoying that she thinks it's all in my head. I know exactly what happened, and it wasn't like it was the first time. None of my white friends get followed around at a store by employees like I do.

"Sure she was," I say bitterly. "Like the guy at the dollar store?"

"I said I was sorry about that. I really thought it was because your bag was so huge."

"Really, Brooke?" I shake my head. "You know one of these days you're going to have to face reality. There are a lot of racist jerks in the world."

"You're right. I'm sorry, Mira. I shouldn't have said that."

165

"It was so embarrassing, and I'm so mad at myself because I froze. I should have said something."

"Hey, that's not on you," Brooke says. "I wish I'd been there with you."

"But that's exactly the point," I say. "I shouldn't have to take reinforcement with me to go shopping while brown."

She doesn't say anything, but she squeezes my arm to let me know she cares.

CHAPTER THREE

"Are you excited for Christmas?" I say to Nadia as we start to take out the ornaments from their boxes. "Here, I found your skates."

"Yay, I've missed these," she says, hanging them on the tree.

Every Christmas, Nadia and I get to choose a new ornament for the tree, and we usually pick something to represent what was important to us that year. For Nadia, it's been ice skating and little musical notes because she loves to play the piano. For me, it's been puppies and kittens because I'm obsessed with animals. It's my favorite time of year, especially decorating the tree while sipping hot chocolate with marshmallows.

"I can't find my treble clef," Nadia says, sounding highly distressed.

"And I can't find the little wooden ornament with all our names on it," Mama says.

"The one Grandpa gave us last year?" I ask.

"Honey, I think there may be another box in the garage," Mom says.

"I'll go and grab it," I volunteer. I pop into the garage,

keeping an eye out for any evil spiders that might be lurking in the dark corners. I climb the stepladder and check the labels on a few of the large boxes in the front, but none of them seem to be hiding any Christmas stuff. I move some around to get to the ones in the back and find a small cardboard box with no label. I pull it out and open it. The garage light isn't really bright enough to tell what's in there, but it's definitely not ornaments. I pick up a spiral-bound planner with *Bloomington High School* printed on the cover and *2000–2001* in gold lettering just underneath. I open it. The name *Ayesha Hameed* is written in cursive on the front page. I'm just about to flip through the pages when I hear Mom calling.

"Mira, did you find it?"

"No, I'm still looking!" I call out.

I don't think I've ever seen this box before, but I'm pretty sure the things inside are my birth mother's. I've never asked my moms her name, but who else could it belong to? Why are Moms hiding it here in the garage? I'm not sure how I feel about this, so I tuck it back in and continue looking for the ornaments. When I find them, I carry them back out into the living room, but for the rest of the evening, my mind keeps going back to the little box in the garage. Just before bed, I sneak back in there and carry it to my room.

I settle on my bed with the box in front of me and take a deep breath. I'm really going to do this. The contents of this box may be the only connection to my birth mother I'll ever have. My hands tremble as I remove the lid and set it on my bed. I peer into the box, trying to decide what to take out first. There's not a whole lot in there, but what catches my eye is a small dark blue velvet pouch. I pick it up and open it. Inside is a delicate neck-lace. It has a small gold heart-shaped pendant hanging on a thin gold chain, the kind that opens up. I open it carefully, and a breath catches in my throat. There's a tiny picture on each side. One is of me as a newborn. I recognize it from the background on Mama's laptop. The other one has to be of my birth mother. I look closely at it, studying the details of her face. I can see myself in her, in the shape of her eyes and the almost-imperceptible bump on the bridge of her nose. My heart aches as I look at this stranger who gave me life but has never been in it. I put the necklace around my neck and fasten the clasp. For some reason, I think I should feel different after putting it on, but I don't. I try to imagine it lying against my mother's skin, and a warmth fills me from inside. I wonder what she was thinking when she added it to this box. Did she imagine that one day, years later, her daughter would wear it and yearn to feel her mother's hands on her, to look into her eyes? I shake it all off. I'm being ridiculous.

I rummage around in the box and find two AMC Theatres movie ticket stubs to *Unbreakable*. Was this a movie both my birth parents watched together? I try to picture them, but I have no reference, no knowledge about them.

I find a purple scrunchie next to the Bloomington High School planner. I pull it out and flip through the pages. The little squares for each day are mostly filled with notes about homework, quizzes, and tests. I count back nine months from my birthday, trying to find something she would have written around the time she must have been with my birth father. Moms had never mentioned anything about him when they first told me I was adopted, so I'm hoping that maybe I'll find a clue in here. But I don't see anything that might hint at his identity, at least nothing that I can recognize.

There's not much else left in the box except a mix CD with a list of songs on the case. I pick it up and discover an envelope beneath it. When I open it, a few photographs fall out. They're of people I don't recognize. They're all brown and look around my moms' age. There's one that looks like a family picture, the parents seated and three young girls standing behind them. Everyone's smiling into the camera. One of them is my mother . . . so these must be my grandparents and aunts.

A million questions explode in my mind, but there's no one here to answer them. Did she leave these things here on purpose, knowing that one day I might find them? Or are they just things forgotten and left behind by someone desperate to sever ties with a part of her life?

My eyes fill with tears as the fist around my heart tightens its grip. I shove the box aside and get under the covers. I don't really know what it is that I was hoping to find. I guess I want to know the circumstances that led to me being born and placed for adoption. The logical part of my brain can empathize with what Ayesha Hameed did. I can't even imagine what I would do if I was ever in that situation. But a different part of me resents having been left with no connection to my roots and family. I feel ungrateful and selfish for even having such feelings, but I can't help it. After all, if Moms wanted me to have these things, they would have given this box to me a long time ago. Maybe it was too painful for them.

I decide it's best if I keep this to myself for now.

CHAPTER FOUR

"So, you're not going to tell your parents at all?" Brooke says the next day after our volunteer shift at the animal shelter. We're grabbing burgers at our favorite place and pick an outdoor table because December in Houston is still nice enough to sit outside. We both got our usuals: a Mexi burger with sweet potato fries for me and a BBQ burger with queso fries for her.

"No," I say, dipping a couple of fries in chipotle mayo. "At least not for now. I'm not even sure how I feel about all of it."

"But you've been thinking about it a lot, though, haven't you?"

"I have, but I was just thinking I'd ask my moms for a little more information about my birth mom. To be honest, holding stuff that belonged to her was kind of . . . weird, I guess."

"Your moms are supercool," Brooke says. "I'm sure they'll understand."

"I know they will," I tell her. "That's why it's so hard. What if it's too much for them?"

"Hmm. I guess you'll have to wait and see how you feel later."

"Did I tell you Nikhil and I are having a Bollywood night tomorrow?" I say, abruptly changing the topic.

"Oh, is that this weekend?"

"Yeah, do you wanna come?" Nikhil and I have been hanging out a lot lately, and I don't want Brooke to feel excluded.

"No, no, you do your thing," she says. "My grandparents are in town, so my weekend's all full."

She takes a bite of her burger and chews thoughtfully for a bit.

"Do you feel different when you're with Nikhil?" she asks.

"Different how?"

"You know, because he's Indian and your birth mom was Indian? I don't know, I was just wondering."

I consider what she said while I munch on my fries.

"I don't know, really." I say. "Maybe a little. I mean his life has been so different from mine, but then, we're kind of from the same background. Not that I really know anything about my background . . ."

She's got me thinking now, and I know it'll be stuck in my head for a while.

● ● ●

Later that night, I'm still trying to figure out if I do feel different. I've grown up in relative comfort in a white, suburban, upper-middle-class neighborhood in Houston. And although the demographics scream diversity, my personal social circle has been remarkably homogenous. And by that, I mean as white as you can imagine. While my moms are both left-leaning liberals, feminists, pro-immigration, and pro-diversity, they do, at the end of the day, default to white when it comes to their friends and families.

I don't really have a full picture of what kind of life Nikhil had in India before he came here. I'm sure it was great, with a mom who works for NASA, and the way that he talks about his life and friends in Mumbai makes me think that it was amazing.

But the great difference in our lives is that he's never had to question whether or not he really belongs in his own life whereas for me that's never been true.

I've questioned my place from the time I was seven years old and we were doing family trees at school. When I was presenting mine, one of the kids asked why I looked so different from the rest of my family. I've never been sure if it was an innocent question or if it was intended as barb, but I could never unhear it and it changed the way I looked at myself within my own family. Obviously, I knew I was different—but I hadn't clued in to the way everyone else noticed it. It made me hyperaware of even the slightest differences and nuances during family gatherings and even my daily interactions with my moms and Nadia. Eventually it was overshadowed by other growing pains, but when I met Nikhil and we became friends, some of those old thoughts returned. It wasn't as if I was out to befriend the first Indian person I could find merely to satisfy some sort of cultural blank space. I mean, I live in Houston, so there were several other kids of Indian origin at my school. But what first drew me to Nikhil was his voice, so full of emotion and depth. It literally stopped me in my tracks as I was walking past the music room. And the song he was singing had so much pain and longing that, even though I couldn't understand a word, the melody tugged at my heartstrings. Of course, it helps that he's sweet and funny and we can make fun of each other without it hurting any feelings. So I don't have any ulterior motives for being his friend, but if I'm being completely honest with myself, I have to admit that I do have an undeniable desire to know what my life would've been like if my Indian birth mother hadn't placed me for adoption.

And along with that comes a sense of shame and guilt for feeling this way.

CHAPTER FIVE

It's Saturday, and I'm ready for my first Bollywood movie night. I'm not entirely sure if it's solely for my benefit or because Nikhil just really loves old Hindi movies, but I'm happy to go along. It turns out that I love the song and dance and drama of it all. It's glorious, and I have decades of movies to catch up on.

Tonight, an old classic is on the menu, *Kabhi Kabhie*, accompanied by a sumptuous dinner made by Nikhil's mom, Sarita Aunty. Nikhil's dad stayed back in Mumbai for work, so it's just the three of us.

I can tell dinner is going to be delicious the moment I step into the foyer of Nikhil's house.

"Whatever your mom's making smells amazing," I say as I take off my shoes and place them neatly in a corner by the door.

"I hope you like mutton biryani," Nikhil says. "Mom went all out when I told her you were coming."

"I love biryani," I say. "My moms take us to eat at Mahek all the time. I swear they can handle spicy food better than I can."

"Well, then you're in luck," Nikhil says with a grin. "I told Mom you're a firangi, so she kept it all mild."

"What's a firangi? And just FYI, I don't appreciate you calling me names in Hindi." I'm only half joking.

"It's not anything bad," he says. "Just refers to white people because, you know, you eat like a white person."

"I do not," I say, narrowing my eyes at him.

"You kind of do," he says with an extremely annoying smirk. "Remember the other day when you took a bite of my samosa and then had to get milk from the cafeteria? I mean, even babies can eat samosas."

"I feel sorry for your future babies."

He's saved from replying when Sarita Aunty walks into the room with a steaming dish in her hands. She puts it down before turning to me.

"How are you, Mira?" she says, enveloping me in a warm hug. "You haven't been over for a while."

"It's been really hectic at school. Plus, I've been taking extra shifts at the animal shelter."

"You must really love being around all the animals," Sarita Aunty says. "Nikhil tells me you're quite the activist."

"Well, I try to do what I can. It's heartbreaking what some people will do to an innocent creature. I can't just sit around and do nothing."

"Plus, she loves bossing people around," Nikhil says, making a face at me.

"I agree," I say smugly. "Especially those who desperately need it."

"You two are so funny." Sarita Aunty serves me some of the biryani. My mouth waters immediately, followed by my eyes as soon as I put a spoonful in my mouth. Is this seriously their idea of mild?

"Nikhil, go and get her a glass of milk, quickly," Sarita Aunty says. "I'm so sorry, Mira. Nikhil told me you love spicy food."

Nikhil returns with a glass of milk, and I resist the urge to throw it in his face. I have to give him credit, though. That was a good one. Now I just have to come up with something equally genius for my revenge.

Sarita Aunty brings out some lentils and roti, which is very soothing once my mouth has stopped burning. She's also made rasmalai, which is now my new favorite dessert. I'm sure Moms will want to try to make it once I tell them about it.

After dinner, we settle down to watch the movie. It's from the '70s, so well before my time. The story line is actually really poignant. I love the songs, and by the end of the movie, I have tears running down my cheeks.

When the credits start to roll, I turn to see Sarita Aunty dabbing her eyes with the end of her sari.

"This movie always gets to me," she says. "No matter how many times I watch it."

"It was really good," I say. "Thank you for inviting me, and for dinner as well."

"Of course. It was our pleasure," she says. "Nikhil, beta, would you go and make some chai for us?"

"Sure." He jumps up and turns to me with a grin. "Mira, would you like some *chai tea*?" He pronounces *chai tea* with an exaggerated American accent.

I roll my eyes at him. "Haha, you really need some new material."

Sarita Aunty shakes her head at us and goes to the kitchen. Nikhil and I follow her, and I help her set out the cups and a platter of snacks.

"Have you had Parle-G biscuits before, Mira?" Sarita Aunty asks, holding out a packet.

"No, I don't think so," I answer.

Nikhil practically snatches them out of his mom's hands, pulls out two cookies, and sticks them in front of my face. "You have to try these," he says, his expression far too excited, but I guess he really has a sweet tooth.

"Okay, calm down, I believe you." I take one, break it in two, and pop one half in my mouth. It is quite delicious.

"So . . . what do you think?" Nikhil looks expectantly at me.

"My god, Nikhil, stop acting as though you made these with your own two hands," Sarita Aunty says.

I'm starting to like this woman more and more every time she takes Nikhil down a peg or two. It's hard being the only one with that responsibility.

"They're really good," I say. "Was this one of your favorite snacks back home or what?"

"Yes, that and all the junk food in the world," Sarita Aunty answers for him.

"It's not my fault that there are so many amazing things to eat back home," Nikhil protests. "Better than your pork rinds and beef jerky."

I secretly agree with him because I don't see the appeal of those either, but I don't want to give him the satisfaction.

"I don't see what's wrong with them," I say.

"Sure, if you say so. But they don't stand a chance against bhelpuri and chanachur and cumin biscuits and, oh my god, mithai." He looks like he's having some sort of a moment there, so his mom and I both just stare at him.

"Okay, okay, baba, I can't win with you," his mom finally says. "Anyway, I have an early morning, so I'm going to bed."

"I should go too," I say, getting up to give her a hug. "Thank you so much—this was a lot of fun."

"You're most welcome anytime, Mira," she says. "Nikhil, you'll drop her off at home, yes?"

"Why? She has legs, doesn't she?" he says with a grin. His mom just ignores him and walks upstairs.

"God, I love your mom," I say, getting my purse off the couch.

Nikhil smiles. "All my friends back home love her. You know when I came out to her, everyone warned me to expect the worst, but she was amazing. So was my dad."

"That had to be hard for you," I say. "I mean, people are pretty close-minded about this stuff over there, aren't they?"

He nods. "No more than here, to be honest. Look what happened with Ryan."

Ryan's a friend of ours from school. When he came out to his parents a couple of months ago, it didn't go well. He ended up having to move in with his best friend Jack's family.

"That's true," I say. "I guess I don't know any other Indian families, really, so I just always assumed it's different in India."

"It's definitely not easy, but there's lots of people like my parents and lots of organizations that help support teens like me."

"I'm really glad your parents are so supportive. My moms are like that too, I guess. I can always talk to them about anything."

"How is it that you've never had any brown friends?" he asks. "This place is full of desi people."

Desi is a new term I've picked up from Nikhil. It refers to South Asian people living abroad and he said it comes from the word *desh*, which means *country*.

I shrug. "I don't know, I guess I've just never found the opportunity to be around them a lot. And my moms have their friends and a couple of them are brown, but they're not super close, so it's not like I've hung around with their kids or anything."

"But what about at school?" he says. "There's Raj and Vivek. And Pooja? She seems nice."

"I don't know. We used to go to elementary school together, but we were never really friends."

"Hmm, maybe if you come to some desi functions with me and my mom, you might meet some people you like."

I narrow my eyes at him. "Why do I get the feeling that you're trying to pawn me off to someone else?"

"Jeez, you're so weird," he says. "I'm just trying to expand your mind. You're welcome."

"Thanks," I say sarcastically. "But my mind is perfectly fine."

"Says the person who's never had Parle-G biscuits before," he mutters under his breath as we walk out to his car.

"For your information, we call them cookies here," I say, poking him playfully in the ribs. "Biscuits are an entirely different thing."

"Pardon me, but I only speak the Queen's English," he says in a haughty British accent.

"You mean the queen you all booted out of India?"

"Yup, that same one," he says, grinning back at me. He puts on his playlist, and suddenly "End Game" by Taylor Swift comes on at full volume and I resist the urge to jump out of the car.

It's great to have someone to talk to about these things. But I also know having Nikhil isn't enough.

I have to talk to my moms about what's going on in my head.

CHAPTER SIX

"Hey, can I talk to you guys about something?" I say hesitantly as I walk into the kitchen. Moms are cleaning up after dinner, and I pretend to help by moving the silverware around. Luckily, they don't have high expectations of me when it comes to doing stuff around the house. Nadia is the one who gets stuck with all that while I help with the errands. We've all come to an uneasy truce after years of fighting and arguing about it.

"Sure, honey, what's up?" Mama says, turning on the dishwasher. "How was Bollywood night?"

"We had wings and fries for dinner," Nadia announces from her corner of the breakfast nook. As usual, she has her nose buried in a book, her feet tucked under her.

"Hey, Nadia, do you mind if I talk to Moms alone for a bit?" I say, knowing full well what's coming.

"Why? What're you going to talk about?" she asks, perking up at the prospect of something juicy.

"Something private, obviously," I say irritably.

"Why can't I hear about it? I'm not a baby," she whines.

"Well, then, maybe you should stop acting like one and leave when someone's asking you nicely."

"Mom!" she screams, her voice so high our neighbor's dog starts barking.

"Nadia, look, you're upsetting Bruno," I say, pretending to be concerned.

"Okay, enough out of both of you," Mom says sternly. "Mira, stop antagonizing your sister. And, Nadia, would you please give us some privacy?"

Nadia gets up and trudges through the kitchen and up the stairs as if she's been unjustly banished for life, but not before throwing me a death glare. She's so dramatic.

Mama takes off her rubber gloves. "Come, help me dry the baking dishes," she says.

Mom begins to wipe down the kitchen island. "What did you want to talk about, honey?"

I pick up a dishcloth and begin to dry. I don't know quite how to tell them.

"I found a box in the garage," I blurt out. "I think it belonged to my birth mom." I stare at the glass dish in my hands, a little nervous to look up at them.

"Okay," Mama says slowly. She sounds fine, so I raise my eyes.

"I'm sorry, I don't want you to be upset," I say.

"We're not upset," Mom tells me.

"How come you never told me about it?"

"We weren't sure, honey," Mama says. "We thought of giving it to you a few times, but we never really knew how you'd feel."

"When did you find it?" Mom asks.

"At Christmastime," I say. "When I was in there looking for ornaments."

"Why didn't you mention it sooner?" Mama says.

"I don't know. I guess I thought since you were hiding it in there, maybe you didn't want me to have it."

"We weren't hiding it, Mira," Mom says. "It's been there for years. We just figured we'd give it to you if you asked about her."

"I've been thinking about it a lot."

"That's perfectly normal," Mama says. "We just wish you'd come to us sooner. We want you to be able to talk to us about anything."

"I know . . . I guess I just want to find out more about where I come from."

"So what would you like to know?" Mom asks.

"Just like . . . stuff about her, what she was like . . ." My voice trails off as I wonder if I've made a huge mistake. The last thing I want is to hurt my moms. I know they're saying that they're fine, but what if they're not?

"Well, she was really sweet and very young," Mom says. "From what she told us, it sounded like she found herself in a situation where she didn't know what else to do."

"But I'm sure she only wanted the best for you," Mama adds hastily.

It feels so weird standing here and talking to Moms about the woman who'd given me life but to whom I feel no connection. She's a complete stranger. Maybe it's just wishful thinking that I see a resemblance between us when I look at the tiny photograph in the locket. Or maybe I've inherited some other trait of hers that I'll never know about. And I realize now that it's the reason I've always felt like there was a part of me missing, that I needed to know her to feel whole. But how could I say that to my moms, who've given me everything, who've held me close after every scraped knee, wiped away my tears, and who've always loved me unconditionally? I can't let them feel, even for a millisecond, that there's something more they could have done, that their love for me isn't enough. Because it is more than enough. It's not about them. It's about me, about my blood and how I feel about myself.

"She was really scared when we met her for the first time," Mama says. She looks at Mom. "Remember, it was at that Denny's in Bloomington?"

"How can I forget?" Mom says. She puts an arm around me. "She was all alone, barely showing, but she was so young, pratically the same age as you are now."

"And I remember thinking how sad it was that she had no one to turn to," Mama says with a faraway look in her eyes.

For the next few moments, they're both silent, and I wish I could look inside their memories. Then they try to tell me everything they remember.

● ● ●

Monday at school, I meet up with Nikhil just before choir.

"Hey, thanks again for the other night," I say as I catch up with him. "It was really fun."

"Yes, it was great," he says. "By the way, my mom loves you."

"Of course she does," I say with a huge grin. "What's not to love?"

He mutters something under his breath, which I choose to ignore because I'm nice like that.

"Hey, listen, can we talk later?"

He stops walking and looks at me. "Sure, is everything okay?"

"Yeah, it's fine. I'll tell you later."

After choir, we hang around until everyone else has left. It's the last class of the day, so in a few minutes, we're alone.

"So, what did you want to talk about?" Nikhil says, planting himself on the piano bench.

"I talked to Moms after you dropped me off," I say, leaning against a table. "I finally told them I want to know more about my birth mom."

"That's intense, Mira. How did they take it?"

"Actually, really well." I tell him about the box.

"So?" he says expectantly. "What was in it?"

I shrug. "I found this necklace." Last night after I talked to Moms, I took out the necklace and put it on again. I've decided to wear it from now on.

He leans in to get a closer look.

"The locket opens," I say.

"Can I look inside?" He's already opening it, and I can see that he thinks it's pretty amazing too.

"Is that you as a baby?"

"No, it's Priyanka Chopra," I say, rolling my eyes. "Of course it's me. And the other one has to be her."

He's still holding the locket, completely mesmerized. "You kind of look like her."

"Right? I was thinking that too."

"Especially your nose. You both have that little bump."

"What bump?" I narrow my eyes at him. "I don't have a bump on my nose. Why would you say I have a bump on my nose?"

"I'm sorry," he covers quickly. "Clearly I need to get my eyes checked."

"Yes, I'll call and make the appointment for you."

"But seriously, what else was there?"

"Just a planner and some old photos. I think they are of her family . . . my family, I guess."

"So, what're you going to do?"

"I don't know. I was hoping there'd be something more informative in there, but that was it. No address or pictures of my father or anything. And my moms only knew her for a few months before I was born. She left right after."

The door to the music room opens, and Pooja Bains walks in. She's a tall, dusky-skinned, raven-haired beauty who's just as much at home with the cheerleading squad as she is performing a classical Indian dance at our school's annual talent show. I've known and disliked her since elementary school. There's something about her that makes me feel bad about myself. Maybe it's the way she flaunts her Indianness in my face like we're both in a competition or it's that she always conveniently forgets to include me in any of the cultural functions she keeps inviting everyone to. Whatever it is, I don't care for her, so seeing her make a beeline toward Nikhil right now doesn't exactly make me feel warm and fuzzy.

"Hey, Nik, what's up?" she says, sidling up to him and turning her back to me. Nikhil smiles at her, the same dazzling one that I noticed the very first time we met.

"Hey, Pooja. Nothing much?" he says. "I didn't see you at Arjun's wedding last weekend."

"Yeah, I was going to come, but then I got the worst headache and I didn't think I could stand all the noise. And you know how everyone's always begging me to do a dance performance and I just knew I wouldn't be up for that." She smiles demurely, and I want to puke.

I wiggle out from between her and the piano and look pointedly at Nikhil, ignoring her completely.

"So, Nikhil, we'll talk later?" I say.

"What's happening later?" Pooja asks before Nikhil can answer.

None of your fucking beeswax, I want to say. But I don't.

"Oh, nothing," he says. "We were just talking."

I feel the blood rushing to my face, and I can't look at him.

"Oh, how sweet," she says, smiling condescendingly. I think she'd make a really good villain in a Bollywood movie. I wish someone would cast her already so she'd stop being one in mine.

"I'll call you later on," Nikhil tells me.

"Let me see what you're working on," Pooja says, grabbing his elbow and guiding him toward the piano bench. I guess I've been dismissed.

It's not until much later that night when I try to fall asleep that I realize something. Nikhil never told Pooja not to call him Nik.

CHAPTER SEVEN

That Friday night I have a dream. I'm standing on an empty road. There's no one there, and I'm tired and scared but not a single car comes by. Finally, I see a woman in the distance. She walks toward me, and when she's close, I see that she's trying to say something, but she can't speak. She's gesturing wildly with her hands and her eyes are wide and panicked but no sound comes out of her mouth. I try to get closer to her, but I can't walk. No matter how hard I try, I can't seem to move. When I look up, she seems to be fading away. I try to scream, but the sound is trapped in my throat and she can't hear me. I try to reach out with my arms, but she's too far away and then she disappears.

I wake up and find that my pillow is damp with my tears. I know without a doubt that the woman in my dreams was my birth mother. And I know she was trying to tell me something.

I grab my phone from the nightstand. It's two in the morning. I turn on the bedside lamp and get the box from where I stashed it underneath my bed.

I open it and look inside. I take out the CD and the photos. When I pick up the planner, something falls out. I look down at the ground and see a couple of envelopes. I pick them up and see my name written in the same cursive that's in the planner. I gently run my finger under the flap of one to break the seal, pull out the folded piece of paper, and lay it on my bedspread. Then I do the same with the other. They're letters, each one hand-written and folded carefully. I pick up the one on top and open it gently.

My sweetest baby girl,

You don't know me now, but I hope and pray that one day you will. Right now, I can feel you inside me, moving about, as if you can't wait to come out and begin your life. I picture you, wide-eyed and eager to learn everything about this world. I hope that even as you learn to trust your own instincts and forge your own path, you also learn to be careful with your heart. I hope that you always protect yourself in friendship and love. I hope that you have the best life and that it's filled with all the love and happiness you deserve. But most of all, I hope that one day you can share your life with me, even though right now I cannot share mine with you. The stars are not aligned for us to be together, but I pray that one day they will be, and we can be close again, the way we are now. As your heart beats within me, I am racked with guilt and uncertainty about many things, but I know you will have a great life with Mel and Sam. Please forgive me for leaving you, but know that in my heart you'll always be here with me.

With all the love in my heart,

Ayesha

I put the letter down as my tears fall on the page right on top of the spots smudged years ago by my mother's tears. The ache in my heart is something I can't describe; it's unlike anything I've felt before. My body is racked with sobs, my pain and sadness flowing out from me, the way they must have flowed from her. I try to picture her as she must have been, in this same house, this bed, swollen with the consequence of a broken trust. How afraid she must have been and how lonely. Almost two decades later, her pain still reverberates within the walls of this room. I have a sudden urge to hold her, comfort her, and tell her it was all right, that her choices didn't hurt me.

I feel like I can't breathe, like the pain and sadness are too much for my heart to hold inside. I open my bedroom window and stand in front of it just taking in huge breaths of the cool night air trying to calm myself. Eventually the tightness in my chest fades and I can breathe normally again. I wander back to bed after a while and try to go back to sleep. But every time I close my eyes, I see her again, the woman from my dream.

Now she has a voice, and I know what she's saying.

• • •

The next morning, I wake up feeling as though I haven't slept at all. A quick glance at my phone tells me it's already noon. For a second, I panic, then remember that it's Saturday. I sit up in bed, rubbing the sleep out of my eyes. Then I pick up the next letter and begin to read.

My sweetest baby girl,
Today I had a dream about you. You were a chubby little girl with dark curls framing your beautiful face. We were together in a park, and you wanted me to push you on the swing. You laughed out loud every time you went high up in the air, and it was the most beautiful sound I've ever heard. Afterward we went to get ice cream, and you wanted sprinkles on yours.

I was just like that when I was a little girl, and my abbu would take me out for ice cream. I'm sad that your nana won't be in your life as you're growing up because he would love you more than anything in the world. I've met your future grandfather, and he is so excited to meet you and spoil you. I wish you both the happiest of times together. As for myself, whenever I miss you, I will close my eyes and imagine you on that swing. The sound of your laughter will make everything good again.

with all the love in my heart,

Ayesha

I don't know if I have any tears left to cry, but my heart is still heavy. My grandpa Mike is the sweetest and most loving person I've ever known, and to know that he's met my mother makes my heart twist in a way I've never felt before. I wish I could travel back in time and meet her, just to let her know that everything is all right, that I have the best life, and that she can stop feeling guilty. I've had the perfect childhood, with family trips and lots of moments to fill my heart with happy memories many times over. But knowing how she must have lived with the guilt of leaving me makes my heart ache.

CHAPTER EIGHT

Hours later, a deep sigh escapes me. I don't feel so good . . . and then I remember that I haven't eaten anything all day. Moms have been trying to get me to come down, but I can't seem to leave my bed, let alone my room. Nadia doesn't know what's going on, and I can hear her pestering Moms for details, but I don't know what they're telling her. Every normal thing in my life seems to have shifted slightly, forcing me to look at it from a different angle. I've always taken my life for granted and never really questioned the cost of it to someone else. Another girl like me, having to make the kinds of life-altering decisions that I've never had to make. She's made sure of it. And now I can't help wondering if by allowing me to have this life, her own may have been destroyed. How can I live with that?

I start to feel nauseous, so I make my way downstairs to the kitchen. It's now four in the afternoon and lunch has long been cleared away, but Moms are sitting at the table having coffee. A covered plate sits on my place mat. They look up when I wander in and grab a glass of water.

"Mira, honey, are you all right?" Mom jumps up and throws her arms around me.

"We've been so worried," Mama says, uncovering my plate. "Here, let me warm up your food."

I shake my head. "It's fine. Don't bother." I don't really have an appetite, but my stomach has a mind of its own. There's a couple of lamb chops with gravy on my plate and roasted potatoes and carrots. Usually I love this, but today I don't really taste anything.

"Sweetie, please tell us what we can do?" Mama says.

"Is it the box?" Mom says. "Did something in it upset you?"

"No," I say, more sharply than I intended. "It's not—"

"Look, whatever it is, you can talk to us about it," Mama says.

"I want to know more about her. I want to know what she was like."

"Of course, honey," Mama says. "Like we told you, we're happy to share whatever we know."

"She was my age, right?" It's been hard for me to imagine her situation when I thought she might have been a little bit older than me, but to think that she was exactly the age I am now makes it even harder.

"She was only eighteen," Mama says softly. "Just a few months older than you."

"How did she find you guys?"

"She went through an agency in Bloomington, Illinois," Mom says. "That's where she was living and going to school."

"And she didn't have any family? I thought you said she was from India. So, she must have had someone, right?"

I can't help but think that if there were any relatives, I might be able to get more information.

"She lived with her aunt and uncle, but she never shared any details about them," Mama says.

"She told us that she was doing this all on her own," Mom says. "She couldn't tell her family. She said she'd come to the US to finish her last year of high school."

"So when did you first meet her?"

"Gosh, it was so long ago," Mom says. "I think she must have been only two months pregnant at that point."

Mama nods. "You're right. She wasn't showing at all. And I remember she told us that all the arrangements had to be made before she started showing. It must have been because of her relatives."

"We felt so bad for her," Mom says. "But we didn't want to push her too much. And she never told us much about her personal life in Bloomington."

"What about my father?" I hadn't found anything in the box about him. Not a single clue or name or anything.

Both Mom and Mama shake their heads. "She didn't tell us anything about him either," Mama says.

"We hoped during all the months she stayed with us that maybe she would share more, but she didn't, and it didn't feel right to ask her." Mom gets up to top off her coffee. "I'm sorry it's taken us so long to talk about this."

"We always kept thinking we should wait until you were a little older," Mama says. "But then you never really asked about her, and there was never a good moment to bring it up."

"It's okay. Don't worry about that," I say. "I'm sorry . . . I know this must be hard for you too."

"Oh gosh, no, Mira, this is perfectly normal. Of course, you'll have questions," Mama says.

"And we promise we'll do whatever we can to fill in the gaps," Mom adds. "We just don't want you to think you're alone in this."

I smile at them, grateful that they're not upset with me. I don't know how much more guilt I can deal with right now.

"She wrote me these letters," I say softly. "It's so heartbreaking, what she was going through, all by herself." I start tearing up again, and Moms both look surprised.

"We didn't realize there were any letters," Mama says. "I wish we'd been able to do more for her."

"She was very sweet, you know, and so quiet, like she wanted to make herself invisible." Mom looks at Mama, a sadness in her eyes.

"We always wondered what she was putting herself through," Mama says. "We tried so hard to get her to open up, but it was like she'd put a wall up around her and didn't trust anyone."

"We never found out how she got pregnant and why she had absolutely no one else to turn to," Mom says.

"But we just wanted her to know that she was safe with us, and we told her if she changed her mind, we would understand," Mama says.

"I'm sure she must have been very grateful to you for that," I tell them. "In the letters she says how happy she was that I'd be part of your family. And she mentions Grandpa Mike. I can't believe that he met her too."

"Yes, Dad was so happy that he'd finally have a little granddaughter to spoil," Mama says with a fond smile.

"I wish she knew my life now," I say. "Maybe if she knew how great it is, she wouldn't feel so guilty."

"We did tell her right from the beginning that she could be a part of your life," Mom says. "We would never keep her away from you."

"But after she graduated and had you, she decided to go back to India," Mama says. "And we had to respect her decision."

I can't believe what I'm hearing. My birth mother *chose* not to be a part of my life. What could possibly have been so awful that she'd never want to see me again?

"Did she say why she decided to go back?"

Mama shakes her head. "No, we did try to ask her, but she was really closed off about it."

"Do you think her family pressured her in some way?"

"I'm not sure, honey," Mom says. "I mean, it's possible."

"She moved out a couple of weeks before you were born," Mom tells me.

"How come?"

"Well, I think she realized we needed to get the nursery ready and wanted to give us the room back," Mama says.

"It must have been hard for her to be around us at the time," Mom adds. "We were so excited about you, and it was all we could think about."

"So where did she go?" I ask.

"She found another place nearby," Mom says. "She asked us to give her some space, and we wanted to respect that."

"But then one night she called us from the grocery store. Her water had broken, and she needed to get to the hospital," Mama says. "After you were born, we got really busy with you and tried to get her to come and visit, but the last time we saw her was when she came to say goodbye."

"We were quite shocked, to tell you the truth," Mom says. "We'd just assumed she'd go to college because she used to talk about Northwestern all the time."

"We know she got in because she showed us the letter before graduation," Mama says.

"We asked her to stay in touch with us when she was in India," Mom continues. "But we never heard from her after that."

"For years, we wondered what happened to her and how she was doing," Mama says. "I hope she found a way to be happy."

It's hard for me to sit here and watch my parents reminisce about the woman who gave me life but then chose not to be in it. I don't know what her circumstances were or why she came to that decision, and I might never know. But it's too difficult to realize that I was the reason for so much heartache.

I need some fresh air, so I go for a long walk around the Oyster Creek Loop. Afterward I sit by the water for a bit, lost in my thoughts. I don't know how to come to terms with the fact that my moms had given my birth mother the opportunity to be a part of my life and that she had decided not to accept it. A resentment begins to build up in me, and I wonder if I was just a huge inconvenience that she had to get rid of. Maybe all the stuff in the letter that she said about wanting me to have a great life was just that and nothing more. It's my own fault for reading more into it than was actually there. I'd been feeling awful this whole time because I thought she didn't have a choice and that it was hurting her to have to give me up. But if that were true, wouldn't she have taken the offer to stay in my life? My moms did so much for her and were happy for her to be part of our family, so why did she still leave without a trace?

I'm beginning to wish I'd never seen that box. Maybe I was better off without her.

I take a deep breath of the evening air and get up to start heading back home. I'm going to put all this behind me and pay attention to the people who *are* in my life. Maybe I need to focus on them and on my future instead of a past I can't control.

When I get home, the first thing I do is give my moms a big hug.

"I'm really sorry I made you worry so much," I say when they've pried free of my death grip. "I guess those letters got to me, but I'll never know why she made the choices she did, so I'm just not going to think about that anymore."

"Well, I think it makes complete sense that you'd want to know more about her, and I wish we could help," Mom says. "But honestly there wasn't much we could do or say once she decided to go back."

"I can tell you, though, that I'm absolutely sure that it was one of the hardest things she'd had to do in her life," Mama says. "It wasn't an easy decision for her."

Nadia walks into the room and looks around. "Why is everyone so serious?" she asks.

I pull her into a hug. "Because we've been seriously wondering where you were," I answer, ruffling her hair. "Hey, want some ice cream?"

"Will you put sprinkles on it?"

"Yup."

"Then yes," she says. "Two scoops, please."

I play a game of Uno with her while we eat our ice cream. It's exactly what I need to feel like my old self again.

CHAPTER NINE

I mostly hang out with Brooke over the next few days, during our shifts at the animal shelter and when we study after. It doesn't leave me much time for Nikhil, which suits me just fine.

Even though Nikhil and I have the kind of friendship where we give each other a hard time, that run-in with Pooja put something into harsh perspective for me. He will always have more in common with someone like Pooja, who, even though she was born here, is totally in touch with her Indian roots in a way I'll never be. Not because I don't want to be, but just because that's not my life. And sometimes I get the distinct impression that maybe Nikhil sort of feels sorry for me because he thinks I feel like a misfit, so he's trying to teach me the basics. And the truth is, strange as it sounds, it's not completely false.

Reading those letters from my birth mother has rekindled all the old questions about where I really belong. I love my moms and my sister, but the fact is that I'll always be the odd one out, at least as far as appearances are concerned. And I'll never fit in with the brown crowd either, because they can't relate with someone who's brown on the outside but white on the inside. I've been called a coconut on more than one occasion, and these days it's starting to bother me in a way it never has before.

I'm glad I have Brooke to talk to because she really gets me. We first became friends in seventh grade on a class field trip to the Houston Museum of Natural Science. We both forgot to get our permission slips signed, so our moms had to rush over to school and sign them. Brooke's mother offered to drive us both there to join the rest of our class, and we've been fast friends since then. In fact, my moms invited her mom over for a glass of wine that evening, and now it's a regular thing for us all to spend time together.

Brooke and I have seen each other through breakups, bad hair days, and problem skin, and she's always been a ray of positivity in my life.

"How's Nikhil doing?" she asks after I've gone a few days without hanging out with him. "Did something happen between you two?"

"Not really . . . I don't know." I tell her about how Pooja had interrupted us in the music room, then say, "I'm so confused. How can he stand Pooja? She's so fake and annoying."

"Maybe he's homesick and she reminds him of India," Brooke says. "He must miss his boyfriend a lot too, right?"

"Yeah, he does," I say hesitantly. "But I doubt that's it. She must have realized that we're good friends, and so she had to ruin it for me. Just like she's always done."

"Okay, I think you're being a little bit dramatic there, Mira. I'm sure it's nothing like that."

"You're just saying that because you're a good person. I'm telling you; she did the same thing to me when I was friends with Ria in third grade. She's always tried to push me out."

"I don't get it," Brooke says. "Why would she want to do that?"

"Because she's evil, Brooke. Pure evil."

Brooke gently takes the coffee cup from my hand. "I think we've had enough caffeine for today."

Later, as we're working on chemistry equations, I wonder if maybe Brooke is right about Nikhil. I mean, he doesn't exactly know about my history with Pooja, so he has no reason to hate her just because I do. I decide to call him when we take a break from studying. I miss hanging out with him, and now I'm feeling guilty because if he's been homesick and hasn't even told me, that means maybe I haven't been a particularly great friend to him.

● ● ●

"I don't think you're giving Pooja a chance," Nikhil says as we're heading to choir practice the next day. "She's not that bad."

"That's because you don't know her as well as I do," I say.

I can't believe Nikhil is defending her. I mean, whose friend is he anyway?

He stops walking and looks down at me.

"Mira, come on—why don't you just hang out with us one time? That's it, just one time, and if you still hate her, I promise I won't ask again."

I hesitate, thinking about what Brooke said to me. Then I say, "Okay, fine. We can hang out. What did you have in mind? A movie and then we can grab some food?"

"Actually, I was thinking more along the lines of a musical evening."

"Okaaay." I'm already not liking this idea. "Like a concert?"

He smiles in a way that does not make me feel better about this at all.

"No, actually it's a classical dance performance," he says.

"Oh. Who's performing?"

"Pooja's been learning classical Indian dance for years, and she and a few others are putting on a show for a children's charity. My mom bought three tickets and asked me to invite you."

"Does Pooja know about this?"

"Well, I kind of talked to her about you the other day, and she said she'd love for you to come too."

I narrow my eyes at him. "What do you mean you talked to her about me?"

"It's no big deal," Nikhil says quickly. "I just noticed some tension between you two, and so I talked to her about it."

I'm fuming. I don't like this one bit. "You know what?" I say. "I don't really want to talk about this right now."

I turn around and walk away. In the music room, I pick a spot as far away from him as I can during choir. And then afterward I leave as quickly as I can.

• • •

I decide I'll make an effort with Pooja because it seems to be important to Nikhil and he's important to me. And as a bonus, I'll get to hobnob with Houston's desi community and possibly start learning something about my heritage.

"Are you sure I look all right?" I ask for the tenth time the night of the charity show.

I'm wearing a traditional Indian outfit, courtesy of Nikhil's mom, who is about my height and petite like me. It's an ankle-length, voluminous skirt called a lehenga with a short, fitted blouse on top called a choli, as well as a matching scarf. The problem is that it leaves my midriff and most of my back bare because that part of the blouse is nothing more than a crisscross of thin straps. I must admit that I've never worn anything so intricately beautiful before. The entire thing is made of burgundy silk and organza with gorgeous embroidery in gold thread all over.

"You look stunning," Mom says. "I can't believe you get to dress up like this."

"You look like a real-life princess," Nadia says, playing with the gold and maroon bangles on my wrists. Sarita Aunty insisted that I borrow all the accessories as well. I'm wearing beautiful little bell-shaped gold earrings and a gold choker with rubies and pearls. Mom let me borrow her golden strappy heels, and I'm practicing walking in them without falling over.

Nikhil's picking me up in just a few minutes, so I quickly put on some light pink lipstick and draw my eyeliner into wings. The last thing is a gold-and-red bindi right in the middle of my forehead, and I'm ready.

The doorbell rings, and Mom goes to answer it. She's back a few seconds later with Nikhil beside her. He looks very different today. He's wearing a dark brown vest with a high collar and a cream-colored silky-looking tunic underneath, as well as cream-colored leggings. Around his neck is a dark-brown-and-gold scarf.

"Wow," I say, uncharacteristically at a loss for further words.

"Wow yourself," he says with a smile. "You look great."

"What do you call your outfit?" Mama asks. "You look so handsome and regal."

"This?" He looks down at himself. "This is called a koti," he says, pointing to the vest. "And underneath is a kurta and the pants are called churidar."

"It looks very nice on you," Mom says.

"Thank you," Nikhil replies. "My mom was so happy to see me in this tonight," he adds. "We don't really get to dress up a lot these days."

"Well, it's awfully nice of her to lend Mira this gorgeous outfit," Mama says.

"It looks great on you, Mira," he says.

"Why, thank you," I say, with a grin and a little dip. "Should we go?"

"Have a great time, you two," Mom says as they usher us out.

"Don't forget to call if you're going to be late." Mama blows a kiss just as we get in Nikhil's car.

● ● ●

When we arrive at the venue, my jaw drops at the opulent decor. It's like something from one of the Bollywood movies I've watched with Nikhil. It looks like everyone is dressed to impress, and I'm glad I didn't change my mind about my outfit at the last minute or else I'd be extremely underdressed. Sarita Aunty is already there and walks over as soon as she spots us. Nikhil takes my coat and goes to check it while his mom gushes over my outfit.

"You have to keep this," she says. "It looks a thousand times better on you, my dear."

"I can't possibly keep it," I say. "It's too much."

"Nonsense. It's yours. Now don't argue with your elders and go find that son of mine and get some food. It's delicious."

Nikhil appears right on cue, and we line up by the buffet for dinner. It's a lavish feast. I don't recognize a lot of the items, but luckily there are little cards in front of each dish with a description. There's lamb biryani, which the card describes as aromatic rice with spicy lamb. Then there's chicken korma, which is chicken in a cream-based sauce. There's an array of vegetable dishes and other meats, and I can't possibly taste them all, so I follow Nikhil's lead and take some of the biryani, along with some vegetable korma and a yogurt salad called raita, which Nikhil says will help temper the heat of the other food. I also grab a piece of buttery naan and vegetable fritters. I'm full just looking at all the food on my plate. Once we're seated, Nikhil pours me a glass from one of the several jugs of a milky-looking drink that are placed around the table. He says it's called lassi and is made from buttermilk. I'm very thankful for the drink a few minutes and several bites of food later because my mouth is on fire. I take a few sips of the lassi, which tastes sweet and creamy. It helps with the burning, and I wait before taking another tentative bite. By the time our plates are cleared away, I've learned that if I take a couple of sips of lassi between every few bites of food, it's not too bad. But to be honest, by the end, I can no longer taste anything. I'm pretty sure all my taste buds have been permanently destroyed, which is a pity because Nikhil brings us a plate of sweets to share and a couple of bowls of rasmalai. I'm sure it's all delicious, but I'll have to take his word for it.

So far there's been no sign of Pooja, and I'm relieved because now I'll get credit for showing up without actually having to deal with her.

Unfortunately, she pops up just as the last of the plates are being cleared.

"Mira, I'm so glad you could make it," she says, leaning over to hug me. I've never been so uncomfortable in my life. What a faker. As if she's ever spared me more than a sneer in all the years we've known each other. But of course, she's performing for Nikhil. Well, I might not have an Oscar, but I will keep up appearances with her as if my life depends on it. No one will be fake nicer than me.

"Hiiii, oh my god, I'm so excited to see you dance," I say, my voice unnaturally high. Nikhil's eyebrows go up slightly, but he recovers quickly.

"How was rehearsal?" he asks her, standing up to offer her his seat since our table's completely full.

"It was good," she replies. "We should be starting pretty soon."

But she sits in his spot anyway, turning to admire my outfit.

"This is gorgeous, Mira," she says breathlessly. "Where did you get it? I didn't think you had any Indian clothes."

Ha. I knew she couldn't hide her true nature.

I turn to look at Nikhil, waiting to see a look of understanding on his face, telling me that now he gets it. But the idiot isn't even listening to us. He seems to have wandered off and is now standing with his mom, gabbing to a bunch of older Indian women. They seem to be having the time of their lives, giggling at something he said. What could he possibly have said that was so hilarious? Why isn't he here witnessing the evil that is Pooja? This is just great.

"Um, yeah, I've had this for a while, you know," I lie. "It was perfect for today. It must be time for you to go backstage, right?"

I've never been happier to see another person leave. I walk over to Nikhil and his mom. She introduces me to all the ladies. It's Mrs. This and Aunty That. I'm trying hard to remember all the names and answer all their questions at the same time.

"So where are you from, Mira?" a Mrs. Gupta asks.

"I'm from right here, in Houston," I say.

"No, of course, but where are you really from?" Pushpa Aunty insists.

"I'm really from here," I say.

"But your parents, they must be from India, or Pakistan, or somewhere, no?" Mrs. Chowdhury asks.

"My mother was from India," I say, and I'm about to tell them that I'm adopted but I begin to feel resentful and hesitate. Why are they being so nosy?

Sarita Aunty comes to my rescue.

"I think it's almost time for the performance to begin," she says, ushering the ladies back to their seats. I throw her a grateful smile before Nikhil and I return to our table.

The performance is breathtaking. The grace and elegance of the motions and the significance behind them as explained in the program are fascinating to me. Much as I dislike Pooja, I have to admit she's an amazing dancer. Watching her face as she matches each movement of her body with the appropriate expression is quite something, as is her intricate footwork. It's not hard to believe that she's had to train for years to be able to do this so well.

After the performance, Nikhil and I go backstage to find her. Nikhil has brought her flowers and hands them to her.

"You were really amazing, Pooja," I force myself to admit out loud.

"Thank you, Mira," she says, sounding a little surprised. "That's very nice of you."

"I mean it," I say. "How long have you been dancing?"

"Only since I was five," she answers with a small laugh. "It's a tradition in my family to train for classical dance."

"My cousin does kathak too," Nikhil chimes in. "She would have loved your performance."

"I take it that was kathak we just watched?" I say.

"Yes, it's like an ancient form of storytelling," Pooja says. "It's a way to share the great epics and stories from mythology across generations. All the women in my family have trained in kathak." Her face lights up as she talks, and I wonder how it must feel to have a connection going so far back.

"This must be really special for you and your family, then," I say. "I'm really glad I came today."

"Me too," she says, with the first genuine smile I've ever seen on her.

"You must be exhausted," Nikhil tells her. "We'll let you get back to your group."

"Thanks for coming back here," she says to us both. "I think we're all going to our guru's house for a little after-party."

Nikhil and I find Sarita Aunty outside, waiting to tell us that we can go on without her. We get our coats and walk out into the cool night. As soon as we've pulled out of the parking lot, Nikhil turns to me.

"That wasn't so bad, was it?" he says.

"No, it was fine," I reply.

"*Fine?* Seriously?"

"Okay, it was great. You were right."

He keeps his eyes on the road, but I can see him smile.

"Look, I know you didn't want to come, and this was hard for you, but I'm really glad you came."

"Actually, I'm glad I came too," I say. "I had a really great time."

"Aaand?"

"And you were right about Pooja too," I say. "She isn't that bad."

A little while later, he pulls into my driveway and turns off the engine.

"Listen," he says, "I'm not saying you have to hang out with us all the time now, but it would be nice if we could do some stuff together."

"What kind of stuff?" I ask warily. I'm still not totally convinced.

"Maybe we can go get some Indian fast food some time, if you're up for it?"

"Like the kind you post on Insta?"

"Yes," he says, suddenly very excited. "That's a great idea. I've been craving it again."

I give him an odd look. "Didn't you all just go the other day?"

"Yes, but you can never have too much pani puri," he says. "Back home, my friends and I go, like, several times a week. We go to Juhu Beach and walk around getting food from different stands."

I raise my hands up defensively at this onslaught of enthusiasm. "Okay, fine, I will go with you."

"Awesome," he says. "I'll ask Pooja and maybe we can go tomorrow."

"Does she have to come?" I venture.

"Mira, c'mon . . ."

"Fine, I'll stop. She can come too."

CHAPTER TEN

Nikhil and I say good night, and as soon as I step inside, Nadia pounces on me. I spend the rest of the evening regaling her and my moms with everything about the evening. Afterward I go up to my room to change into my pajamas and get ready for bed. But as I lie there trying to go to sleep, something keeps coming back to me.

At the event tonight among all those Indian people, I realized that it was the first time I was in a room full of others who looked just like me, where I wasn't one of just a handful of brown bodies. It felt different somehow. In a good way. Like I was part of something that I belonged to. It's strange to feel like this about a group of people I've just met, but I can't deny it. I felt at home there in a way I haven't felt before. And I can't help wondering why it's taken me so long to feel this way. When I look in the mirror, a brown girl looks back at me every single time. But on the inside, I feel white, like my moms and my sister. And most of my friends.

My mind goes back to when I overheard Pooja calling me a coconut. Normally I ignore comments about how I don't exactly fit in with the rest of my family, but what Pooja said really stung for some reason. Now I can't help wondering if maybe it's because there's more than a grain of truth in it. I have no sense of being Indian in any way, but I am, whether I choose to acknowledge that part of me or not. When people say things about me not really belonging with the rest of my family, I just ignore it or chalk it up to racism because I know exactly how much my family loves me. But having roots in a culture I barely know about is something else.

I sit up. It's pointless trying to go to sleep now. I tiptoe down the stairs to get some water and find Moms watching *Law & Order: SVU*, one of their favorite shows.

"Hey, honey—what's wrong?" Mama asks.

"Just can't sleep."

"Come sit here with us." Mom holds out her arm for me to snuggle into.

I watch with them until the show's over, then stand up to stretch.

"Sweetie, are you sure you're okay?" Mom asks.

I shrug and slump back onto the couch.

"Okay, c'mon, out with it," Mama says in her no-nonsense voice.

"It's nothing, really." I'm hesitant to share my feelings about tonight. I'm not sure they'll understand where I'm coming from.

"It's obviously something," Mom says. I know it's pointless to try to fool them. They can read my face too well.

"It's just . . . Tonight when I was at the thing with all those Indian people, it felt different."

"What felt different?" Mama says.

"Just how I fit in with them, you know?" I look at my mothers, willing them to get what I'm saying.

But I don't think they do. Yet.

"I think it's normal, Mira," Mom finally says.

Mama nods.

"I mean, you've never really been around a lot of Indian people, even though we live here in Houston," she says.

"It's kind of our fault," Mom says. "It's not like we don't have Indian friends, but really no one that we're particularly close to."

"How come?" I say. "I mean, Mama, you know Mrs. Rasheed from work, and, Mom, you know Pooja's dad, right?"

Moms look at each other. I'm starting to wish I hadn't stirred this particular pot, but I can't stop now.

"I don't know," Mom says. "I guess we just never needed to because we already had our group of friends that we're close with."

Mama takes my face in her hands.

"Honey, if you feel like you need to be around more Indian people and get to know them, then of course we're going to do everything we can to make that happen," she says.

"Yes, and we can go out to Indian places more and maybe attend some cultural events, you know," Mom adds.

I nod, not knowing what else to say. I don't know how to explain to them that cultural events and food and dinner parties are all great, but they're not going to be enough to fill this hole I've suddenly discovered in myself.

What if I never feel at home in my own life again?

• • •

Hours later, I'm tossing and turning in bed, once again unable to go to sleep. Finally, I lean over the edge of my bed and pull out the box from underneath. I settle onto the floor and take out the items one by one. Once the box is completely empty, I turn it over and shake it. An envelope falls out. It's

211

sealed like the others and must have been lodged into the corners of the cardboard. I take out the letter, smooth it out, and begin to read.

My sweetest baby girl,

As I write this, you are still safe inside me and I can only see you with my heart. I picture you as strong and beautiful, bringing joy to everyone around you. By the time you are old enough to read this, I'll be far away, but you'll never be too far from me. I only hope that your heart will still be open for me and that you will find it in yourself to forgive me and to understand why I had to do what I did. It will be the hardest thing I will ever do in my life, and I draw strength from the knowledge that it is what's best for you. I'm ashamed to admit that I don't have the courage to stay with you and face the consequences of my actions. But know that you will always be the most precious thing in my life, no matter how much time has passed or how far we are from each other. I'll carry you in my heart until the day I die. But there is something I have to ask you to do, even though I know I have no right. On your 18th birthday, I will wait for you at the Flora Fountain in Mumbai at 4 p.m. If after reading this, you decide you want nothing to do with me, I'll understand completely. But if there's any part of you that feels that there's even the slightest chance that we can reconnect, please come to me. I'll be waiting.

With all the love in my heart,

Your mother, Ayesha

I put the letter down, my heart racing and sweat making my palms tingle. This has to be a sign. All this time I've been worried that my birth mother didn't want me in her life, and now I find this letter, this invitation from her. But right away doubts cloud the new sense of hope that's barely had a chance to take root.

She wrote this letter eighteen years ago.

Who knows what's happened in her life since then?

CHAPTER ELEVEN

After a restless night, I show up at school the next morning bleary-eyed and cranky. Upon waking, I realized that talking to my moms last night may not have been the best move because I couldn't help noticing how guarded they suddenly were around me. As if they were afraid to say the wrong thing and of hurting my feelings. Nadia is the only one who is oblivious to what is going on, and for that I am thankful.

"You look like you didn't get any sleep," Brooke says as soon as she sees me by our lockers. "How late did the event go?"

"Not too late," I say, grabbing my math textbook and my graphing calculator. "I just couldn't sleep."

"But did you at least have a good time?"

"Yes, actually I had a great time," I say. "Pooja was amazing. You should see her dance sometime."

"Well, I'm glad you decided to go after all."

Just then Pooja passes us in the hallway and gives me a little wave. I wave back in shock, because in all the years we've been at school together, she has never really acknowledged my existence.

"Wow, what was that?" Brooke says, clearly as shocked as I am.

"I know, right? I suppose my appearance at her performance yesterday sealed our friendship." I make a face at Brooke. "Guess I'll have to be nice to her from now on."

"Stop being so cynical, Mira," Brooke says. "It can't be that bad."

"Ugh, you have no idea. Now Nikhil wants the three of us to hang out together."

"So what's wrong with that?"

"I'll tell you what's wrong with that. Pooja just wants to be the center of attention as usual, and she can't stand that Nikhil and I are good friends."

"Even if that's true, which I don't think it is, maybe once you get to know her, you'll realize she's quite nice."

"I don't know," I say. "I told Nikhil I'll go out with them tonight, so I guess we'll find out."

"I'm sure you'll have a lot of fun."

"Do you want to come with us?" I think to ask, grabbing her hand. "Please say you'll come."

"I wish I could," she says. "But I have softball practice. Maybe I can join you guys next time."

"Okay, then pray for me," I say, clutching her hands to my chest. "Goodbye forever."

Brooke walks away shaking her head.

• • •

After school, Nikhil and I meet up in the music room to practice the Hindi song we've been working on. It's from the *Kabhi Kabhie* soundtrack, and Nikhil has transliterated the Hindi lyrics for me so I can sing it too.

We're just in the middle of practicing when Pooja walks in.

"Is that what I think it is?" she cries, coming up on the stage and sitting down next to Nikhil. And then she proceeds to belt out the whole song while Nikhil plays it on the piano.

Great. Just great.

"Wow, you're such a good singer," I say when she's done.

"Thanks. You're quite good too," she says.

Thank you, I think?

I mumble a thank-you, wishing I was anywhere but here.

"So, are we still on for tonight?" she asks, smiling brightly at Nikhil.

I wonder if she knows he's gay and that he has a boyfriend back home. I'm not sure how deep their friendship goes, and maybe she likes him and thinks I'm the competition.

Nikhil doesn't talk about his boyfriend much, and so far all I know is that he exists, that his name is Ashish, and that they miss each other a whole lot. So there's a good possibility that Pooja doesn't know and thinks that he and I are more than friends. I guess I'll have to make sure to show her we're not.

● ● ●

That evening, Pooja drives us to Hillcroft Street for chaat, which she and Nikhil explain to me is an umbrella term for savory, spicy street food in India. Apparently Chowpatty House has the best pani puri, and since I've never had any, I'm quite excited to try it for the first time. Once we're seated, Pooja and Nikhil order a variety of dishes without even looking at the menu. Going by the enthusiastic greetings we got as we entered, it seems like they're both regulars here. It's a good thing no one put me in charge of ordering because the items on the menu are a complete mystery to me. But I'm not worried. Soon, I too would become an expert on desi street food, and I can show off when I bring Nadia and my moms here.

The first things to arrive are three platters of pani puri, one for each of us. There are six small, ball-shaped things on my plate. They're crispy and hollow, filled with a spicy potato mixture. I follow Pooja and Nikhil closely, watching carefully as they dip one hollow piece into a brown liquid and pop the whole thing in their mouths. I do the same, but as soon as I bite into it, the very spicy, tangy liquid explodes in my mouth and goes down my airway. I start coughing and soon my nose is running and there's a mess on my plate.

"How did you two just bite into it like that?" I sputter once I can talk again. My throat is still burning, and I gulp down half a glass of water.

"Maybe you should start with something less violent," Pooja says, smirking a little.

"Like what?" I glare at Nikhil, but he's busy stuffing his face.

"Huh?" He looks up at me. "Oh, sorry. Are you okay?"

Do I look okay? I could have died.

"We're just saying that maybe she should start with some dahi puri," Pooja says.

"What's that?" I ask as the waiter puts three more plates on the table.

"It's a flat version of the pani puri, minus the water but with yogurt on top," she says. "Try it—I think you'll really like this one."

I pull one of the small plates toward me and use my spoon to pick up a piece. I put it tentatively in my mouth . . . and luckily this one doesn't attack me.

"Mmm, this is so good," I say as I munch on the crunchy puri, enjoying the tangy, sweet, and spicy sauce on it. The cool yogurt takes some of the bite out of it.

"I told you you'd like it," Pooja says, acting as though she made it for me with her own two hands. I'm too busy relishing the flavor to be annoyed with her.

Next, we have some bun kebabs, which are spicy meat patties on buns with a delicious tamarind chutney, tastier than anything I've ever had before. Nikhil has the foresight to order me some sweet mango lassi, and a few sips of the cool buttermilk drink keeps the burning at bay. Afterward we practically have to roll out of the restaurant because we're way too full. But it was all so good, and I can't wait to bring Moms and Nadia here soon.

"So, what do you want to do next?" Nikhil says as we step out into the cool evening. It's Houston in January, so it's not exactly sweater weather, but there's definitely a little nip in the air.

"Ooh, should we get some chai?" Pooja says. "And then we can go look at the Christmas lights at Avenida Houston."

"Yes, let's do that," I say. "I think today might be the last day the lights are up."

We pop into another Indian shop to get some chai and walk back to Pooja's car to head over to Avenida Houston.

The lights are spectacular as always. I kind of wish Nadia was here to enjoy them with me because she loves this as much as I do. There's something magical about them, and as we slowly walk along, sipping our chai, I'm really happy that Nikhil pestered me to come out tonight.

CHAPTER TWELVE

A few weeks later, Nikhil, Pooja, and I are hanging out at the library doing research for a class project. Nikhil reads something in an article and leans over to show it to Pooja. He tells her something in Hindi, and she giggles. I'm sitting right there, and suddenly I feel really left out, but I don't say anything because I don't want to make a big deal out of it. Things have been going so well with the three of us and I don't want to seem super needy, but I can't deny that it really hurts. Especially that Nikhil doesn't even notice. And it's not like I can tell him he's not allowed to speak his mother tongue just because I don't speak it. Even though Pooja was born here like I was, she speaks fluent Hindi. I feel so awkward whenever they do that, and this isn't the first time. But it just doesn't feel right to bring it up. And I know I should be more mature about this and that Nikhil and Pooja probably don't mean to hurt me, but the fact is that no matter how much I try there's no particular bubble I fit in and I never will. Not unless I find a few other brown girls who've been adopted by white parents. They must be somewhere out there in the world, but for now this is all I've got. But it's just not enough anymore. I want something more, a sense of real belonging.

"Okay, then," I say suddenly, startling Nikhil and Pooja. "Who wants to help me learn Hindi?"

They both look at me in confusion at first, but Pooja recovers quickly.

"Hey, sorry, we're being rude, aren't we?"

"No, it's not that," I say. "It's just . . . To be honest, it just feels weird when you guys start talking in Hindi and I don't get a word of what you're saying."

"Sorry," Nikhil says. "I guess I didn't realize, but you're right."

"So?" I smile. "Anyone up for helping me learn?"

They both look at each other, and Pooja rubs her hands.

"Sure," she says with a big smile. "I'm in."

Nikhil lets out a big sigh. "Oh, thank god," he says. "I was really scared I'd get stuck doing it." He grins at Pooja. "You're going to have so much fun."

"Hey," I say, kicking him under the table. "I'm right here."

"Ouch!" He glares at me. "What did I say?"

"I'm so excited," Pooja says, completely ignoring him. "I can't wait."

"Awesome," I say. "So, when do we begin?"

"I want to take an oath first," Nikhil says, his face dead serious.

"An oath? What kind of oath?" Pooja asks.

"I solemnly swear that I will never ever make fun of Mira's firangi accent when she speaks Hindi."

I stare at him, not sure if this is a joke or if he actually means it.

But then he bursts out laughing, which earns him a glare from a couple of people trying to read in peace. Clearly, he suffers from the delusion that he's extremely hilarious.

Pooja doesn't look amused, and I think for the first time I can truly start liking her after all.

"Nikhil, stop it," she tells him sternly. "It's not funny."

"That's because you haven't heard her yet," he says, still grinning from ear to ear.

"You know what?" I say, gathering my things and standing up. "If this is what—"

"No, no, please wait, I'm sorry," he says, grabbing my arm across the table. "I promise I'll be good."

I hesitate, pinning him with a withering glare. Then I sit down slowly.

"Okay," I say. "But I swear if you make fun of me even once, I'm never going to talk to you again."

"I promise, really," he says. "I'll be good."

"Don't worry, Mira," Pooja says. "If he steps out of line, he'll have to deal with me too."

I smile at her and throw Nikhil a smug look.

"Okay, you know what, I don't think I like this anymore," he says, but he's still smiling.

"Why don't you come over to my place on Saturday?" Pooja says. "We can do a lesson and see how it goes."

"Okay," I say hesitantly. "Should I download an app or something?"

"No need. I can teach you everything. Whenever I go to India for the summer, my grandmother and I volunteer at the orphanage and I help the kids learn how to read and write."

How have I never seen this side of Pooja before?

"Okay, well then, thank you. I'm really excited to get started."

"I can't make it this Saturday," Nikhil says.

"Sounds good to me," I say, making a face at him.

• • •

Back at home, I tell Moms about our plan, and I can tell that they're relieved to hear about it.

"I think that's really nice of your friends to do that for you," Mom says. "Let's make sure to invite them over for dinner and a movie night or something soon."

"Are you excited, honey?" Mama asks.

"So excited," I say. "I always feel jealous that Nikhil and Pooja both speak three languages."

"English, Hindi, and what else?" Mama asks.

"Nikhil also speaks Marathi, and Pooja speaks Punjabi," I tell her.

"Oh, so other dialects," Mom says.

I shake my head. "No, that's what I thought too at first, but then Nikhil told me they're completely different languages, with like their own script and everything."

"This is so interesting," Mama says, looking up from her phone. "I just googled this, and it says there are twenty-six different languages spoken in India."

"That's a lot of languages for one country," Mom says.

"Well, India wasn't always one country," Mama observes. "It used to be different kingdoms."

"I've been looking up college courses for next year, and I definitely want to take some on Indian history," I say. "I think that'll be so interesting."

"If you still want to major in anthropology, then you could minor in Asian Studies or something," Mom says.

"That's a great idea," I tell her. "I still have to narrow down my top choices, so I can look up their course offerings before I do that."

"Well, let me know if I can help you with that, okay?" Mom says.

She's a guidance counselor at a private high school, so this is what she does for a living. Having spent a great deal of my childhood listening to her talk about her work has prepared me quite well.

"Thanks, Mom," I say, running up the stairs to download a language app so I can get started on my own. I'm not about to go to Pooja's completely unprepared.

I spend the next hour or so before bed learning some basic words. Nikhil is going to have to eat his words when he hears my very accurate pronunciation because I am a keen learner when it comes to anything new.

• • •

A couple of days later, I'm in Pooja's living room. Clearly, I have grossly underestimated how invested she is in this. The table in front of us is covered with workbooks, index cards, and markers. We've already gone over pronunciation techniques for sounds that aren't used in English as well as basic pronouns. I've learned that there are many different words for relatives. For example, maternal aunts and uncles and paternal aunts and uncles each have their own titles. The same goes for grandparents and cousins. It seems confusing at first, but I get the hang of it pretty quickly. I'm having the time of my life, so I don't realize how late it's gotten until Pooja's mom walks in.

"How is it going, girls?" she asks. "You look like you've been working very hard."

"It's going great," I say. "Pooja's a great teacher."

I'm not even being fake. She really has a knack for making things easy to understand.

"Yes, our Pooja has always wanted to be a teacher," her mom says with a smile. "Even as a little girl, she would line up all her toys and teach them something or other."

"Mom, please stop," Pooja says, her cheeks turning red.

"Mira, would you like to stay for dinner?" her mom says. "It's nothing fancy, but we'd love for you to join us."

I look at Pooja. I'm not sure if she wants me to hang out for that long, now that we're done with our lessons.

"Please stay, Mira. You can show off what you learned today," she says with a smile.

I call my moms to let them know I'm staying for dinner, and then Pooja takes me upstairs to her room while we wait for dinner to be ready.

Her room is very neat, way better than mine. On a shelf in one corner are all sorts of awards and trophies. But I'm drawn immediately to an array of photos on the wall next to the window. There are many of her in her dance outfits, performing, receiving awards, and others with large groups of people.

"Is this all your family?" I say, turning to look at her.

"Yes, these are from our summer vacations in India. This is my nani." She points to an older woman standing beside her in the middle of the group.

"Wait, Nani—that's your maternal grandmother, right?" I say.

"Yes, that's right. And these are all my cousins." She points to about five or six young girls who look around twelve to fifteen years old.

"Wow, you have a lot of relatives," I say. "It must be so much fun when you go there."

She looks wistfully at the pictures. "I love it more than anything. I can't wait to go there again this summer."

"What's it like?" I ask.

"Have you never been?"

"No. But my moms talk about going there for a vacation one day."

"Can I ask you something? You don't have to answer if you don't want to."

"No, it's fine."

"Do you ever wonder about your birth parents?"

I don't answer right away, and Pooja looks uncomfortable.

"I'm sorry, I shouldn't have said anything," she tells me. "It's none of my business."

"No, it's okay . . . It's just funny that you ask because lately it feels like that's all I've been thinking about."

"Do you want to talk about it?" she says.

Of all the people in the world, I can say with complete honesty that I never ever thought I'd be sitting on Pooja Bains's bed wondering if I should share my deepest, heaviest thoughts with her. But I guess the universe is having a good laugh right now, because as it turns out, it's really easy to confide in Pooja.

"I've sort of started to feel like I'm a guest in my own life," I say. "Does that make any sense?"

"Kind of," she says. "I guess it must be hard not to have anyone who gets where you come from."

"Exactly. I mean, don't get me wrong, my moms are the best. And they can't help that they're not Indian."

"You know when we were little, I used to be jealous of you," she says.

"Seriously?" I find that hard to believe, given the

225

snooty way in which she had always acted toward me.

"I thought your moms were so cool and my parents were, you know, not," Pooja confides. "Kids would always make fun of their accent and the lunches my mom made me."

"That's horrible," I say, reaching out to touch her arm.

"*I* was horrible. I was so embarrassed of my own parents, I didn't want them to come to parent-teacher nights. I never stopped to think of how much they sacrificed and struggled to build a life here."

"But you were a kid," I say. "You didn't understand all that back then."

Pooja nods. "And I was awful to you too, wasn't I?"

"Honestly?" I say with a smile. "Yes, you were pretty horrible."

She smiles back and squeezes my arm. "I used to wish my parents were white too so no one would make fun of them. And I hated that you got to have that."

I lie back on her bed. It's so weird hearing Pooja say these things after years of putting up with her.

"I love my moms so much," I say. "And when I was little, I never understood that to other people I looked out of place when I was with my family."

"Until people started telling you," Pooja says softly. "I was one of them." She looks a little sad, but I feel worse for my ten-year-old self than I do for her at this moment, so at first I say nothing.

Then, after a moment's thought, I tell her, "You know, I think you might be the reason I started to question everything about my life."

"I'm so sorry," she says.

"No, I'm not trying to make you feel bad. It's not really about you."

"What do you mean?"

"I was too young at the time," I say. "I started wondering about stuff, but then I got distracted by life and sort of forgot about it."

"I guess that makes sense. We were only ten, I think."

"Exactly. But then, last year in history class, Mrs. Williams asked me something during the India unit, and I didn't have a clue."

"Of course, she asked you because as a brown person you are naturally endowed with all the knowledge about India," Pooja says sarcastically.

"I know, right? But to be honest, I felt bad for not knowing the answer, and I realized that I'd never even made an effort."

"So, did you start looking stuff up?"

"Yup. I googled everything I could think of, so now I'm pretty much a walking encyclopedia on facts about India."

"But there's so much more to being Indian," Pooja says.

"I was so happy, thinking that I knew so much, and for a while, it was enough. But then I became friends with Nikhil right after he came here, and I started realizing how much I don't get."

Pooja shakes her head. "That Nikhil, always making trouble wherever he goes."

"We have so much fun together, but he reminds me of everything that's missing in me. You know, everything that makes me desi."

"Did he teach you that word too?" Pooja asks.

"One of the first things."

"So why didn't hanging out with him help?"

"It did. But you know he made me see myself in a different

way. Like I was finding all these gaps in myself, all these spaces I didn't know how to fill."

Pooja raises her eyebrows. "That's deep, man. I never thought about it that way, but I think I get it. It's like you're looking at a selfie, but there are all these holes in it."

"Exactly. And the more I hang out with him and with you, the more empty spaces I find."

"I guess Bollywood songs and spicy food can only fill you up so much."

"I tried to talk to my moms about this," I say. "But I just don't think they get it."

"Because they're white?"

"Kind of. Mostly because I don't think they've ever had to question their right to be exactly where they are. They can own their lives."

"I mean, you can own your life too," Pooja points out. "You have a great relationship with your moms and your sister, right?"

"I do," I say. "But it's different for me. I mean, when people look at me with my family they have questions, you know? Like, how did I end up with them? And where am I really from? It's not like that for Nadia. She looks like them, so she automatically belongs."

"Yeah, you don't have to explain that to me," Pooja says. "I mean, hello, I'm a brown girl with brown parents living in the US, so we all know a little bit about not belonging."

"And that's why you get what I'm saying?"

She nods. "I do, totally. But I think I'm starting to appreciate how much more complicated it is for you."

We both sit silently for some time. I never realized how Pooja felt about me as a kid, and now that I know, everything she did makes a lot more sense. It doesn't excuse any of it, but at least now I understand.

"Thanks for listening," I say, sitting up and smoothing down my hair.

"Thank you for sharing," she says. "I know we have some bad history, but I really hope we can move on from that. I'd really like for us to be friends."

"I think after what I just dumped on you, we can officially say that we are," I say with a little laugh.

She reaches over to hug me, and for the first time in a long time, I feel a real connection. It's a great feeling.

"Have you ever tried to find your birth parents?" Pooja asks, scooting all the way up on her bed.

"Not really," I admit. "When I was about five, my moms told me that I was adopted and that my birth mother was a young student from India who couldn't keep me. And so she placed me for adoption because she knew they would love me."

"That must have been really difficult to hear."

"Not really. I think I just sort of took that information and stuck it somewhere deep inside. I had a great childhood, so it was just something that happened, and they told me about it and that was that."

"I guess at five it's not like you could really process it any more than that," Pooja observes.

"But I have been thinking about it a lot recently," I say.

"I'm sure they'll understand. I mean, it's normal for you to wonder about it, right?"

"No, that's not what I'm worried about. I just don't want them to start thinking that I'm unhappy or that it's their fault or something like that."

229

"Do you think she's still here?" Pooja asks. "Your birth-mother? Like in the US?"

"She went back to India after I was born."

"Would you want to meet her?"

"I don't know, to be honest," I say, getting off the bed. "You know, you should think about a career in investigative journalism."

"I'm so sorry," she says. "I overstepped, didn't I?"

"Nah, it's okay," I tell her. "I just shared my deepest, darkest secrets with you, so I guess that gives you a pass."

Pooja's mom calls out to let us know that dinner is ready.

I walk downstairs fully expecting another culinary adventure for my mouth, but to my relief and slight disappointment, I see that we're having fish tacos for dinner.

"I've kept the hot sauce on the side," Pooja's mom says. "I heard about the incident at the chaat place."

"Thanks a lot," I mumble to Pooja as I take a seat at the table.

Dinner is fun, with Pooja's mom regaling us with stories from her childhood, growing up in Delhi.

"It's a good thing that Pooja's father is as fond of eighties music as I am," she says. "When my parents told me that he would make a good match for me, my first question was about his taste in music."

"So it was an arranged marriage?" I ask.

"Yes," she says, placing another platter of tacos in front of me. "My parents always made sure they asked that question before they entertained any marriage proposal."

"Was it scary to get married to someone you didn't know?"

"Everyone thinks that arranged marriages are something draconian," Pooja says. "Actually, it's just like meeting someone on a dating app, except there's an aunty or uncle in the middle."

"I never really thought of it like that, but yeah, that makes sense, I guess," I say.

"Whenever someone brought a proposal for me, my parents would always ask me first," Pooja's mom says. "I figured they knew me better than anyone else, so it made sense that they could find someone best suited for me."

"Yeah, I can't imagine anyone else who loves to go dancing as much as my parents," Pooja says. "They're always the first ones on the dance floor and the last ones to leave at any party. Even now."

"What do you mean, *even now*?" Pooja's mom asks in mock indignation. "We're young at heart, and there's no age limit for dancing," she adds with a smile.

"Yes, Pooja," I say, grinning at her. "So that's why you're so good. You got a double dose of the dance gene."

"Actually, Pooja is very dedicated at whatever she does," her mom says. "When she was younger, she would practice for hours while other kids were playing outside."

"Wow, that sounds really intense," I say. "Do you think you'll keep doing it even when you're in college?"

"I hope so," she says. "I'd like to teach dance to young kids when I'm older."

"I'm sure you'll be an amazing teacher," I say.

● ● ●

At home over the weekend, I can't stop thinking about my conversation with Pooja and her mom. I've always just sort of gone along with the kind of thinking I grew up with. Conversations about other cultures always went the same way. Our ways of doing things here in the US were always the better ones, the ones that made the most sense.

Arranged marriage is a topic that has come up in

conversation both with my moms and at school with my white friends. It's something most of them consider oppressive, a situation in which the women involved are unwitting victims of circumstance. I wonder how many other things I've been blind to. I'm not so naive as to think that many of the traditions and customs in all cultures don't exist to benefit the patriarchy, but why do we as Americans always think we know best? My moms are educated and liberal-minded, but even they speak about these sorts of things with a certain amount of condescension, and I'm beginning to question a lot of my own perspectives. I realize now that although I'm brown, I still have many privileges because I've been raised in a white family. My time with Pooja has given me a lot to think about. It's time to reground myself.

CHAPTER THIRTEEN

For the next few days, I'm too busy with schoolwork and my Hindi lessons with Pooja to think about my birth mother again. At least that's what I tell myself every time I remember the exact words she wrote to me in her letters.

Also, I haven't really had a lot of time to hang out with Nikhil, and the few times I've seen him at choir, he was unusually distant. Today I catch up with him after school just before he has a chance to disappear.

"Hey, stranger!" I call out to his retreating back.

He turns to look at me. "Hey, Mira, what's up?"

"What's up? C'mon, dude, you can do better than that."

He walks over to me, and up close I can tell that something's definitely not right.

"Are you okay?" I ask. "Let's go grab some food and talk."

I grab his elbow and point him in the direction of my car. He doesn't resist, and a few minutes later, we're sitting in a corner booth at IHOP. I order banana-and-strawberry pancakes. He gets Swedish crepes.

"Do you want to talk about it?" I say.

He doesn't answer at first, but I press on.

"Is it Ashish?"

Still nothing.

"C'mon, Nikhil, tell me what's going on?"

"Ashish called."

Finally.

"And? What did he say?"

"He said it's too hard, being so far away from each other."

"Okay, but you're going home to visit this summer, aren't you?"

He nods. "He's just having a really rough time. He misses me a lot, and with the time difference, there's never really a good time to talk."

"Okay, so make the time," I say. "Tell him how much you miss him. And maybe he can visit you here."

"It's not that easy," Nikhil insists. "He won't be able to get a visa just like that. It's really tough."

"Why not?"

He looks at me with a strange expression on his face. "You really have no clue, do you?"

"What's that supposed to mean?"

"You know people like us can't just walk up to the US embassy in India and ask for a visa, right?"

"Well, no, I'm sure there's a process and it takes a bit of time, but I mean, he *can* get one." I don't get what the big deal is.

"Mira, you have no idea how hard it is," he says. "You have to provide proof of your finances, and most of the time you get rejected anyway."

"But why?"

"There are so many people who want to come here, and US immigration officials are always suspicious that they won't

234

leave. Not everyone has sufficient funds to prove that they can support themselves when they're here. And that's just a couple of the reasons they're refused entry."

"Wow, I really had no idea it was that hard."

"Most people here don't," he says. "I realized that when I first moved here. People really have no clue what life is like for others around the world."

"It sounds really hard." I'm not really sure what the right thing to say is here, because I'm just as guilty of this as everyone else. And he's right. I don't know a lot about anything outside my own bubble of privilege.

"It's okay. I'm sorry I came down so hard on you." Nikhil looks really sad, and I feel for him. I don't think I've ever really been in love the way he seems to be, and certainly not with anyone so far away.

"No, you're right," I say. "I didn't stop to think that things aren't the same for everyone or as easy as they are for us here. I mean, I'm pretty sure I can travel to most places in the world with my US passport without any hassle."

"It's not just that. It's the notion that we are so desperate to come here that we would lie and cheat our way here. When really sometimes people just want to visit and then go back home to their families."

I wish I could do something to help, but all I can think of is how miserable he looks right now, and I can't stand it.

"There's gotta be something you can do." I reach over to touch his hand.

"Maybe I can go and visit him over spring break," he says, in a tone that makes me realize he's trying to believe it.

"That's a great idea," I say. "It's going to be all right. And hey, listen, I'm sorry I haven't been around much."

"I see that you and Pooja have been hitting it off lately," he says, smiling for the first time since we started talking.

"She's actually been really great, helping me learn Hindi, and we've been talking a lot and stuff."

"That's great, I'm happy for you."

By the time we're done eating, he's grilled me on all my newly learned vocabulary. He's also managed to poke fun at my accent, but seeing as he's been so sad about Ashish, I let it slide.

It's the least I can do for being a lousy friend.

● ● ●

The next day, it's Brooke who's the cause for my concern.

"Hey, are you okay?" I ask her when I see her by the lockers at school. There's a heaviness in her shoulders I don't usually see there.

"Sure," she says, but I can tell from the look in her eyes that things are not okay. "Why do you ask?"

"So, here's the thing," I tell her. "I've been really distracted lately, and I just want to say I'm sorry that we haven't been hanging out that much."

She shrugs. "It's fine, don't worry about it."

"No, it's not fine, not really."

"Well, I don't know what you want me to say."

"Can't you just get mad at me or something?" I know I'm being ridiculous, but I don't know what else to do.

"You know what? You're right. I get that you've been think-ing a lot about your mom lately and about being Indian and all that, but you didn't have to blow me off just to hang out with Nikhil and Pooja."

"I wasn't blowing you off. I—"

"Call it whatever you want, but you've been hanging out

with them a lot lately, and you didn't even ask if I wanted to come too." She's tearing up, and I feel awful. Plus, she's absolutely right. After that first time, I haven't asked her to join us again.

"I'm so sorry. I just didn't think you'd want to come with us."

"Why? Because I'm not Indian like the rest of you? So what? We're supposed to be best friends."

"Brooke, listen to me," I say firmly. "You and I are always going to be best friends, okay. I screwed up, and I'm sorry. I should have thought about how I was making you feel, but I was too caught up in my own stuff to see that."

She takes the Kleenex I offer her and dabs her face with it. Then she looks at me with her big, blue, watery eyes. "I'm sorry, I know I'm being a baby, and I was trying to understand what you were going through, but—"

"No, you don't have anything to be sorry for." I throw my arms around her and squeeze tight.

She squeezes back, and I pull away for a second to look at her.

"Let me just warn you, though," I say with a grin. "Those two are all about spicy food. My stomach lining is probably damaged forever, but you can take your chances."

CHAPTER FOURTEEN

Pooja and I have another Hindi lesson together after school that day, and this time I've invited her over to my place. I take her up to my room, and after we're done, I bring up some snacks and drinks.

"So, I've been meaning to tell you something," I say once we've settled in. "Back around Christmas, I found a box of my birth mother's things."

"Oh my god, really?" She looks stunned. "What was in it?"

"I found this necklace." I show her the pictures in the locket.

"You look so much like her," she says. "Especially your eyes." She leans in closer to my face. "Huh, you have the same bump on your nose."

What is it with people's fascination with my nose? I make a face at her, and she grins.

"So, what else did you find out?" she asks.

"Well, her name's Ayesha, and she was eighteen at the time."

"Oh, so she was Muslim."

"Really? How can you tell?"

"Desi names are like that," she informs me. "Hindu names

are usually from Sanskrit or sometimes the names of gods and goddesses, and Muslim names are pretty easy to tell as well. They're often Arabic."

"I had no idea. Her last name was Hameed."

"Yup, definitely Muslim."

"Interesting," I say. "I mean, it doesn't matter—my moms are atheist, and they've always said it's completely up to me and my sister when it comes to faith."

"Was it weird to see all of her stuff like this?" Pooja asks.

"Honestly, yeah, it's really weird. I found a few letters addressed to me."

"What do you mean?" she says, her eyes wide. "She actually wrote them to you?"

"I know, right? They're from before I was born."

"Did you read them?"

"Well, duh, of course," I say. "But I kind of wish I hadn't."

"How come?" Pooja asks. "Did they say something bad?"

I shake my head. "No, not bad, just . . . they made me really sad."

"They must have been hard to read. Listen, Mira, we don't have to talk about this."

"No, I want to," I tell her.

"So, what is it that's making you feel sad?"

"At first it was just making me feel sad for her because my moms told me she was my age." I look at her. "Can you imagine being pregnant right now and not having anyone there for you?"

"Not at all," she says. "I wouldn't have a clue how to handle it even with my whole family there."

"She must have been so scared. But I don't understand why she couldn't tell her parents. I mean, sure, they would have been pissed, but eventually they'd understand, don't you think?"

"Are you kidding me?" Pooja looks at me with the same expression that was on Nikhil's face when I talked about visas.

"No, I'm just saying they were her parents. They wouldn't just abandon her."

"Mira, people have done worse than just abandon their unmarried daughters for getting pregnant," Pooja tells me. "Trust me, it's a lot more complicated than you think."

"Okay, so explain it to me." I'm still not convinced that there was no way she could have told her family.

"Well, first of all, there's the family's reputation," she says. "It's a huge deal back home and even here in the desi community. Once you lose that, then you're finished."

"Seriously?"

"Seriously. Especially when it comes to unmarried daughters."

"That's such a double standard," I point out.

"Yup, it is. But it's very real, whether we like it or not."

"But it's so unfair. Why did she have to make such a big sacrifice?"

"That's exactly why you might want to reconsider the way you're judging her," Pooja says gently. "I can't claim to understand everything you're going through, but I'll bet that whatever choices she had to make were a lot harder."

I don't know what to say. Hearing Pooja say these words is like cold water to my face. She's absolutely right. Once again, I've been looking at everything through a veil of privilege. I'm judging my birth mother's actions based on my assumptions that everyone's parents and family are as accepting and open as my moms are. I've been so busy trying to find the missing parts of me that I've failed to understand how, almost eighteen years ago, another young girl just like me had to erase a part of herself just so I would have the love of a good family.

"I've been such an idiot," I say slowly, as the realization creeps in. "You're so right, Pooja. I've been looking at this all wrong."

"Hey, I'm sorry if I was too harsh, but—"

"No, actually you've given me a lot to think about," I say.

She stands and gathers her things. "I think you need some space, so I'm going to leave. But if you want to talk, I'm here for you."

She squeezes my shoulder gently on her way out. A little bit later, Moms and Nadia are back from piano lessons.

"Mira, we ran into Mr. Barnes from up the road," Mom says. "He told us there's a lost dog running around the neighborhood."

"We told him to post it on our neighborhood Facebook page," Mama says.

I jump up and grab my laptop off the coffee table.

"Let me just post on the rescue group's page as well," I say, quickly checking the post and sharing it. "I'll call Brooke, and then can you drive us around to look?"

"Of course," Mom says. She looks at Mama. "I'll take them. Nadia still has to study for her math test, right?"

Mama nods. "I'll get dinner ready for you guys."

A short while later, we're walking around with flashlights calling out for Roxy, the little rescue Chihuahua who wiggled out of her harness and ran off. As our group page suggests, the owners have brought some of her chew toys to create a scent trail. It's dark out, and we get a lot of coyotes in our area at nighttime, so it's vital that we find her quickly. Brooke has brought her mom and brother as well, and a few other neighbors have joined us, so there are quite a few people out searching with us.

Moms have never let us have a dog because Mama and Nadia are both super allergic and so I've channeled my love for animals into volunteer work. I enjoy managing the rescue shelter's social media page, but most of all, I love actually being around the animals, mostly dogs and cats but also the occasional ferret. Brooke and I do this together, and when we started out a couple of years ago, we would clean out cages and take the dogs for walks, but now we have more responsibilities. We organize fundraisers at our school to collect beds and toys for the animals, as well as money that goes toward food and medications for them.

"I had a long talk with Pooja earlier," I say to Brooke as we walk through the park trail, carrying a well-chewed stuffed lamb. "Roxyyyy. Roxyyy." I point my flashlight into the bushes, but there's no sign of her.

"About what?" Brooke asks. She stops to take a swig from her water bottle.

"Just those letters," I say. "She made me realize I'm being a jerk."

Just then we hear one of the other searchers calling out. They've found Roxy. This has to be one of the quickest rescues ever, but that's a good thing.

We run to where the owners are cradling the little pup, who seems to be fine. The search party disperses, and we all head back to our vehicles. Brooke and I walk slowly behind our moms and talk in hushed voices so that they don't hear.

"What were you saying about you being a jerk?" Brooke grins at me in the light of the streetlamps.

I make a face at her. "I was just really upset earlier when my moms told me that she'd chosen to leave even though my moms said she could be a part of my life."

"Your birth mom?" Brooke says loudly.

"Hey, can you speak up? I don't think the entire neighborhood heard you."

"Sorry," she whispers. "So, you think she should have stayed and been in your life?"

"That's what I was thinking. But then Pooja sort of gave me a lecture on how difficult it can be for some people."

"I'm sure she must have had a good reason for leaving," Brooke says.

"Honestly, I was just thinking of how it all affected me, not how awful it must have been for her."

"So what are you going to do now?"

I move closer to her. "In one of her letters, she asked me to meet her in Mumbai on my birthday."

"In India? Just like that? How? Are you going to go?" Brooke's looking at me like I've lost my mind or something.

"I'm thinking about it. Obviously, I don't have it all planned out yet," I say, a little irritated that she isn't immediately excited for me. "But I will."

We're at our cars and have to stop talking about this. Back at home, I can barely wait to get through dinner before running upstairs with my laptop so that I can do a little research. That night I sleep like a baby after a long string of restless nights.

CHAPTER FIFTEEN

Everything seems to be falling into place. There's only one problem: I haven't worked up the courage to tell Moms yet about what I want to do. Obviously, I'm expecting there to be some resistance, but I have my strategy all laid out. Mama's the overprotective one in our house, so the plan is to convince Mom first and then enlist her to convince Mama. If everything goes according to plan, and there's absolutely no reason why it shouldn't, then in a few months I'll be basking in the sun in Mumbai and hopefully chatting it up with my birth mom. Of course, I'm fully aware that there's a good possibility that she may not even show up. Lots of things can change in eighteen years. But either way, I'm choosing to focus on the positive.

● ● ●

I think it will be a lot better to approach my moms once I have some concrete information. Like maybe an address or a phone number or something. I can't exactly show up at Flora Fountain in Mumbai and call out her name. I get out of bed and open my laptop. I log on to my Facebook account and search for Ayesha Hameed. There are more than a dozen results. Not helpful since they almost all have dark hair and dark eyes. I narrow it down to women who look like they're in their thirties, but it's really hard to tell from the profile pics. I search her name on Google. Again, there are like three pages of results and more images to sift through, but no luck.

I'm not even sure she still goes by the last name Hameed. Maybe she got married and changed her name like a lot of women do. It's not something I ever plan to do because my name is part of my identity and it feels weird to change it just because you marry someone. In my head, I go off on a rant about all the reasons it's ridiculous to give up something so personal. Then my mind eventually wanders back to what I'm looking for, but it's pointless. I can't find anything. But over the last hour, I've come to realize one thing. I'm going to take the plunge and just go. Even if she doesn't show up, at least I'll know I tried.

• • •

I wake up the next morning with a knot in my stomach. I can't wait to tell Moms about the letter and my trip, but at the same time, I'm really nervous about their reaction. I brush my teeth and rush downstairs, bursting into the kitchen. Moms look up in surprise, probably because I've been moping around for the past couple of weeks.

I give them each a tight hug and then wrap my arms around Nadia.

"You're in a good mood today, honey," Mama says, pouring pancake batter onto the griddle.

"Yes, who are you and what have you done to Mopey Mira?" Mom comments with a grin.

"I have something very important to tell you," I announce,

grabbing a plate and holding it out for some pancakes.

"What?" Nadia says, drowning her pancakes in syrup.

I make a face at her. "Would you like some pancakes with your syrup?"

"So what's up, sweetie?" Mama says. She pours herself a mug of coffee and joins us at the table.

"I want to go to India this summer," I say.

"Okay," Mom says slowly.

"Ooh, India," Nadia says. "I wanna come."

"Does this have anything to do with the letters?" Mama asks.

"What letters?" Nadia butts in.

"Honey, why don't you go watch some TV," Mom tells her. "You can take your pancakes and finish up over there."

Nadia opens her mouth, undoubtedly to protest, but the prospect of unscheduled TV time is too tempting. She carries her plate off to sit on the couch.

"I found another letter," I say, barely able to contain my excitement. "From my birth mom."

Moms look at each other, but I can't tell what they're thinking. They've mastered these blank expressions for all the times I ask them something they're not sure about. But that's okay because I'm prepared for this. It's not like I expected them to jump with joy at the prospect of me going to India. They're going to have to warm up to it, and I will give them all the time they need. This isn't the first time I've come up with an outrageous idea.

"And what did it say exactly?" Mom asks.

"Just that she hopes I'll be able to forgive her and that she didn't have a choice but that she knows I'll have a great life with you."

Step One: Flattery. It always works.

"And?" Mama needs more information, as usual.

"And that she'll always keep a part of me in her heart."

Mama's eyes begin to glisten.

Step Two: Appeal to their emotions. Already working.

"She was so young," Mama whispers, almost to herself.

"I wish we'd been able to help her more," Mom says.

And now for the hardest part.

Step Three: Go in for the kill.

"She wants me to meet her. In Mumbai."

"What? When?" Mom says.

"On August sixth. At Flora Fountain at four p.m."

"But . . . that's your birthday." Mama seems at a loss for words. She reaches for Mom's hand.

I'm beginning to feel that this was not one of my best ideas. It's not like that time I asked if I could go for an overnight trip with the family of a friend I'd just met or to get my nose pierced. This was much harder. For all of us. But it was too late to back down now.

"Please, Moms," I say. "I really need to do this."

"I thought you wanted to celebrate your eighteenth with Brooke in Cancún," Mom said. "We've already put down a deposit for the trip."

"Can't we get a refund or something?" I ask. "This is really important to me."

Mom opens her mouth to say something, but Mama stops her. She puts a hand out to rub my shoulder. "Of course we understand what you're feeling. But give us a little time to think about it, okay? This is a pretty big ask."

I guess this conversation is over for now, and it's only fair to give them a little time to get used to the idea.

"Okay," I say. There's no point in pushing them because then Mom will shut down and just say no and Mama will get mad at her for being too hard on me and it'll all be my fault. Better to let them think about it. They've always cared about stuff that's important to me, so I'm hoping they'll come around.

CHAPTER SIXTEEN

"Wait, what? You're going *this* summer? Like, in three months?" Nikhil stares at me in disbelief.

It's a few nights later, and we're at his house, eating some desi snacks from Mumbai. He's opened a few different brightly colored foil bags and emptied the contents into little bowls. There are spicy fried chickpeas and peanuts mixed in with raisins and other crunchy ingredients I can't identify. But they're yummy, so I don't care.

I catch him up on everything.

"Wow, so she really wants to meet you, then? How exactly are you going to go to India all by yourself?"

"I'm going to buy a ticket and then get on a plane."

"You know what I mean," he says. "How're you going to get around? You don't know anyone over there, do you?"

"Well, they have Airbnb and Uber, right?"

"Yes, of course, but it's not that easy," he insists. "It's a big city, and it can be really confusing if you don't know your way around. Especially because everyone will know you're not from there."

"So what? I'm sure most people speak English there," I say. "How hard can it be?"

He shakes his head. "I don't think it's a good idea for you to go alone for the very first time."

"Oh my god, you're so annoying, Nikhil," I say. "Why can't you be happy for me?"

"I am happy for you," he says. "I'm just being realistic."

"I just want to meet her," I say softly. "Why is everyone being so weird about that?"

"What did your moms say?"

"That they'll think about it." I'm starting to think that if even Nikhil thinks it's a bad idea, then the chance that Moms will let me go is pretty slim.

"Well, maybe they'll be okay with it and it'll all be fine," he says, but I can tell from his voice that he's just trying to placate me.

"Maybe," I say, wishing he would be a little more supportive. "Anyway, tell me everything about you and Ashish."

"It's been a little weird, to be honest. Remember how I told you we've sort of been having a lot of arguments lately, but we weren't really talking? Anyway, I told him how much he meant to me, and how I'd be back in the summer and that it's going to be amazing. We don't usually talk like that. It's usually more joking. But this time, it was good to let our hearts speak. And even though it's not the same as being in the same place, it's a promise of something better, at least."

• • •

When I get back home, it's almost dinnertime. I help Moms without even being asked. We're having seafood risotto, and I chop the ingredients for a salad while Mama adds a liberal amount of fresh Parmesan to the steaming dish.

Soon we're sitting around the table enjoying our meal, and I'm waiting for Moms to bring up my trip to India.

And waiting. And waiting. By the time we get to dessert, we've talked about Nadia's upcoming piano recital, living arrangements for me and Brooke for the fall, and how Mrs. Grayson up the street just got a landscaper in to fix her front yard. No mention of India. This does not bode well for me. It's not until after Nadia has gone upstairs to her room and I've finished loading the dishwasher that Moms ask me to come and sit with them.

"Honey, we thought about what you said," Mom starts. "And here's what we think. Why don't we all plan a family trip to India maybe next year?"

"That way we'll all be together and it's much better that way, don't you think, sweetie?" Mama says.

"But what about the letter?" I can't wait until next year. Then she'll think I don't want to meet her. And how am I supposed to track her down after that?

"We just don't think it's such a good idea for you to go there all by yourself and meet her," Mama says gently. "What if something happens to you?"

"Like what?" I say. "What do you think will happen to me?"

"Honey, anything can happen," Mom says. "You don't know your way around, and you'd be a young girl in a strange country. It can be dangerous."

"Really? So what about all the things you've always said about taking chances and having adventures and living my life to the fullest? Was that all just talk?"

"Of course not," Mama replies. "But that doesn't mean knowingly putting yourself in a dangerous situation."

"Especially when we're not there to help you," Mom adds.

"So what?" I glare at them. "I'm supposed to never go anywhere unless you two are right there to save me? That's ridiculous."

"Mira, what's ridiculous is that you think you can talk to us like that," Mom responds angrily. "If you can't talk about this in a mature and rational manner, then maybe you need to go to your room and cool off."

"Fine, whatever." I storm out of the kitchen and up the stairs to my room. I slam the door extra hard and fling myself on my bed. Hot angry tears flow down my face as I think of how my mother will feel when she's waiting for me at the fountain and I never show up.

CHAPTER SEVENTEEN

I'm sitting on my bed making notes for my upcoming biology test. All night I've been listening to Moms going back and forth, arguing. Even though they're trying to be discreet, it's a little hard not to hear them. There's a knock on my door, and Nadia peeks her head in. Her huge eyes seem bigger than usual, and I can tell that she's worried. I wave for her to come in and sit on my bed.

"What's wrong, Nadia?" I ask, wrapping a few of her curls around my finger. I let go and they spring right back.

"Moms are fighting. Why did you have to make them so angry?" Her eyes fill with tears.

"I didn't mean to make them angry," I say. "I just want to go to India before I start college."

"But I heard them talk about someone called Ayesha. Is that your birth mommy?"

For all our efforts to protect Nadia from certain things, she doesn't really miss much of what goes on in our house.

"Yes, Ayesha is my birth mommy," I say with a smile. "And she wrote me a letter when I was in her tummy and said she'd like to meet me when I'm eighteen."

"Can I come with you?" she asks. "I don't want you to go all by yourself. Moms say it's dangerous."

I shake my head. "We'll all go there together someday," I say. "But this time I have to go by myself. So I can check everything out for you."

"Will you bring me back something?" she asks.

"Anything you want." I put my arms around her and squeeze tightly. "I promise."

After she leaves, I try to figure out what I should do now. I don't want Moms to fight because of me. I hate arguing with them, but this is too important to me.

I decide to go downstairs and see if I can convince them. Mom is sitting at one end of the table with a glass of wine. Mama is standing in front of the cabinets, unnecessarily rearranging the coffee mugs.

Mom looks up when I walk into the kitchen. "Do you want anything to eat?"

I shake my head. "No thanks."

"Oh, look, she can talk." Mama stops messing around with the mugs. "So are we done with the silent treatment, then?"

This is worse than I thought. No wonder Nadia was worried.

"Look, I don't want to fight with you guys," I tell them. "But I still think that you should trust me and let me go."

"Oh, honey, it's not that we don't trust *you*," Mom says. "It's everyone else we don't trust."

"But I'm going to be eighteen soon and I know how to take care of myself," I say. "You need to trust that I can use my own judgment and not put myself in dangerous situations."

"The thing is, Mira," Mama says, "you'll be in an

unfamiliar place among people you don't know, and a lot could happen."

"What about when I go away to college, huh?" My voice has risen a couple of octaves, but I don't even care anymore. They're being ridiculous. "What're you going to do then? Move into my dorm room with me and Brooke?"

"Mira, be reasonable." Mom's voice has a hard edge to it. "You're going to college forty-five minutes away. You'll be sharing a room with your best friend in the city you grew up in."

"That's hardly the same as flying halfway across the world to a country where everything is new to you and meeting a woman you don't know." Mama's voice is shaking a little, the way it does when she's really angry.

"And have you considered the fact that she wrote that letter almost eighteen years ago?" Mom says. "How do you know that she even remembers? We don't know anything about her life since then."

"But what if she *does* remember?" I'm yelling now. "What if she waits for me there and I don't show up? How can I do that to her?"

"Look, Mira, the bottom line is that it's our job to keep you safe," Mama says. "And there's no way we can let you go over there like this."

"I promise you, we'll plan a trip there next year," Mom says. "I'm sure you can meet her then."

"Oh my god, do you hear yourselves? How am I supposed to find her there? If I don't go this time, I'll never see her." I'm screaming, and tears are running down my face. "I can't believe you're doing this to me. It's like you're afraid of me meeting her!"

I don't wait around to see the damage my words have done. I turn on my heels, run upstairs, and throw a change of clothes into my backpack. Then I go back down and storm out of the house.

CHAPTER EIGHTEEN

I ring the doorbell frantically until the door flings open, and Nikhil stares at me in surprise.

"What happened?" he asks, taking in my tearstained face and disheveled hair.

"I had a huge fight with my moms," I say, bursting into tears again. "Can I stay here with you?"

He pulls me in and shuts the door. "Yes, of course, but are you okay?"

I drop my backpack on the floor and trudge over to the couch.

"They refuse to let me go and meet my birth mom," I say, wiping my tears on the sleeve of my T-shirt. "They just don't get it."

"Mira, it'll be okay," Nikhil says, awkwardly patting my shoulder. "Just give them some time."

"I don't have time! If I don't meet my mom at Flora Fountain on my birthday at four o'clock, I might never find her again."

"Is there no other way to contact her? Maybe you can email her or something?"

"No, you don't get it," I wail. "That's the only way I'm ever gonna see her."

The door opens, and Nikhil's mom walks in.

"Hi, Mira. How—"

"Mom, can we talk really quick over here?" Nikhil jumps up and pulls his mother aside. They talk in urgent whispers while I blow my nose loudly. I haven't been this overwhelmed with anger and frustration before, and it takes me a few moments to remember my manners.

"Sarita Aunty, I'm sorry about all this," I say when they come back. "I'll get out of your hair." I start walking toward the door, but Sarita Aunty gently pulls me back.

"Mira, please, you're not a bother at all," she says with a smile. She strokes my hair softly. "Why don't we sit and talk about it?"

"I'll grab us something to eat," Nikhil says, disappearing into the kitchen.

I sit back on the couch, and Sarita Aunty sits down next to me.

"Nikhil says you've had a fight with your parents?" she says.

"Yes, it was really bad."

"Well, they must be pretty worried about you, so why don't I call them and let them know that you're here and safe and that you'll stay for a bit?"

I nod. My moms must be freaking out by now. In my hurry to leave, I left my phone at home, so they don't have any way to reach me.

Sarita Aunty makes the call, talking in hushed tones before hanging up and coming back to me.

"They want you to come home, but I've asked them to give you time."

"Thank you," I say. "I'm so sorry about all this."

"Do you want to talk about it?"

"I don't know if Nikhil's told you about my birth mom in India."

"He has told me. It must be quite a difficult thing you're going through."

"I just want to go and meet her this summer. But my moms don't think it's safe."

"They're not wrong, you know. I would probably say the same thing if I were in their shoes."

"But it's the only chance I'll ever get to meet her." Why is it so hard for everyone to understand that?

"Are you sure that's what you want?" she asks. "It was a very long time ago. Things might have changed. What if she's not there when you go?"

"Then I'll enjoy my time in Mumbai and come back," I say.

Sarita Aunty doesn't respond immediately. I'm beginning to think it was a bad idea to show up here like this.

"You know," she says after some thought, "we were planning to go back next month for a quick visit."

I perk up. Nikhil walks in with snacks and iced tea.

"Can you postpone your trip?" he asks.

Sarita Aunty nods slowly. "That's what I was just thinking. I can push my trip to August and then Mira can come with us. Provided, of course, that her mothers are okay with it," she adds quickly.

Now that I've calmed down a little, I'm remembering what I said to Moms before I left. I have no idea what I'll be walking into back at home, but I know I have a lot of groveling to do.

"Can you talk to them about it?" I ask. "They're pretty mad at me right now."

"Yes, of course," Sarita Aunty says, then goes off to make the call.

She comes back a short while later. "They want you to go home first," she reports. "I think that's best for now."

"I can drive you," Nikhil says. "It'll be fine. My mom's really good at convincing people."

We walk out to his car. "I hope so," I say. I am in an intense shame spiral, and I don't know how I'm going to face my moms after the way I stormed out earlier. "I said some really awful things to them, Nikhil. I don't think they'll ever forgive me."

"Of course they will," he says as he pulls out of the driveway. "Just apologize and give them some time."

"You don't know them," I tell him. "Especially Mom. She really knows how to hold a grudge."

"Then you'll just have to be super patient," he says. "Do you want to come to Mumbai with us or not?"

"Obviously, I do."

"So do whatever it takes to convince them." Once we get to my house, he turns to me and advises, "Just think of how badly you want it and don't get into it with them until summer."

"You're right," I say. "And listen . . . thanks for everything. I owe you big-time."

"Sure thing," he says. "You're going to have a blast in Mumbai. I can't wait."

I step out of the car and walk slowly toward my front door. I turn briefly to wave goodbye to Nikhil and take a deep breath before walking inside.

It's quieter than usual for a weekday evening in our house. Normally Nadia would be practicing piano and Moms would be catching each other up on their respective days. But today only silence greets me as I walk in the door.

260

I walk up the stairs quietly and go to Nadia's room. I need to find out what happened after I left.

I knock softly on her door and open it. She's sitting on her bed, holding her favorite stuffie, a tattered light brown puppy that has seen better days. She hasn't done that since she was ten.

"Hey," I say, walking in and closing the door behind me. "Where are Moms?"

She looks at me, and I can tell that she's been crying. She's always been the sensitive one in this family, deeply affected by what everyone else is feeling.

"Mom left a while ago," she says. "And Mama's in her room."

"Are you okay?"

"Why did you have to fight with them?" she asks, her eyes huge in her face as a couple of fat tears roll down her cheeks. I rush to envelop her in a tight hug.

"I'm so sorry, bug." I've never been so mad at myself. "I was just really angry at them."

"Because they won't let you go and see your birth mom?" she says.

"Yes, but that doesn't change the fact that *they're* my moms. I just wanted to meet my birth mom, that's all."

I get up from her bed. "I'm going to go talk to Mama now, okay?"

"But you can't yell at her."

"No, I won't, I promise." I leave her and go over to Moms' bedroom. I knock softly and wait for an answer. Nothing. I open the door slightly and peek in. Mama's curled up on an armchair by the window, gazing out at the setting sun. It's turned the sky into a blazing orange, and somehow I know I'll never forget how my mother looks at this very moment. Beautiful and heartbroken, her curly brown hair falling on her shoulders and hand clutching an old blanket. I recognize it immediately. It's one that I carried around with me for years, and Moms finally had to hide it from me so I wouldn't take it to preschool. My eyes fill with tears of shame and regret because I can never take back what I said, no matter how hard I try. But I will still try.

I walk over to her and touch her gently on the shoulder. She startles and looks up. Her eyes are swimming with tears, and I fall to my knees in front of her.

"Mama, I'm so sorry," I say, my shoulders heaving as I put my arms around her waist and hold on tight. I'm afraid she'll push me away, which is what I deserve, so I hold on as tight as I can. But she turns toward me and puts her chin on top of my head. Her tears mingle with mine, and after a while, I look up at her.

"I didn't mean it, Mama," I say. "I love you so much, and I'm so sorry."

"I know, sweetie," Mama says, stroking my hair.

The door opens, and Mom walks in. I freeze when I see her, not sure how she's going to react. She doesn't come toward me, rooted to the ground by the door. I get up and go to her. She doesn't resist when I put my arms around her, but she doesn't return my embrace either. I step back and look her in the eyes.

"Mom, I'm so sorry for what I said. I didn't mean any of it. I was just so angry."

She looks at me for a moment without saying anything and I know that I've hurt her like never before.

"Mom, please say something," I say. "Yell at me. As much as you want."

She sighs deeply. "I don't want to yell at you, Mira." She

walks over to Mama. "What you said . . . I don't understand. You're our daughter and we love you, you were our miracle baby, and we know that nothing is going to change that, even if . . ." Her voice trails off as her emotions overwhelm her. Mama puts a hand on her arm.

"Mira, is that what you really think?" Mama says. "That we're afraid we're going to lose you as a daughter?"

"Of course not, Mama. Please . . . I was just being stupid and selfish. I didn't mean any of it."

"Well, I don't know," Mom says. "Maybe it's our fault. We shouldn't have tried to keep you from seeing her."

"I don't care about all that anymore," I say, surprising myself. It's true, I realize. Right now, the only thing I care about is that I've hurt my moms and I have to fix it somehow.

"Either way," Mom says, "if you want to go, we won't stop you. After all, you'll be eighteen and you can make your own decisions."

Mama doesn't say anything, and it feels like I've been dismissed.

I stand in front of them, not sure what to do. No one says anything and the silence becomes uncomfortable, so I leave and go back to my room. So that's it, I guess. They've given up on me, and I can't really say that I blame them. I change and get under the covers, but I can't sleep. I fear that in searching for a connection to the past, I may have jeopardized my relationship with my moms in my real life. And I'm afraid that this wound will never heal completely.

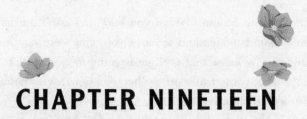

CHAPTER NINETEEN

Somehow, it's already May, and in a few short weeks, my friends and I will be graduating. Things at home have been strange over the last month. On the surface, everything seems perfectly normal, but something has definitely changed. Moms are carrying on as usual, but I can sense a hesitation, an uncertainty in all our interactions. It's as if they're still afraid that the foundation on which they built our family has been shaken and everything is suddenly fragile.

Mama has been easier to talk to than Mom. I get the distinct feeling that Mom's avoiding being alone with me, as if she's afraid she might say the wrong thing to me if Mama isn't there to be a buffer. It's been difficult to navigate this new dynamic at home especially with graduation and all the stuff associated with that. Nikhil, Pooja, Brooke, and I are all going to prom together, so it's a lot of fun shopping and preparing for that. Nikhil and Pooja have also decided where they're going to college, and while Pooja got into Stanford, Nikhil is going to Rice, so he'll still be close. Things are getting hectic, and it's a good thing because it helps to keep my mind off my upcoming birthday and the fact that I won't be meeting my birth mom. I try my best not to let it get me down, but whenever I have a quiet moment to myself, I feel a deep sadness and I have to work hard to get over it each time. Brooke and I have been excitedly planning out our living situation, and it's been so strange and exciting to be connecting with student groups at Baylor on social media.

Finally, the big day is here, and I'm getting ready for prom. My new turquoise dress is laid out on the bed, and my silver strappy heels are on my feet as I try to break them in before all the dancing commences. Mama gave me her silver teardrop earrings to wear, and I'm just finishing with my makeup when she and Mom knock on the door.

"Mira, honey, we want to talk to you for a minute," Mama says. They both walk in and sit on my bed. A little knot forms in my stomach, and I hope it's nothing bad.

"We have something for you," Mom says, handing me a thick envelope. "It's a graduation present."

A smile lights up my face as I take the envelope from her. "What is it?"

"Open it," Mama says. She has the same look on her face as Nadia does on Christmas morning.

I open the envelope and pull out a folded piece of paper. But I don't get a chance to read what it says because Mama is practically bouncing.

"It's a plane ticket to Mumbai," she blurts out.

Mom scowls at her. "You're the worst secret keeper in the world, honey," she says, pulling Mama closer.

"Oh my god, Moms, really? I don't believe it."

I look at the paper in my hand. It's a printout of an electronic ticket for a flight from Houston to Mumbai, India.

"Look, it's for August 1, leaving at two p.m. You're flying out with Nikhil and his mom," Mama says.

"We arranged it all with them a month ago, and it's been so hard keeping it from you," Mom adds. "We didn't think we could hold out until your actual graduation . . . so tonight seemed like the best occasion."

I am completely in shock and don't know what to say, so of course I start sobbing. My moms look alarmed, but then I'm smiling and throwing my arms around them both.

"I love you so much. You guys are the best." I'm a blubbering mess and I know I'll have to apply my makeup all over again, but I don't care. Then something occurs to me.

"So wait," I say, pulling back. "Are you saying Nikhil's known this whole time?"

"Yup, he's really good at keeping secrets," Mom says. "We've been talking to Sarita quite a bit about the trip, and we're really grateful that she's offered to look after you while you're there. And Nikhil says he'll show you around, so you won't feel like just a tourist."

"We think it's going to be a very special experience," Mama says. "And we hope that you get to meet Ayesha."

"We should have been more understanding when you first told us," Mom says. "But it's not easy for us to think that you feel as though something is missing in your life."

"But we realized we weren't being fair to you," Mama says.

"You have nothing to worry about," I tell them, tears running down my face. "There's nothing that will ever change the way I feel about you. You'll always be my moms. I just need to do this. To know where I came from."

"I know, honey," Mom says. "It's just that when you came

into our lives, you gave us so much hope for the future and you made us a family."

"You were our miracle baby," Mama says. "And just the thought of losing you made us a little insecure."

"You're not getting rid of me that easily," I assure them. "No one can ever take your place. But I just don't want to have any regrets, you know. If I miss this opportunity, I might never find her again, and then I'll always wonder."

"I'm just so relieved that Sarita and Nikhil will be with you," Mama says. "If you were there alone, I wouldn't be able to sleep at night."

"Oh my god, I'm so excited," I say. "I can't wait to tell Brooke. She's going to die." I rush over to grab my phone and message her.

"I guess that's our cue to leave," Mama says.

"Don't take too long to get ready," Mom calls out as they shut the door behind them.

I have to take a moment and sit on the edge of my bed to let it all sink in.

I'm actually going to India. And I'm going to meet my birth mom.

CHAPTER TWENTY

We're standing in the departure terminal at George Bush Intercontinental Airport in Houston, and there are huge butterflies in my stomach. Moms have driven us all to the airport in the van, and we're all checked in and just waiting around until it's time to say goodbye. Nadia is reminding me of all the things she wants me to bring back for her room. I made the mistake of showing her a website with lots of cool stuff to hang on her door and walls, and now I have a long list on my phone. Moms have reminded me a million times to make sure I keep my passport and money safe whenever I'm outside. The last weeks have been full of shots and travel meds and visa applications, and somehow I've been able to fit my clothes and personal items in a carry-on despite the ridiculous amount of disinfectant wipes, hand sanitizers, and over-the-counter medicines that Moms are forcing me to take with me. Apparently, all the germs in India have been put on alert for my imminent arrival. But I know how difficult this is for them, and I'm not about to make them worry even more by being cavalier about the dangers of rogue viruses and savvy pickpockets.

Nikhil and his mom have to check their luggage, two huge suitcases each.

"It's all gifts," Nikhil says when I stare at their bags. "So many gifts." He rolls his eyes. "It's been a while since we've gone back, and we have a lot of relatives."

"What kind of gifts?" I ask.

"Lots of toiletries, chocolates, and Texas souvenirs," he says. "I have a lot of cousins my age, and they like makeup."

"Is that why you've been running into Sephora and Ulta every time we go to the mall?"

He nods. "Yup. But, Mira, look—I packed a huge Toblerone for the flight." He unzips his backpack to show me.

"I can take that off your hands if you like, you know," I say. "Just so your bag isn't too heavy."

"Ha, nice try. I'm not falling for that again."

"Hey, for real, though, how stoked are you for this trip?" I say, while we wait for my moms to finish looking over their multiple checklists.

"I can't wait to show you all the cool spots," he says. "You're going to love it."

"I bet you can't wait to see Ashish."

He gives me a bashful smile. "You have no idea."

"I can't wait to meet him. Have I told you how thrilled I am that we're going to Mumbai together?"

"Only about a hundred times," he replies. "Look, I know I'm amazing, but you don't have to keep telling me."

Then it's time for us to go. Mom and Mama pull me aside for a minute.

"Honey, listen, when you get there, you'll have to switch out your SIM card," Mama says. "Make sure to do that right away and call us, okay?"

"And don't forget to take your Emergen-C every day," Mama reminds me. "I put in two boxes. They're on the right side, under your jeans."

"Moms, I'm only going for three weeks, not three months." I smile at them as they stand in front of me looking utterly bereft. "Guys, I love you so much," I say, throwing my arms around them both. "Please don't worry about me, I'll do everything on your list. I promise."

Nadia wants in on our hug, and we just stand there for a minute, holding each other.

"Don't forget to bring me the little hanging elephants thingy for my ceiling fan, okay?" Nadia says.

I smile down at her. "I won't forget a single thing, trust me."

"And, sweetie, we'll FaceTime every night, so you won't even know that Mira's gone," Mama says.

"But there's a twelve-hour time difference," Nadia points out. "I googled it. So, will it be night for us or for Mira?"

"It'll be morning for us and night for Mira, honey," Mom says.

Nikhil and his mom are looking antsy. I guess it's time to go.

"Okay, guys, I have to leave now. I'll call as soon as I can," I say, giving big kisses to my moms and Nadia. After a few last hugs, I join Nikhil and his mom to go through security. We're flying with Emirates airline, so with two connections, one at JFK and the other in Dubai, we'll be landing in Mumbai almost twenty-seven hours after we take off from Houston. I've packed lots of snacks and have enough movies and books on my iPhone to keep me busy. The first few hours go by quickly, but by hour ten of the flight from JFK to Dubai, I'm restless and itching to get off. It doesn't help that Nikhil is fast asleep with his head on my shoulder, mouth-breathing the whole time while I'm stuck looking out the window at nothing but clouds. My head hurts, so I can't even stand to look at my phone, and I'm running low on snacks because Nikhil scarfed down most of my potato chips. His backpack is under the seat, out of my reach, so I'm stuck without any chocolate to keep me alive. Eventually I end up falling asleep only to wake up as we're taxiing on the runway at the airport in Dubai. We have a layover there before getting on the last leg of our trip to Mumbai. It's only a couple of hours, and I can't wait to finally reach our destination.

Approximately three hours after we take off again, I'm standing in a line at immigration at Chhatrapati Shivaji Maharaj Airport in Mumbai. I'm enthralled by the crowd of people, because as soon as I step off the plane, the first thing I notice is that for the first time in my life almost everyone around me is brown. It's a little weird, like coming home to a place you've never been to before but where you belong without question. I stand in the pretty long line designated for foreign nationals. It seems like there are a lot of people like me, of Indian origin but who hold a different nationality. Nikhil and his mom are in the line for Indian citizens, and I can't help marveling at the randomness of it all. Under different circumstances I might have been born right here in India like Nikhil, standing in the same line at the airport, not wide-eyed at the controlled chaos around me. Soon enough we're walking out the exit. I'm immediately engulfed by humidity and heat, and nothing could have prepared me for it. Houston gets pretty hot and humid too, but in Mumbai, it's on a whole other level. Sarita Aunty's driver flags us down and puts our bags in the car while I slide gratefully into the cool air-conditioned interior of their car. Traffic is an unimaginably traumatic experience for me, and my legs are shaking when we finally arrive at their apartment. I have never seen such erratic driving or such crowds, both on the sides of the streets and on the highway as well. It's quite an assault to the senses, and I breathe a sigh of relief when we make it to the house in one piece.

A woman who looks about thirty comes out to greet us, and together with Nikhil and the driver, they bring all the luggage into the house. My head is throbbing, and I want nothing more than to take a cool shower and go to sleep.

"So, Mira, here we are," Sarita Aunty says. "I'm sure you're exhausted, so Meghna will show you to your room and get you whatever you need."

She instructs Meghna in Hindi, and I'm thrilled that I can understand a few snippets of the conversation.

Meghna refuses to let me roll my own bags to the room, and I don't want to offend her, so I follow her to one of the bed-rooms. I enter to see a four-poster bed with a batik-printed bedspread in the middle of the room and a small desk by the window. A tall, dark-brown armoire stands on one side of the room. It's dim in here, which is just what I need right now. I thank Meghna, and after she leaves, I immediately jump into the shower. It's almost evening here now, and I want to adjust to the jet lag as quickly as possible, so after my shower I resist the temptation to collapse on the inviting bed. Instead, I go back out into the living area, where I can hear Nikhil and his mom chatting.

"How do you like your room, Mira?" Sarita Aunty asks.

"It's great. Thank you so much," I say, sitting down next to her on the couch.

"Please let me know if you need anything at all, okay?" she

says. "I want you to feel completely at home here. I know it's not much by Texas standards, but we've lived here ever since Nikhil was a baby, so this will always be home."

"I really appreciate you letting me stay here, Aunty," I say. "I know my moms are so relieved that I came with you."

"Of course," she says. "It's our pleasure, and I know Nikhil is so happy that you could come."

"When do I get to meet Ashish?" I ask Nikhil.

"He had to go out of town for a family thing," he says. "He should be back in a few days."

"I can't wait. I want to know *all* your secrets."

He makes a face at me. "He's too loyal, dude. You're not going to get anything out of him."

"Oh, but I will. I have mad skills, trust me."

"Nikhil, why don't you show Mira your room?" Sarita Aunty asks.

Nikhil lets out a deep sigh and grins at me. "Fine, I might as well get it over with."

I follow him down the hall to his room. The first thing I see is a poster of Sridevi on the wall next to the window. I know her from *Mr. India*, one of the movies we watched together.

I turn to him with as much of a straight face as I can muster. "You never told me you were such a big fan," I say, my lips twitching uncontrollably.

"Shut up," he says. "And don't even think of telling Pooja."

"Hey, I don't know if I can promise such a thing," I say, taking a quick picture with my phone.

"It's cool," he says. "I mean, Sridevi was only one of the biggest Bollywood stars of all time."

"And what do we have here?" I walk across the room to where a few framed photos sit on top of a dresser. "Is that you?" I point to one of an adorable little boy with thick curls and glasses dressed in a kurta and turban.

"That was at my uncle's wedding," Nikhil says. "I think I was four."

Up on the wall are numerous certificates and awards, mostly for music competitions.

"How come you never told me you've won all these?"

"How come you've never asked?"

I'm about to come up with a clever retort when Sarita Aunty peeks her head around the door. "Shall we go and eat something now?" she says. "I've asked Meghna to make something light and simple."

Clearly *light and simple* means something different here because the spread on the table is hardly that. There's spiced couscous, hummus and pita, samosas, curried chickpeas and naan, and bowls of cut-up mango and ice cream. I can only eat a little of everything before I can feel myself nodding off.

A bit later, I'm in bed thinking how strange it is that just yesterday I was half a world away and now I'm here in Mumbai. The letter from my birth mom is safely stashed in my purse, and as I drift off to sleep, I have a feeling that my life is about to change forever.

CHAPTER TWENTY-ONE

The bright rays of the sun streaming aggressively through the curtains wake me up the next morning, and it takes a few minutes for me to remember where I am. But then it all comes back, and I stretch languorously in bed, my body slightly sore from hours of sitting in a cramped airplane seat. The day seems full of possibilities as I wash up and get dressed.

Sarita Aunty and Nikhil are already at the breakfast table, and Meghna brings out delicious deep-fried puffy bread and some kind of potatoes along with fried eggs.

"What kind of potatoes are these?" I say after I've taken a big bite. "They're delicious."

"This is zeera aloo," Sarita Aunty says. "Potatoes with cumin. And the bread is called poori. It's one of Nikhil's favorites."

"It's so good." I reach over to grab a couple more pooris. "So, what's the plan for today?"

"Well, I thought I'd take you around today," Nikhil said. "Do you want to check out some shops?"

"Ooh, that sounds great," I say. "Can we go to some place that sells those pretty bangles? I want to get some for my moms and Nadia."

"You can take her to Colaba," Sarita Aunty says. "That way you all can shop and eat there. And Mira can see the Gateway of India."

"I read about that before we came," I say. "I'd love that."

Nikhil helps himself to another heaping spoonful of potatoes and three pooris.

"Let's do it," he says with a grin. "Let's introduce you to some street food."

"Nikhil," Sarita Aunty says in a warning tone. "We don't want her getting sick right away, so maybe for today stay away from street food."

"Why? She has to get sick at least once, so we might as well get it over with."

"Thank you, Aunty, for saving me," I say, getting up to give her a hug while simultaneously shooting a death glare in Nikhil's direction.

A short while later, I'm ready to go, dressed in a cotton T-shirt and jeans. Sarita Aunty warned me it would be hot, so I'm prepared. Traffic is a nightmare, and once again I hang on for dear life. But when we arrive at the Colaba Causeway, I forget all that. There is a stunning array of products on display in the shops lining both sides of the street. Everything ranging from costume jewelry to sunglasses is available, and I'm practically drooling. I squeal a little every time I see yet another cute pair of dangly earrings. I'm about to buy ten different pairs when Nikhil pulls me aside.

"Okay, so I should've warned you," he says. "You can't shop here like this."

"What d'you mean?" I'm eyeing a particularly gorgeous silver necklace.

"You have to haggle," he says. "These guys can tell that you're not from here, so they're going to overcharge you."

"But it's all so cheap," I say. "I can never get these at the mall for so little."

"True, but I'm just saying, you have to bargain a little."

"Okay, so show me how it's done."

And show me, he does. It's quite fascinating watching him start at half the price quoted by the shopkeepers and seeing how they land in the middle. Since Nikhil's doing all the work, I'm able to just take in everything going on around me. It's invigorating, the colors, the sounds of Bollywood songs blaring from speakers, the different accents from all the people walking about. I hear a lot of Hindi, but also a lot of English, which surprises me.

"How come so many people speak English here?" I ask Nikhil when we pop into a place called Leopold Cafe for some food.

"Mumbai's kind of a melting pot," he says. "People come from all over the country to make a life here, and they all have different mother tongues. And English is like the one common language they all speak."

"That's so cool," I say. "And so weird at the same time. I mean, who would have thought English of all languages would be the one they all speak?"

"That's colonialism for you," Nikhil says. "You know India used to be all different kingdoms, right?"

"Yeah, I read about that," I say. "I honestly want to spend more time here, you know. Like, live here and study the history."

"Maybe one day you can," Nikhil says. "Speaking of history, after we eat, I'll take you to the Gateway of India. You'll love it."

The menu here at Leopold is overwhelming to say the least. They offer everything from fries and sandwiches to tandoori chicken to pasta and risotto. I'm still a little jet-lagged, and after all the shopping, I end up ordering fries and a grilled cheese sandwich because I just can't decide.

"Wow," Nikhil says after I tell him what I want. "You came all the way to India for a grilled cheese and fries?"

"I know it's stupid, but look at all this," I say. "How am I supposed to decide?"

"Okay, fine, you can have your white-people comfort food this time, but please promise me you're going to be a little more adventurous for dinner?"

"Yes, I promise. Now can we please eat and go?" I'm dying to see the Gateway, especially after reading so much about it.

The images on the internet do not do it justice. At all. There's just no way to capture the essence of the crowds, the British Raj architecture of the buildings around, and, of course, the Gateway itself. It's an arch-monument that was built in honor of the first British monarchs to visit India in person. Except according to Google, it wasn't actually built until years later but became a symbol of British colonization. Apparently, it was also the point of departure for the British troops when they left after India won its independence. Looking out at the Gateway with the Arabian Sea in the background, I'm filled with awe, thinking about the historical significance of where I'm standing at this very moment and what brought me here. I have an overwhelming desire to absorb everything somehow so I can carry it all back with me.

We spend over an hour just wandering around, and I'm grateful that Nikhil doesn't rush me or start acting bored after a while. He's grown up in Mumbai, and I'm sure he's been here dozens of times, but he's letting me take it all in and I love him for it. As I stand here, I can't help wondering how often my birth mother has walked along these very streets, looking at the same view. I imagine she's one of the many people milling about, unaware that a letter she'd written eighteen years ago has brought someone halfway across the world to try to reconnect with her. She might even be close by at this very moment. Does she remember writing the letter? Does she still think about me or is my memory too painful? It occurs to me that I might be on a journey that'll end up presenting more questions than answers.

"Why're you looking at me like that?" I say when I notice Nikhil staring at me.

He shrugs. "No reason," he says. "Just, it's pretty cool to watch you seeing this for the first time."

"Do you remember the first time you came here?"

He shakes his head. "I don't know. I'm sure my parents brought me here when I was pretty small."

"Yeah, I guess it's not a big deal if you live here."

He smiles at me. "Well, I'm glad I get to be here with you now."

He throws an arm over my shoulder, and as we stand here together watching the sun set over the Arabian Sea, I'm happy that I get to share this special moment with him.

• • •

When we get back that evening, Sarita Aunty has a surprise waiting for us. We have company, and I only need to look at the tender and joyful expression on Nikhil's face as soon as we walk in to know who it is.

"Ashish . . ." There's a catch in Nikhil's voice, and I walk over to join Sarita Aunty in the kitchen to give the two of them some privacy. But I can't help stealing a glance at the guy who's made my friend's face light up like this. He's slightly taller than Nikhil, and his hair is longer and wavier. They make a striking couple, and as I walk away, I see Ashish reaching for Nikhil's hand even as Nikhil steps closer to him.

"He's so cute," I whisper to Sarita Aunty as I hop up to sit on the kitchen counter.

"He's a very sweet boy," she says. "Actually, I've invited his parents for dinner, since we haven't seen each other for quite some time."

Nikhil calls me back out into the living room after a while, and I join the two of them, eager to talk to Ashish.

"It's so great to finally meet you." I move in to give him a hug. "Nikhil won't shut up about you, so I feel like I already know you."

"Same here." I love how he puts his arm around Nikhil's waist and pulls him closer. "I'm so glad you decided to visit Mumbai."

"Yes, we've had the best time today. I'm sorry if we made you wait."

"Not at all. I wanted to surprise him." He smiles at Nikhil, who's actually blushing.

I hook my arm around Ashish's free one and pretend to lead him away.

"I think we need to talk. I have a lot of questions about our boy Nikhil here."

Ashish grins at me. "And I have a lot to tell you." He pries away his arm from around Nikhil's waist and we start walking away, but Nikhil pulls him back.

"Don't you dare." He narrows his eyes at me. "Would you please leave my boyfriend alone?"

I nod at Ashish. "We'll talk later."

He winks at me. "Later."

I like him immediately. His slightly crooked smile and dark eyes that literally twinkle completely win me over. Not that I need much convincing. After all, if Nikhil loves him so much, he has to be a good guy. What I really love though is watching the two of them together. There's something really special here, and I'm glad they got everything sorted out earlier in the year.

"So how did you like Colaba?" Ashish says as we sit down to dinner after his parents join us.

"I loved it," I say as I recount our day to them. "I don't think I'm ever going to want to leave."

"Did you know that Mumbai once belonged to the Portuguese?" Ashish's dad, Vikram, says. Nikhil has told me that he's a professor of history, and I warm to him immediately.

"Really? I had no idea," I say.

"Yes, the Mumbai you see now used to be a group of seven islands. They were given to King Charles II as dowry when he married Catherine of Braganza in 1661."

"So how did all the islands come together?" I ask. I think I've just outed myself as a history nerd. I can see Nikhil giving me a weird look, and Ashish is mouthing something in my direction.

"Arre, Vikram, these poor children are still jet-lagged," Ashish's mom, Neha, says. "You'll have to forgive my husband," she adds, turning to me with an apologetic smile.

"Oh my god, no, please, I love this stuff," I say. "I was just telling my moms that I might declare a major in history when I go to college in September."

"Aha, you see, not everyone finds this boring," Vikram Uncle declares triumphantly.

Nikhil and Ashish exchange a look, but I ignore them.

"Please, Uncle, continue," I say. "I'm just so fascinated by all this."

Vikram Uncle looks around the table and then at me with a rueful smile.

"I'm afraid we've been outvoted, my dear," he says. "Perhaps while you're here, I can accompany you to Elephanta Island, if you'd like."

My eyes widen. "I read about that too," I say.

"Actually, I wouldn't mind going as well," Sarita Aunty says. "It's been a long time since I went."

"Why don't we all go and make a day out of it?" Neha Aunty says.

"That sounds great," Ashish says. "Let's do it."

"Okay, but can we go to high tea at the Taj before we head out there?" Nikhil asks.

"Oh yes, that sounds like a great idea," Sarita Aunty says.

"Okay, well, then it's settled," Vikram Uncle announces. "Then Mira and I can talk without all of you making such bored faces at us."

The others all mumble denials, but everyone is smiling. I know I've just met Ashish and his family, but I already love them.

After everyone leaves, Nikhil and I sit on the screened verandah with a bowl of pistachios and some ice-cold lemonade, listening to the sounds of the city below. The sky is barely visible through all the smog, but I imagine that the stars are twinkling in the sky. I feel very content in this moment.

"Hey, Nikhil, I just want to tell you that you don't have to hang out with me the whole time I'm here," I say. "I mean you and Ashish don't get to see each other, so please don't feel like you have to babysit me or anything."

"Thanks, but no, it's fine," he says. "We'll have lots of time, plus we just got here. You need more than a day to find your way around Mumbai by yourself."

"Sure, but maybe after a few days, I can start figuring it out," I say. "I mean, I have my phone and most people speak English, so it's not like I'm helpless."

"Let's see how you feel after a couple of days, and then you can decide."

"By the way, I really like Ashish," I say. "I can see why you're so crazy about him."

"He likes you too," Nikhil says, and I swear he's blushing a little.

"What I can't figure out, though, is how did the poor guy end up with you?" I throw Nikhil an evil grin, and he throws a pistachio at my head.

Later, I video chat with Moms and Nadia and tell them everything about my day.

"We miss you so much, honey," Mama says. "It's been so quiet around here."

"I can't believe I'm saying this, but I miss cleaning up your messes around the house," Mom says. "Everything is so neat and clean without you. It's weird."

"Hey, I thought I was calling my loving family and instead I get this?" I say, grinning at them. "Wow."

"Did you buy my stuff from the list yet?" Nadia says.

"Jeez, Nadia, I've been here for *one* day."

"I'm just saying, so you don't forget."

"I won't forget, I promise."

I tell them all about the plan to visit Elephanta Island, and as I listen to them tell me about their days, I wish they could all be here to share this amazing trip with me. But then again, I'm sure I'll be coming back here with them. This particular journey has to be one I make alone. I hope that when I return home, I'll have found that part of me that's always been missing.

CHAPTER TWENTY-TWO

I've been here a few days, and Nikhil, Ashish, and I have been traipsing all over Mumbai eating like there's no tomorrow. So far, I haven't gotten sick, so I'm thankful for that because I wouldn't want to miss all the amazing shopping. Back home I like to go to the mall every now and then, but the shopping experience here is on a whole other level. After that first day in Colaba, Nikhil and Ashish have taken me to several other places, and each time it's like no other. I've posted more pictures on Instagram in one week than I have ever before. Brooke and Pooja are so jealous, but they love following along with my daily adventures. There are street vendors who have their wares set out on mats on the ground and sell beautiful art and other decorative items. There are food carts at Elco Market, where I got to eat some of the tastiest food I've ever eaten. In the evenings, Sarita Aunty or Ashish's parents have taken us out to fancy restaurants. And a couple of times, the three of us have hung out with Nikhil's school buddies from before he left for Houston. Through it all, the thought of meeting my birth mother is never far from my mind. I'm sort of glad that I'm getting to see a lot of Mumbai before then because I have no idea how I'm going to feel after my birthday.

This evening Nikhil, Ashish, and I decide to go to Juhu Beach. It's the perfect time to go, just as the sun is setting, and despite the crowds and the garbage that litters the beach, the sky with its deep orange glow is breathtaking. We walk along the water, chatting to Ashish about our lives in Houston.

"Nikhil told me you got into UPenn," I say. "You must be thrilled."

"It's not Texas, but at least it's closer than Mumbai." Ashish puts his arm around Nikhil's shoulder, and they exchange a smile.

"It'll be so much easier to visit than from here," I point out. "I'm so happy for you both."

"So, who wants to get golas?" Nikhil says as we approach some food carts.

"What're golas?" I'm already intrigued by the colorful cups lined up on the first cart.

"They're like snow cones," he says.

"But on steroids," Ashish adds.

"Well, of course now I have to try one," I say.

We go to one of the stands with the colorful displays. The large clear plastic cups are filled with shaved ice in a rainbow of colors and topped with cream, nuts, and dried fruits and finished off with little paper umbrellas. I pick mango, and the first bite is pure ecstasy. It's sweet and tangy all at once, an instant fix for the heat and humidity even at this late hour.

"Ashish," I say. "When you visit Houston, we'll take you to the best Tex-Mex place in town. They have these amazing steak fajitas and the best nachos."

"That sounds amazing," Ashish says. "I've never been to Texas."

"You'll love it," I say.

We stroll along the beach for a little while longer before returning home to help Sarita Aunty prepare for our trip to Elephanta Island the next day.

● ● ●

We all go for high tea at the Taj, an ornate hotel right across from the Gateway. I feel very fancy as we enjoy the delectable scones and pastries along with a huge selection of teas. I can't help wondering what my life would be like if my birth mother had brought me to India with her. Would we have mother-daughter rituals like coming to the Taj for high tea? Or would we spend evenings at Juhu Beach eating golas and playing in the surf? But if that had happened, my life and all my memories with my moms and Nadia wouldn't exist. There's a dull ache in my heart at the thought of that, and I wonder if it'll ever go away.

After high tea, we stand at the Gateway of India once again. This is where we'll catch a ferry to Elephanta Island. It's an hour-long ride, and when we arrive, I'm astounded by all the monkeys scampering about, completely comfortable with all the tourists who are already here. It's quiet and peaceful away from the noise and crowds of the city. We start walking toward the entrance of the caves, and I pull out my plastic water bottle to take a drink before we go in. All of a sudden, a monkey appears out of nowhere and tugs at my water bottle. I scream, and for some reason, I can't seem to let go. We engage in a tug-of-war for the bottle, but the monkey wins and runs away.

"Hey, that's my water!" I scream after him while Nikhil and

Ashish just stand there laughing and recording it all on their phones.

The little thief has stopped just a short distance away from us, and I can't believe my eyes as it unscrews the cap from the bottle and chugs the water until its done. Then it flings the bottle back in my direction. Unbelievable.

"I told you we should have warned her about the monkeys," Ashish says disapprovingly to Nikhil.

I glare at Nikhil, who just shrugs. "I owed her one," he says, casually walking away.

"I won't forget this!" I shout after him, but he's still laughing, this time looking at his phone, and I know he can't wait to post the video.

"You kids are funny," Sarita Aunty says as we enter the caves. They're a UNESCO World Heritage site, and the interior is simply stunning. There is a huge statue of the three aspects of the Hindu god Shiva. Inside there are numerous sculptures and reliefs all dedicated to Shiva, created almost 1,500 years ago. I walk around with wide eyes and my mouth hanging open. Vikram Uncle joins me, playing tour guide, and after a couple of hours I am more enthralled than ever with the history of this place. It strikes me just how bizarre my life has become. This history should have been mine as well. I should have already known it, like most of the people here. I'm like a transplanted tree with roots here and also far away, not quite sure where I really belong. I wonder if I'll ever feel differently.

CHAPTER TWENTY-THREE

It's my birthday today, and I wake up full of trepidation. All my previous excitement at the prospect of finally meeting my birth mother has been replaced by a paralyzing fear that she won't show. I don't know if I have it in me to deal with that. What if Moms were right and this has all been a huge mistake? I wonder for the hundredth time if I should just enjoy the rest of my trip exploring Mumbai and then fly back to my real life in Houston. I mean, what am I expecting will happen even if she does come today? I'm sure she's moved on with her life and has a family of her own. How is she going to explain me to them? If she couldn't parent me all those years ago, what could have changed by now? I'll just be a painful reminder of a very difficult time in her life. I'm not sure I want to be that.

Would she have even returned here if it hadn't been for me?

I ponder all this as I get dressed, and by the time I come to the dining room for breakfast, I'm no closer to a decision.

Sarita Aunty puts her arms around me in a tight hug. "Happy birthday, Mira." She kisses both my cheeks. "I've made Bombay toast for you. I hope you like it."

"Thank you so much, Aunty. It smells amazing."

Nikhil saunters into the room with his arms behind his back.

"Happy birthday, dork." He punches me lightly in the arm.

"OW. That better be for me." I point my chin at whatever he's hiding rather unsuccessfully.

"Give it to me." Sarita Aunty practically snatches the package from his hands and hands it to me. "Open it."

I carefully remove the colorful wrapping to reveal a royal-blue velvet box. I open the clasp and gasp when I see the beautiful necklace inside.

"Aunty, this is gorgeous." I look up at her with a huge smile. The necklace is a stunning choker with pearls and nine different colored stones.

"Do you like it?" Sarita Aunty says.

"I love it, but it's too much."

"Nonsense. It will go beautifully with the lehenga set you wore to the dance performance."

I get up to give her a big hug.

"Hey, how come I don't get a thank-you?" Nikhil says.

In reply, I punch him playfully in the arm, just a little harder than he did.

"So, Mira, how are you feeling about today?" Sarita Aunty asks as I load my plate with Bombay toast, my newest favorite breakfast food. "A little bit nervous?"

I nod as I finish chewing on the delicious crunchy toast fried with egg, onions, and cilantro. Then I confess, "I'm really scared."

"Are you worried she won't show?" Nikhil asks.

"A bit . . . but mostly, what if it's really weird, you know?"

"I think you should be prepared for that," Sarita Aunty says. "It's been so many years. But, Mira, you know you can change your mind if you don't feel comfortable."

"Do you want me to come with you?" Nikhil says. "I could take you there and wait for you."

"Really?" I say. "It wouldn't be too much?"

"No, not at all. I can meet Ashish, and we can hang around until you're ready."

"Actually, that would be great. Thank you." I had said all along I wanted to do this by myself, but now I realize I need someone else there.

"No problem," he says, grabbing the last piece of toast just as I reach out to take it.

"Wow."

"Can I just say, I'm so happy that you two are so close," Sarita Aunty says. "Nikhil always wanted a sibling, and this is just how I imagine it would be."

"Eww, Mom, I didn't mean like *her*," Nikhil says, talking with his mouth full of my Bombay toast.

"Sarita Aunty, I'm so sorry you've had to deal with him all these years." I keep my face completely serious. "I can't even imagine how annoying he must have been as a child."

"I wasn't a brat like you," he says. "I mean, I didn't know you then, but I do now, so I can tell."

Sarita Aunty just shakes her head at us as she finishes her chai.

"I talked to your moms yesterday," Sarita Aunty says. "They sounded worried about you."

"I know," I say. "I figured they would be. I think they didn't want to bring it up, but I could tell."

"I told them they had nothing to worry about. We're all here for you, no matter how it goes. And of course they will be calling you later for your birthday."

"Thank you, Aunty." I reach out to touch her hands. "I'm really grateful for everything."

"Nonsense, dear. You're family now, so no need for thank-you and all that." She pats my hand affectionately while Nikhil makes a gagging sound.

I try to kick him under the table, but he moves his leg before I can make contact. I'll have to figure out a way to get back at him.

To distract me from worrying about this afternoon, Nikhil takes me shopping to Linking Road, which is a haven for someone like me. Stalls line both sides of the road, selling the most gorgeous embroidered Bohemian-style handbags and beautiful scarves. There are also shoes and sandals in colorful designs, and it's the perfect way to spend the morning. I manage to pick up gifts for Moms, Nadia, Brooke, and Pooja, and I'm so excited because I know they'll love them.

At the last minute, I decide to pick up a beautifully embroidered purse for my birth mom. Today is all about being positive. A thought crosses my mind, and I immediately feel ridiculous. Will she bring me a gift for my birthday?

We pop into a fast-food joint for a quick lunch of burgers and fries before going to Sancha, a specialty tea boutique where I pick up some lovely gift sets for Moms and also for Sarita Aunty as a thank-you for everything she's doing for me.

Then, somehow, it's almost four, and we head over to Flora Fountain, which is just a short walk away.

"Are you sure you don't want me to stay?" Nikhil asks for the third time.

"No, really, I'm good. But thanks, though," I say. "And listen, Nikhil, I forgive you."

"For what?" He looks utterly confused.

"For the whole monkey thing," I say, putting on my most hurt expression. "And this morning when your mom was saying that thing about us being like brother and sister. It really hurt me, you know." I look down at my hands because I can't let him see that I'm trying so hard not to laugh. But I can't resist peeking at his face. His expression is priceless. He looks so worried and guilty. Mission accomplished.

"Mira . . . I'm so sorry," he says, looking extremely remorseful. "You know I didn't mean . . . OH MY GOD, Mira, you suck!"

He catches my grin and glares at me.

"Dude, you're so gullible," I say, opening the car door. "Thanks for the ride," I call out as I walk toward the fountain, my heart in my mouth. It was nice to mess with Nikhil's head, to not focus on the giant knot in my stomach for a little bit, but there's no more avoiding it. The moment I've been waiting for is finally here, and whatever happens, at least I won't have to keep wondering for the rest of my life.

I check the time on my phone. It's almost four. I find a spot to stand by the fence surrounding the lush green around the fountain. I have no idea which direction to look in, so I keep moving. I want to be able to see her as soon as she comes. If she comes at all. What if I don't recognize her? Or, even worse, what if she comes here and changes her mind? What if she doesn't even live in India anymore? I'm beginning to think that this was all a huge mistake and that I should have listened to my parents.

Fifteen minutes later, she's still not here, and I'm a mess. The knot in my stomach has dissolved and has been replaced by nausea. I don't know what to do. Should I wait or just leave? What if she's almost here or stuck in traffic? I mean, from what

293

I've seen of Mumbai traffic, it's a miracle anyone makes it anywhere on time. And also, Nikhil and Ashish have introduced me to the concept of Indian Standard Time. Apparently as someone of South Asian origin, I'm going to be late to everything. This makes me feel a lot better about my chronic tardiness since I now know it's not my fault. It's just genetics. I wonder if this logic will work on Moms the next time they're yelling at me for taking so long.

Ten further minutes later, I take a deep breath and decide to leave. I can't do this. It's been hard enough just convincing myself that this won't be a disaster without waiting like this, not knowing if she'll even come. I'm about to stand up when I notice a woman approaching, clearly looking around for someone. She's wearing jeans and a beige tunic with a black scarf wrapped loosely around her neck. A pair of sunglasses are perched on the top of her head. I touch the heart pendant that's nestled in the hollow of my neck. She looks exactly like the picture of her that's inside. Her hair is longer but just as black, and as her eyes settle on me, an expression crosses her face that I can't quite describe.

She smiles hesitantly and starts to walk toward me. I smile back, rooted to the ground, my body unable to move.

Then she's standing in front of me, but she doesn't feel real, this flesh-and-blood woman who gave birth to me and who I've imagined a million times in my mind.

"Mira?" she says softly, and I nod. My name on her lips sounds nice, like it belongs there. "I'm Ayesha."

"You came," I say.

"I'm so sorry I'm late," she says. "To be honest, I was scared. I didn't know if you'd read my letters. Or if you'd come."

"Of course I had to come."

"How are you?" she says. She studies my face, her smile uncertain but her eyes unwavering.

"I'm good," I say. "How are you?"

"Better now."

I can't take my eyes off her. I want to absorb every detail of her appearance. It's kind of surreal looking at her and recognizing parts of myself in her smile, the tilt of her head, the way her nose crinkled just a little when she smiled.

I realize I've just been staring at her and that it's getting weird.

"Would you like to go get a coffee?" she asks. "There's a Starbucks very close by here."

"Sure, that'd be great," I say.

We start walking, not even trying to make small talk. A few minutes later, we're sitting at a table by the window. The whole time I have the urge to simultaneously scream and laugh. I'm afraid I might be losing it. After all the drama of the last couple of months, it would be just like me to scare my birth mother off by behaving like a lunatic.

"Is there anything you'd like to ask me?" she says. "I'm sure you must have a lot of questions."

"Should we get some coffee or something first?" I ask. I can't believe with everything else going on, I'm still worried that we can't just occupy a table and not order anything.

"Sure, what would you like?" she asks, pulling out her wallet from her purse.

"No, it's fine, thanks. I can get it."

"Please, Mira," she says with a smile. "You came halfway across the world for me. Let me buy you a cup of coffee."

A few minutes later, we have our drinks and are sitting at the table again. As I look at her, I marvel at how young she is. Even though I know she was only eighteen when she had me, I'm still a little surprised now that she's sitting in front of me. But most of my fears and unease have disappeared. It feels right to be sitting here with her like this, trying to reconnect and hopefully get back some of what we both missed out on over the past eighteen years. I'm glad I came here. It was the right thing to do.

"I don't know where to begin," I say. "I've spent most of my life wondering about so many things, and . . . now you're here."

"Are you happy?" she asks softly. "Were you happy growing up?"

I don't hesitate. "Yes, very. My moms are amazing."

"I knew they would be. I think that was the only reason I was able to leave you."

It's almost like I'm outside my body, watching. I can't believe this moment has come. The question I've carried with me for so many years—I never really believed I'd get a chance to ask it, but now that chance is here, and the words are right there where they've been all along. I ask her, "Why did you have to go?"

She doesn't say anything for a long time, and I don't know what to do. Maybe I shouldn't have asked her that.

"I was so afraid," she says, almost to herself. "I didn't have anyone to turn to."

"Were you scared of your parents finding out?"

She nods. "But there were so many other things as well." She closes her eyes for a minute, and I know it must be incredibly painful for her to talk about this. "Your father . . . he never came back."

"Who was he?"

"We met in high school, at a friend's party. We didn't know

each other for that long, just a few months, but we loved each other. At least that's what I thought."

I am afraid to ask too many questions, terrified that if I put too much stress on the conversation, it will collapse entirely. But at the same time, I don't know if I'll ever have this chance again. I have to keep going, one question at a time.

"Was he from India too?" I ask.

"Yes, from right here in Mumbai. He left one day because his father was sick, and then he just never came back."

"Did you ever look for him?"

"I tried so many times, back when I was still in Bloomington. Every time I called, his mother would pick up . . . and then after a while I stopped calling. I had to figure out what I was going to do."

"And that's when you met my moms?"

"They were wonderful to me," she says. "I'll never be able to repay them for what they did. But I had to leave." Her eyes are filling with tears, and my heart is breaking for the scared young girl she must have been, all alone with nowhere to go and a baby on the way.

"Did you ever think about me?" I hate that I can't stop the words, but I have to know.

She looks at me, and her eyes are full of regret. "Every moment of every day," she says. "A day didn't go by when I wasn't imagining what you must be doing, how big you must be. Every time I had to remind myself that you were better off just to keep going without me in your life."

My eyes are full of tears now too, and she reaches for my hand. She holds it gently, close to her heart. "Please forgive me," she whispers. "I'm so sorry."

I feel like my heart is breaking into a thousand pieces. All the memories I didn't get to make with her, all the love she couldn't give me, it's all too much. I don't care that people around us are turning to look. It doesn't matter. I don't even know what I'm feeling anymore. I have no way to define this avalanche of emotions that is coming down on me at this moment. I get up and run out of the café and take in huge gulps of air outside.

Suddenly I have an overwhelming desire to be back in my room at home in Houston, sitting on my own bed with Moms right there so I can talk this through. But instead, I'm thousands of miles away in a strange city trying to find a connection with a mother who is nothing but a stranger to me. Yet there is something intangible that binds us together, and I don't know what it is. I try to think about what Moms would say if they were here right now. Mom would tell me to take a few deep breaths and remember that I don't have to do anything I'm not comfortable with. And Mama would say that I have a big heart and that she knows I will figure out a way to make a connection because I always do.

My heartbeat has slowed down, and the pounding in my ears has stopped. I take a couple of deep breaths and square my shoulders. I can do this. I've come this far, and I'm not going to run away now because things are uncomfortable. I'm going to be a grown-up about this just like I told Moms I was. Even though I know that it's a big, fat lie.

CHAPTER TWENTY-FOUR

I walk back inside and join Ayesha at the table. She looks very worried and confused.

"I'm so sorry, Mira," she says as soon as I sit down. "I completely understand if you want to leave. Maybe this wasn't such a good idea."

"No . . . it's fine," I assure her. "I'm sorry, I shouldn't have run out like that."

"No, Mira, listen . . . I can't imagine how difficult this must be for you. I'm just so happy that you came and that I can see what a beautiful young woman you've grown up to be."

I blush a little at this unexpected praise.

"I'm glad I came too," I say softly.

We sit in awkward silence for a while, but then Ayesha gets up abruptly.

"Shall we get something to eat?" she says. "They make a really good reshmi kebab roll here."

"Sure, that sounds great," I say. I start taking out my wallet but stop when I see the stern look on her face. I smile at her. "Thank you."

I check my phone while she goes to place the order.

How's it going?

It's Nikhil. I'm sure he's dying to hear all about this.

Going great!

She comes back in a little bit and sits back down.

"Would you tell me something about yourself?" she says.

"What would you like to know?" I don't even know where to start with this highlight reel of my life.

"Well, maybe tell me what your plans are now that you're done with high school," she says.

"I got into Baylor, so that's where I'm going when I get back."

"And what are you going to major in?"

"I'm not sure yet, but I'm leaning toward history. And I really want to focus my studies on India."

"You like history, huh? And what do you see yourself doing in, say, five years or so?"

"I think I'll get my master's and then teach."

"Your grandmother was a teacher as well," she says.

It feels weird to hear her mention my grandmother in such an offhand way, as if she's someone I already know.

"Mom used to be a teacher back home," I say.

"Yes, I remember. Sam used to talk about her students when I was staying with them."

"She's a guidance counselor now."

I try to picture Ayesha in my home, the same house where all my memories were built, but I can't. She doesn't fit in our lives, and for some reason, that makes me feel a little bit guilty.

"So when did you move in with them?" I ask.

"Soon after I met them," she says. "I don't think they ever knew what they did for me."

300

"They mentioned an aunt you used to live with in Bloomington. Does she still live there?"

"Salma Aunty. Yes, she and Hafeez Uncle still live there. And their daughter, Reshma, lives in Chicago."

I need a moment to let that sink in. I've had family in the US my whole life. "And they never found out?"

She shakes her head slowly. "I made sure that no one ever knew," she says. Then she lets out a hollow laugh. "I did a great job protecting my family's reputation. As far as they were concerned, I was still their golden daughter."

"Is that why you did it? To protect them?"

In a way, I can understand that. I would do anything to protect my moms and Nadia. And although I've never lived in India, I know things are different here. Pooja helped me understand that.

"My friend told me that sometimes protecting your family means destroying your own dreams," I say, Pooja's words running through my mind.

"Your friend is right," she says. "But it's also true that some people are strong enough to fight for their dreams." She looks at me, and there's a sorrow in her eyes I can't bear to look at. "I wasn't one of the strong ones."

I've always considered myself a pretty tough person, but I don't know what I would have done in that situation if I didn't have an open and honest relationship with my moms. If I were to get pregnant now, I can't imagine that they'd be thrilled, but they would stand by me and help me decide the best way to move forward. I would still feel loved and supported. And the idea that Ayesha at eighteen didn't have those kinds of parents and that she had to make such a drastic and life-altering decision all by herself makes me incredibly sad. Ever since I found the letters, I've been judging her, vacillating between pity and resentment. But now, maybe for the first time, I can really understand just how difficult it must have been and how fortunate I am to have my moms.

I put my hand over hers, and she looks at me in surprise but doesn't say anything.

"Did you ever get married?" I ask.

"I did," she says. "But it didn't work out."

"How come?"

"Well . . . he wanted children and I . . ."

"You didn't want any more?"

I want to ask her why, whether her decision not to have any more children had anything to do with me, but I'm not sure if I should ask.

"Listen, Mira," she says. "If you like, could we do this again maybe?"

I hesitate. "I'm only here for two more weeks," I say.

"That's okay," she says. "I'd love to get to know you a little better while you're here."

"I'd like that too," I say.

"Is there anything special you'd like to do? I can clear my schedule so we can do whatever you like."

"There is something I'd like to do," I say.

"Of course," she says. "What is it?"

"I'd like to find my father."

CHAPTER TWENTY-FIVE

I can't really read her face right now, so I don't know if I've made a mistake by bringing up my father. The thing is, though, I may not get another shot to find him, and so I have to take this one.

"I haven't spoken to him since our last phone call eighteen years ago," Ayesha says.

"Do you know where he lives?" I ask.

"Yes. He lives right here in Mumbai."

"And does he know about me?"

There's a fleeting sadness in her eyes, but it's quickly replaced by something cold.

"He knew I was pregnant," she says, a slight bitterness tingeing her voice. "I'm sorry, Mira. I wish I had a better answer for you."

"No . . . I'm sorry," I say. "I didn't mean to . . . I don't want to cause you any more pain."

"You're not the one causing me pain," she says. "I'm very grateful to you for coming to meet me here today." Her eyes become moist. "It's more than I deserve."

A new kind of emotion courses through me. I feel protective toward my mother. Suddenly I picture her calling and waiting for my father to call her back, desperate for him to be there for her. What kind of person deserts someone at a time like that? Shouldn't he have taken some responsibility? I mean, it wasn't like she got pregnant all by herself. He owed it to her to at least reply to her messages.

"Did you love him?"

"I did," she says. "And I thought he loved me too."

I've never really been in love, at least not the way I think love is supposed to feel, but I imagine that Ayesha must have felt something real for my father if their relationship went as far as it did. And to be betrayed like that must have been incredibly devastating.

"Are you upset that I'm asking about him?" I'm starting to feel like this isn't worth making her relive all the hurtful moments from that time.

"No, Mira, not at all," she says, squeezing my hand. "You have every right to know who he is. Look, I won't lie to you. It is hard talking about him, but it was all so long ago."

"I feel really bad for asking about him."

"I knew what I was doing, and I know *my* feelings were real. It took me a long time to find a way to move on with my life, but there was always a big part of me that felt ashamed and guilty for what I did to you."

"You don't need to feel that way at all," I say. "I've had a great life so far, and now we have a chance to get to know each other."

She touches my cheek gently. "You don't know how much it means to hear that," she says. "To be honest, I wasn't sure if you'd come. I prepared myself for that possibility, but I was really hoping that you would have forgiven me." She lowers her gaze. "I don't think I can ever forgive myself."

We both have tears running down our faces, and I smile through mine.

"I have to admit when I first found your letters, I was angry." Shame spirals through me as I remember my early reactions. "I didn't understand why you'd left without me. But now . . . I don't know what I would have done in your situation. I'm not sure I would have been strong enough to do what you did."

Ayesha looks at me, her eyes swimming in tears. "I've spent years wondering . . . what you would think, if you ever missed me. And the ache never really went away, no matter how many times I told myself that I did what was best for you."

I don't know what to say. How do I erase years of regret and worry from my mother's heart without also erasing everything that led to this moment?

"We're going to get banned from this place," I say with a little laugh.

"That's okay—I know a lot of cool places around here." She reaches into her purse and takes out a pack of tissues. She hands me one and takes one for herself. "Look, we have so much to talk about, and I'm sure you still have a lot of questions."

"When can we meet again?" I ask.

"How about the day after tomorrow, in the afternoon? I can come and pick you up." She looks a little uncertain. "Is that okay? Where are you staying?"

"I'm staying with a friend and his family," I tell her. "And yes, that would be totally fine. They'd love to meet you."

We exchange phone numbers, and she promises to text me when she's heading over to pick me up. I decline her offer for a ride back home and text Nikhil that I'm ready.

"How did it go?" Nikhil asks as soon as I slide into the passenger seat. He takes in my tearstained face and reaches over to take my hand. "Are you okay?"

"Yeah, I'm fine," I say, smiling reassuringly at him. "It was really nice, actually."

"Do you want to talk about it?"

"Yes, but can we go home first?" I say. "I just want to take a shower and change."

"Sure thing," he says as we pull into the vortex that is Mumbai traffic.

• • •

Later that night, I get on a video call with my moms. I know they've been worried, and I doubt they got any sleep at all. It's early morning in Houston when I reach them.

"Mira, happy birthday, honey. Are you okay?" Mama's sleepy voice doesn't fool me. Her eyes look tired, and I'm sure she's been sitting in her chair by the window for most of the night. Her night.

"Thank you, Mama. I'm good." My face is puffy from all the crying, and after Mom joins the call, I rush to tell them everything.

"I don't know what to say." Mom reacts when I'm done. Both she and Mama are really emotional. "I can't even imagine what she must have gone through all those years."

"I feel so awful for all the things I said about her."

"You didn't know. And at least now you've met and she knows about your life here." Mama is always one to look at the bright side of things, and today it's exactly what I need.

"I don't think I ever apologized properly for the things I said to you when I first found the letters." I figure this day has been one for clearing the air, so why stop now?

Moms are getting teary now too, and I feel I should get some sort of prize for making the most people cry in one day.

"Honey, you did apologize, and there's no need to talk about that anymore." Mom gives me a watery smile. "Besides, we know you'll always be our little cuddle bug. No matter what happens."

The waterworks start again, and I'm starting to feel dehydrated. I blow them kisses and remind them to hug Nadia for me before ending the call.

• • •

The next day, I'm cradling a hot cup of chai in my hands as Nikhil and I sit in his living room. I've caught him up on everything, and now we're trying to decide on how I'm going to approach my father.

"Did she say she'll tell you how to contact him?" Nikhil says.

"Kind of . . . Well, she didn't say she wouldn't."

"You know we could try and find him ourselves, right?"

"You mean, like stalk him on social media?"

"Yeah, exactly like that."

"That's a great idea, except I don't even know his name."

"Well, can't you ask your mother?"

"Actually, she's coming here tomorrow to pick me up," I say. "Do you want to meet her?"

"Yeah I want to meet her," he says. "Mom's going to be here too. She's actually been a little worried about you, so I think it'll be great for them to meet in person."

"I think so too. Okay. So I'll ask her about my dad again and then you can do your stalker thing?"

"Sure. And thanks for making me sound really creepy," he says.

"Anytime," I graciously respond.

I realize that I'm very excited to see Ayesha again the next day. But at the same time, I have no idea how she's going to fit into my life in the long term or how I'm going to fit into hers. For one, we live on different continents. But physical distance aside, I'm not sure what kind of relationship we're going to have. I already have parents. So, what exactly are we doing? After going around in circles in my head, I decide that for now I'm just going to enjoy the time I have with Ayesha and leave the worrying for later.

CHAPTER TWENTY-SIX

"Suresh Khanna," Ayesha says when I ask her for my father's name. "He's a big business tycoon now. That's how I found him."

"What do you mean?" We're sitting in the restaurant at Elco Market and having the most delicious pani puri, which is now officially my favorite food.

"About three years ago, I saw an article about him in this magazine. It was a thirty-under-thirty-five list of people in business, and there he was."

"Wow, that's . . . something. Did you try to contact him?"

"No," she says. "I had no reason to."

"Listen . . ."

I realize I don't know what to call her. *Mom* seems completely weird, and I'm not too sure about calling her by her first name.

"You can call me Ayesha," she says, reading my mind. "Look, I know this is very strange, so let's not get hung up on formalities."

"Okay, thanks . . . Ayesha." I try it out and I guess it'll take some time to feel normal, but it is what it is.

"Mira, I'm perfectly okay with you contacting your father, if that's what you want," she says. "I just want to make sure that you're prepared."

"For what?"

"Honestly, I don't know. I just don't want you to get hurt."

"I'll be fine," I say. "It's not like I need anything from him. I just want to know who he is." And the part I don't tell her is that I want him to know what he missed out on when he so callously ghosted Ayesha eighteen years ago, leaving her pregnant and alone. I don't see why he gets to just live his life while she had to live with the secret for so long.

"There's something I need to tell you, Mira." Ayesha looks a little worried, and I can feel a knot forming in my stomach.

"What is it?"

"My parents still don't know about you," she says. "I wanted to tell them so many times over the years, but every time I lost the nerve."

"You don't have to say anything to them if you don't want to," I say. I don't want to be the reason for any discord in her family.

"No, that's just the thing," she says. "I want to tell them now. I wanted to wait and see if you would come, and now that you're here, I want them to know."

"Are you sure?"

Her eyes glisten. "Yes, I really, really am. I don't care what anyone thinks. I want everyone to know that you're my daughter."

I don't know what to say. Her words are like a balm, soothing that part of me that always wondered why she didn't want me. Now that I've spent a little time with her, I know that it must be incredibly difficult for her to tell her family. But the fact that she's choosing to do it now, finally, means more to me than I could have imagined.

"I'd really like that," I say softly.

"And about your father . . . I'm sorry, but I think you'll have to see him by yourself. I don't think I'm ready for that." She looks at me and tucks a strand of hair behind my ear. "But I support your decision, whatever it is."

"Oh my god, of course, I completely understand," I say hastily. "I would never ask you to do that."

"Thank you for understanding," she says. "But remember, no matter what happens, I'll be here for you."

I learn a lot about her as we order more delectable dishes. She's a social worker and works for a nonprofit that helps pregnant teens with housing, education, and job skills. I can't help noticing how her eyes light up when she talks about her work, and it's clear that she's found her calling. She tells me about how young women are stigmatized simply for exploring their sexuality, especially when they come from lower-middle-class families and the double standard that exists. She's made it her life's work to advocate for them, and my heart swells with pride as I listen to her. At the same time, I feel a resentment growing as I think about how unfair it is that she had to leave me and bury that part of her life while my father made no sacrifices whatsoever.

I'm fuming by the time Ayesha drops me off at Nikhil's place. I texted him my father's name and told him about the article as well, and he has news for me.

"You know it's so unfair," I say when Nikhil opens the door. "Ayesha was telling me about everything that she had to deal with when she got pregnant with me. And then she finds out a few years ago that my birth father has this great life and never had to take any responsibility."

"It's just wrong," Nikhil agrees. "Didn't you say that he never even replied to any of her messages? Who does that?"

"A selfish coward, that's who." I'm so angry, I want to go over right now and confront him. "So, what did you find out?"

"You're not going to believe this—he lives right here in Bandra. His building's like fifteen minutes from here."

"But it'll take, like, two hours to get there, right?" Since I've been here, I've spent more time in the back of a car stuck in traffic than anywhere else.

"Probably," he says with a rueful grin. "I can take you there tonight if you want."

"Okay," I say, my palms suddenly sweaty. I look at him. "I'm really going to do this."

"Do you want me to stay with you?" Nikhil offers.

"Thank you, but I have to do this on my own," I tell him. "He might not even be there."

"Okay. Let's do this, then," he says, and once again, I can't help feeling incredibly thankful for his friendship. And I can't believe that I'm finally going to be face-to-face with my birth father.

CHAPTER TWENTY-SEVEN

I approach the gate of the building my father lives in and stop in front of the security guard. Nikhil is here with me and tells the guard my name and explains I've come all the way from America to meet Mr. Suresh Khanna. The security guard calls and relays the message. I'm sure my father has no earthly clue who I am and I'm not sure why he agrees to see me, but the guard ushers me in. I turn to give Nikhil a little wave before walking in. My earlier bravado has turned to trepidation, but I'm here now, so I might as well meet him.

I take the elevator to the penthouse apartment and ring the bell. There's an ornate brass sign on the wall with the name *Khanna* on it in black lettering. The building looks very posh and well maintained, with marble floors in the lobby and intricately designed furniture. I hear footsteps inside before the door opens. A young man, too young to be my father, stands there and invites me in. He asks me to take a seat and then disappears. I decide to stand, walking over to the large windows. From up here, the view is quite mesmerizing, people looking like ants, scurrying about everywhere, dodging taxis, auto-rickshaws, and buses. It's organized chaos, because somehow, completely defying logic, everything runs along smoothly. I hear footsteps and turn toward the sound. A man walks in, maybe in his thirties, tall and trim, with thick black hair and glasses.

"I'm Suresh Khanna," he announces. "What can I do for you?"

"I'm Mira," I say, not quite sure how to proceed now that he's actually standing right in front of me.

"Hello, Mira," he says. He looks understandably confused. "Have we met before? The guard said you've come from the States?"

"Yes . . . I'm from Houston." My brain seems to be stalling, and I'm unable to form the words that will tell him what I need to say. "I came here to meet my mother."

I'm not sure why I choose these words because it's not like he can read my mind. I should probably make myself clear before he gets nervous about my presence in his home. I know this doesn't look good, some strange young girl showing up at his house this late in the evening.

"Ayesha," I blurt out. "My mother's name is Ayesha. You knew her a long time ago."

The blood rushes from his face. He looks at me in stunned silence.

"Ayesha," he says, almost to himself, running his hand through his hair.

"I'm your daughter." There. I said it.

He stares at me in disbelief. "What . . . ? How . . . ? Who are you again?"

"My name is Mira Jensen. My birth mother, Ayesha Hameed, placed me for adoption eighteen years ago. I've come to Mumbai to meet her, and I wanted to meet you too."

He stumbles a little and sort of falls back into an armchair. I'm a little alarmed, but some of my anger is returning. Why is he so shocked? I mean, he must have known that this could happen someday. But he seems genuinely stunned.

"You knew about me, right?" I continue. "Ayesha told you she was pregnant."

"No . . . I mean, yes, I knew she was pregnant, but . . ." Suddenly he looks up at me. "How do I know you're telling the truth?"

"I really don't know what to tell you. I don't want anything from you. I just wanted to meet you," I say. "Do you even remember her?"

"What?" He looks at me in disbelief. "Of course I remember her. The last time we spoke she was still in Bloomington. So you're saying she lives here in Mumbai now?" His eyes get a little misty.

"Yes. I met her two days ago for the first time. I know all about your relationship and how you had to leave Bloomington to take care of your parents and that you just ghosted her."

"I didn't—"

"You left her pregnant and alone," I say. I'm not really interested in his excuses. "She couldn't tell her family, and you couldn't be bothered to stand by her." I'm crying now, but I don't even care anymore.

"I need to talk to her," he says. "I have to explain." He turns to me, and there's a look of desperation in his eyes. "Please. You have to help me. I have to see her."

Something about him, the way he looks so forlorn, makes me think that maybe there's more to the story than what I know. But will Ayesha even want to talk to him?

"I'm not sure how she'll feel about that," I tell him.

"Please. You don't understand. This is all a huge mistake. I . . . I have to explain."

He has tears in his eyes as he pleads with me, and my heart goes out to him.

I shrug. "Okay, look, I can try. But I'm not promising anything."

"That's all I'm asking." He points to the sofa across from him. "Would you like to stay and talk?"

I hesitate but only for a moment. "Sure, I can stay for a little bit."

"Can I ask you something?" he says. "Please don't be offended."

"Sure."

"I want to trust you, but I have to ask. You're telling me the truth, right? This is not some sort of a scam?"

I can't help smiling at his earnestness. "I'm telling the truth. I'm not here for anything other than I just wanted to meet my father. That's all."

"You know, I can see a lot of Ayesha in you," he tells me. "You have her eyes and her nose too. That little bump." He smiles for the first time. "How did you find me?"

"She mentioned an article about you, and the rest was all social media. It wasn't that hard."

"So, she's known I was here all along? And she never came looking for me?"

"Well, you sort of made things clear the last time you talked to her," I said sharply.

"I didn't disappear. I went back looking for her, but she was gone."

"That's not how she remembers it," I say. "Look, I think it's best if I leave now."

"But—"

"I'll tell her that you want to talk, and I'll call you."

He pulls out a business card from his wallet and scribbles something on the back.

"Here's my direct number," he says. "You can call me anytime, night or day."

"Okay. I will, I promise."

He smiles at me again. "I'm not sure how to do this," he says. "I've never had a daughter before. But I can promise you that I had no idea."

"It's . . . I don't know. It's hard for me too." I feel bad leaving him like this. "I have to go."

"Do you think we could have lunch together soon? There's so much I want to know about you." His eyes are tender as he looks at me, but I'm not ready to feel anything for him. Not yet. Not until Ayesha's talked to him first.

"Can I think about it?"

He nods. "Of course."

I walk out the door, to where Nikhil is waiting for me in his car.

"How was it? Did you tell him? What did he say?"

Nikhil has to be the most impatient person I know.

"It was weird, and yes, I told him, and he said he had no idea."

"Wow, really?" It's dark out, but I can feel Nikhil rolling his eyes.

"I actually believe him," I say.

"Okay, but isn't that exactly what someone would say if they didn't want to take responsibility?"

"I know, but you didn't see him. He was really shocked. And he said he just wants to talk to Ayesha. He said he went looking for her, but she was already gone."

"Wait, you mean he went back?"

"He came here to take care of his dad or something, and then he went back to Bloomington and found out that she was gone."

"But what about all her calls?"

"I don't know. When I told him, he was so shocked, I'm not sure he was thinking clearly."

"Okay, so then they should talk, right?"

"I think so, but I don't know if Ayesha will want to. She sounded really sad when she spoke about him. And I don't want to push her."

"No, I totally get that," Nikhil says. "So, what're you going to do?"

"I think I'll just tell her everything that happened and let her decide."

There is nothing else for me to do until I see her again. I desperately hope she'll agree to see him. Call me a romantic, but I get a strong feeling their story isn't finished yet.

CHAPTER TWENTY-EIGHT

My palms are sweating, and my stomach is in knots as I ring the doorbell. I can't believe I've actually talked Ayesha into coming here tonight, but when she saw how much I wanted this, she couldn't deny me. It means the world to me that she's willing to put herself through this for me.

The door opens, and my father's standing there. They look at each other, my mother and my father, and it's as if the years fall away and they're seventeen again and deeply in love with each other.

"Ayesha." His voice breaks as he says her name, and my heart aches for both of them. In my mind, they've never stopped loving each other. "Please, come in."

We walk in, and he closes the door behind us.

"Ayesha, I can't . . . I have so much to tell you," he says. "It's been so long. How are you?"

It's surreal, being in the same room with them like this. After inviting us to sit and offering us drinks, my father seems to have forgotten that I'm here too. It's as if I've disappeared and they only have eyes for each other. I move away to the window to give them some space as they talk in hushed tones. I can see the city below me, and this apartment is so insulated from all of it.

"Ayesha," my father says. "Why didn't you tell me?"

She stares at him in utter disbelief.

"I did tell you," she says. "I tried so hard to get in touch with you after our last call, to tell you what I was going to do. You never called back. You didn't even care what happened to me. I was all alone."

"I remember what I said to you the last time we talked," he says. "And I've been ashamed of myself for that ever since. When you said you'd take care of it, I thought . . . And with my dad being so sick, it was just too much. I just couldn't handle it. But I should have been there for you. I'll never forgive myself for that."

"It doesn't matter," she says. "It's all in the past now and we can't change anything, so I don't see the point of rehashing it."

"It matters to me, Ayesha. You don't know how hard it was for me to go back and find out that you were gone. No one knew where you'd moved to. I didn't even know where to start looking."

"I don't understand, Suresh," she says, her voice a little sharper now. "What happened to all the emails I sent? How could you not have seen them?"

"By the time I saw them, it was too late. You'd already left." He runs his hands through his hair, visibly distressed now. "To be honest, I don't know what I would have done if I'd found you then. I was such a mess—my father was getting worse every day, my mother was falling apart, the business, everything. It was all too much." He looks at her intently for a moment before continuing. "But if I'd known for one moment that you had decided to have our baby . . . You don't think I would have dropped everything and come straight to you? I loved you, Ayesha."

He sits down on the sofa with his head in his hands, and I'm not sure what to do. I feel like an intruder, listening to a very private conversation, but Ayesha made me swear I would stay with her the whole time. So that's exactly what I'm going to do.

"You know a woman picked up your phone the last two times I called," she says.

"What woman?" he says, looking up.

She shrugs. "I don't know. I assumed it was your mother. She sounded annoyed. She asked who I was, but I got scared, so I hung up."

He doesn't say anything, lost in thought until Ayesha clears her throat awkwardly.

"I think we should go?" she says.

I don't want her to leave him like this. I think they should keep talking and figure things out. But it's not my place to say anything, so I continue to stare silently out the window.

"No, please, Ayesha, don't go," he says, jumping up and grabbing her hands.

She pulls them back immediately, and he tenses and steps away.

"I'm sorry, I . . . I shouldn't have done that." Then he looks at her. "Does your family know about us? And Mira?"

She shakes her head. "No one knows."

"You had to go through this all alone," he says, mostly to himself. "I'm so sorry. You have no idea how sorry I am."

"Well, there's nothing much we can do about it now," she says. It's hard to ignore the bitterness in her voice, and I can't even begin to understand what they're both going through at this moment.

"I'm going to go now," she says, and this time she follows through, walking out the door with me at her heels.

• • •

Back in her apartment, she finally breaks down. The pain and loneliness from all the years must have been so much and seeing my father now had to be devastating.

"You know," she says as I hold her in my arms, "I always told myself that he must not have ever truly cared about me and that seeing him again would have reinforced that. But I never thought that he would still be the same person I fell in love with all those years ago. He hasn't changed."

I stroke her hair and rock her back and forth gently, wanting desperately to comfort her and take away her pain.

"When you said you were going to meet him that first time, I was so afraid that he would cause you nothing but hurt," she says. "But then the way you spoke about him sounded so familiar. It's how I used to feel about him, until he abandoned me."

"Do you think he's telling the truth?" I ask.

"He sounded so earnest," she says. "And in my heart, I want desperately to believe that he's telling the truth."

"But it sounds unlikely. I get it."

"You know when I was there and he was looking into my eyes, I remembered how he used to make me feel so safe."

I try to imagine how she must be feeling after so many years of keeping this secret, afraid to let anyone look into the chasm of loss and despair that has become a part of her. But now her carefully orchestrated life is threatening to fall apart. And once again, I'm the reason that her life is all messed up.

"I'm so sorry," I say. "I shouldn't have pushed you to see him. Everything in your life was fine until I came here."

She gently puts a hand on my cheek.

"Mira, seeing you all grown up into a beautiful, strong young woman has been so reaffirming for me. All the doubts and fears over the years about what I did, leaving you behind, are gone because I know now that I made the right decision. Knowing what a great life you've had means everything to me."

Her words make my eyes fill with tears, and I hold her close. We sit together like this, drawing comfort and solace from each other, and right now, there's nowhere I'd rather be.

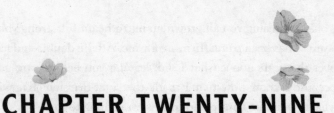

CHAPTER TWENTY-NINE

The next day, we return to my father's apartment.

Ayesha called me last night and said he'd asked to see both of us and that it was important. So here we are, all together again, and all I can think of is how my life has turned into a Bollywood movie. For someone who started out just wanting to be more in touch with my Indian roots, things have sure taken an interesting turn.

"I have something to tell you, and I wanted to say it to both of you," Suresh says once we've all sat down. "Since you both left yesterday, I haven't been able to stop thinking about what I did back then."

Ayesha shifts in her chair. "You mean why you never tried to find me?"

He hangs his head. "I'm ashamed to admit this, but I want to be honest with you both." He raises his head, but he's not looking at us. He seems to be lost in his own anguish. "I was a coward. I didn't know how to deal with everything that was happening with you, Ayesha, so I didn't deal with it at all."

He looks her directly in the eye. "When you said you were

going to take care of things, I took the easy way out. Things were so messed up at home, and I was too selfish to take on anything else. It was easier just to drown myself in work and pretend that my whole time in Bloomington was behind me."

"So, you just erased me from your life? Everything we had, all the promises, meant nothing," Ayesha says quietly.

Suresh moves next to her on the sofa and takes her hands in his.

"Ayesha, I'm so sorry," he says, tears running down his face. "There's no excuse for what I did, but you have to believe me when I say that I could never erase you from my life or my heart. I was stupid and selfish and scared back then. I know I don't deserve your forgiveness, but . . ."

Tears are streaming down both their faces, and my heart is breaking as I watch them try to piece back their love for each other.

"Forgive you?" She stares at him in disbelief, and then she's standing. "I had to leave my child because you couldn't be bothered to call me back or help me. Do you understand what I went through? No. You have *no idea*."

She's crying too, but she sounds so angry and of course I don't blame her. I hate my father for what he did to her. How did he just put her out of his mind like that?

Ayesha pulls at my arm. "I have to go," she says, and I don't hesitate for a second. I can see that my father is struggling, but my loyalties lie with Ayesha.

Once we get outside, she's quiet, and her silence is deafening. It's as if she's screaming on the inside, at the cruel twist of fate her life has been, and I can do nothing but stay close to her in case she needs to lean on me. It's as if I can see her thoughts, an avalanche of emotions as she tries to reconcile her anger at the man she thought had abandoned her, with the young boy who at eighteen had just not known how to do the right thing. I wonder if she'll ever forgive him.

"I don't know what to do," she says at last, turning to me, her eyes weary and so full of sadness. "I don't know if I can ever forgive him, but at the same time, I think about all the years we've lost."

"Do you still love him?" I ask hesitantly, afraid to upset her further.

She doesn't answer right away, and after a few minutes, I don't think she will.

"I don't think I ever stopped," she says eventually. "I think a part of me knows that he thought I was getting an abortion when I told him I'd take care of things." She turns to look at me with concern. "Is it awful of me to say that to you?"

"That you considered having an abortion?" I can't say it's not a little strange to think that if things had gone differently, I might not be standing here at all. But I can't even begin to understand what she had gone through. "Honestly, I don't know what I would have done in your situation," I tell her. "So, no, I don't think that's awful. I think you're brave, and that you did what you thought was best for me."

She bursts into tears and clings to me, and suddenly it's as if she's eighteen again, frightened and lost. So, I hold her tight, as the pain and hurt from all the years come pouring out, and in a way, I feel lucky that I'm here to be what she needs right now.

I don't know how long we've been sitting here like this. She seems calmer now, just her shoulders shuddering every now and then from the aftershock. My leg is cramping from being in the same position for so long, but I don't want to move. I want her to have this time, this outlet, so that she can finally breathe freely.

It must have been so hard for her, carrying so much anger and pain for all those years without any closure. I saw it in both my birth parents' eyes earlier, an unfulfilled longing they must have felt for each other for all those years.

● ● ●

I lie in my bed at Nikhil's place that night. Everyone has gone to bed, and I stare at the ceiling, wondering if I've made a huge mistake by even coming here. If I had just stayed, maybe it would have spared Ayesha some of the agony of seeing my father again, of having those old wounds reopened. Here in Mumbai, my old life seems so far away, so unreal somehow. The old me back in Houston seems like someone I knew a long time ago. I can't help thinking what Ayesha's life would have been like if she hadn't decided to give birth to me at all. Would she have been able to move on and have a good life if she didn't always have memories of her child growing up as someone else's? It's like my very existence continues to bring her nothing but unhappiness.

When I wake up the next morning, my pillow is damp from my tears and my heart is heavy. For the next couple days, I don't hear from Ayesha or Suresh. I want to give her space, and I don't know what to say to him, so I don't contact either of them. Nikhil and his mom try to keep me distracted by taking me shopping but my heart's not in it.

I tell Moms everything about that evening at my father's place and how terrible I'm feeling. They rush to reassure me that it might not be the worst thing for both Ayesha and Suresh to get some closure. I know they always try to protect me from harsh truths, but this time I'm not so sure that I made the right decision after all.

Then, on the third day, my phone rings just as we get home.

It's Ayesha, and she wants to pick me up and go with her to meet Suresh.

Her face lights up when she sees me walking to her car. She leans over to kiss me on the cheek as soon as I get in.

"I'm so sorry I haven't called," she says. "I've just been going over everything in my mind, and I just needed some time."

"Of course," I say quickly. "What are you going to say to him?"

"You know, that's exactly what I've been going over and over in my head since the last time we talked. We've lost all this time, and even though it was terrible going through all of it at the time, I can't stop feeling grateful that you're here now and that your father is here and we can be in each other's lives again."

"So, you'll just forgive him, then?" I'm a little shocked, but I'm trying to keep an open mind.

"I don't know if I can ever completely forgive him," she says. "But I think I can forgive the young boy he was at the time." She turns to me. "And I think I need to forgive the young me as well." She places a hand gently on my cheek. "You're so beautiful and amazing, and you're here. It's more than I could ever have dreamed of."

My face crumples as I burst into tears. Ayesha looks alarmed, but I shake my head as I try to reassure her that these are tears of relief.

"I was so worried that coming here just made everything worse for you," I say, taking the tissue Ayesha hands me.

"Oh my goodness, Mira, please never think that," she says, her eyes full of love for me. "I can't believe that you're here, that I can talk to you and hold you. You have no idea how happy you've made me by coming here."

"Really?" I say as the waterworks continue.

"Yes, really," she says. "Come on now, let's go to your father and talk to him."

When we arrive at Suresh's front door, he's already standing there. We walk in, and he offers us tea and coffee, which we politely refuse.

"Ayesha," Suresh begins. "I was so happy when you called me back. I know I have no right to expect anything from you, but if you just give me a chance—"

"It's okay, Suresh," Ayesha says softly. "I've had some time to think about what you said. And I believe we've lost so much time already. So, what are we going to accomplish by living in the past and wasting the time we have now?" She walks over to him and puts her arms around him.

My father is sobbing now and clinging to my mother as they both face the horrible truth. They lost their chance at happiness and of having a family. All because of circumstances and misunderstandings and because they were both so young and far away from each other. But fate has brought them together again. It's brought us all together.

They both turn to me, as if suddenly remembering that I'm still in the room. My father holds his arms out, and I run into them. He wraps me in a tight embrace, and then I feel my mother's hand on my head, gently stroking my hair. My heart is so full of sadness for all the memories we never got to make, even though I remain grateful for all the ones I made with my moms and Nadia.

The three of us stand together crying for a long time.

I don't know how long we stay like this, but eventually we break our embrace and take a step back.

"Ayesha, I should have tried harder," Suresh says. "I should never have stopped looking for you."

Ayesha takes a deep, shaky breath. "How could you have known?" She dabs her eyes with a tissue. "I was so angry and heartbroken, I told Natasha not to tell you if you ever came back, and I knew my aunt and uncle would never say anything."

"I would have come back right away if I'd known," he says. "You believe me, don't you?"

She looks into his eyes for a long time before replying. "I do," she murmurs.

Once again, it's as if they've forgotten about me, and I don't mind a bit because I can feel whatever it was that was between them all those years ago. It's tangible, this ghost of the love they had for each other, and I can feel the empty spaces in my heart melt away as they're replaced with the memories that should have been there in the first place.

● ● ●

It's almost my last week in Mumbai, and Nikhil has decided that we're going to spend the day in Chor Bazaar, which literally translates to "Thieves Market," and I'm thrilled and terrified at the same time. Apparently, this is the place to get anything from antique furniture to rare used car parts and possibly some dubiously acquired wares as well. According to Nikhil, there's an urban legend about this place that says if you lose anything in Mumbai, you can buy it back in Chor Bazaar.

"So is that why it's called Chor Bazaar?" I say.

"Actually, it used to be called Shor Bazaar, which means 'Noisy Market,'" he says. "But the British got confused and called it Chor Bazaar, and the name stuck. Or at least that's the story I heard growing up."

Needless to say, once we get there and walk around, I'm obsessed. We start out at an antique camera store that's almost a hundred years old. The store owner lets us look around as he tells us a little bit about the different cameras he has. The most fascinating to me is a really old wooden Kodak camera that actually still works. Next, we go into a furniture store that has some very intricately carved antique teak headboards that I love. I promise myself to bring Moms here one day. They would absolutely love the stuff in here, and the store owner assures me that customers from abroad frequently buy stuff here and have it shipped to their homes.

My favorite is an old music store where I discover original records of vintage Bollywood hits. I pick out a few to take back with me and listen to on my moms' record player at home. We also find a place that sells classic movie posters, and I find some I love and can't wait to hang up in my room at home. As we walk along the crowded lanes, I can't help thinking how strange it is that I feel so connected to this city even though I've only been here for such a short time. Houston will always be my home, but this city is where I've finally been able to find my roots, to connect to my heritage, and that's something I've been searching for all my life.

It's been an amazing day, and by the time we get home, we're tired and I want nothing more than to wash the city off my skin and take a nap. Nikhil's mom is home setting the table for dinner, and something smells really delicious.

"Aunty, what did you make? It's smells so good," I say, taking off my shoes outside the door before walking in.

"I made mutton biryani and rogan josh," she says. "I promise I didn't make them too spicy," she adds with a smile.

"Aunty, you know I'm used to it by now," I say.

"Yeah, Mom, she really is," Nikhil chimes in. "You should have seen her at Elco Market."

"Why don't you wash up and then we'll all sit down to eat," Sarita Aunty says.

I walk over to my room, open the door, and scream at the top of my lungs.

Sitting on my bed, grinning at me, are my moms. I blink, unable to believe my eyes.

"Surprise!" they sing in unison, and behind me, Sarita Aunty and Nikhil are standing there clapping gleefully.

I run to my moms and throw my arms around them.

"What are you doing here? Oh my god, how . . . ? When did this happen?"

"Well, Nikhil promised to keep you out all day, and Sarita was kind enough to pick us up at the airport . . . and so here we are," Mama says. She gives me a big squeeze.

"I'm so happy to see you." I collapse on the bed beside them, still in shock. "Aunty, I can't believe you pulled this off," I say, smiling at her. "And, Nikhil, wow, I don't even know what to say. You should be, like, a spy or something, because you sure know how to keep a secret."

He grins at me and for once doesn't say anything snarky.

"So," Mom says. "I know things have been difficult, but I'm so glad you're also having a great time."

"It's been great," I say. "I guess I've only been telling you the bad parts. But now that you're here, it's going to be even better. I can't believe you're actually sitting here right now."

"Why don't we all catch up over dinner?" Sarita Aunty suggests, and I rush to get cleaned up.

Dinner is delicious, and Moms can't stop thanking Aunty and Nikhil for their hospitality. But then I'm finally alone with Moms in my room, and we're all snuggled up together. I'm over the moon that they decided to surprise me like this, and I can't wait to tell them everything that's happened.

"How did you manage to leave without Nadia?" I ask.

"It wasn't easy," Mama says. "But then Grandpa said he would come over and stay the whole time we were here, and you know how Nadia loves him."

Our grandfather is the most loving and fun person *and* he also happens to spoil us completely, so I'm not surprised that Nadia was happy to know he'd be there.

"So, honey, did anything more happen with Ayesha?" Mom says.

"Yes, the last time we spoke, you told us that things didn't go well between Ayesha and your father," Mama says.

I'd planned to call Moms tonight about the latest development, but now they're here and it's so much easier.

"I think they both needed a bit of time, especially Ayesha. But then we all met again and they talked, and I think they'll be okay."

Mama gently strokes my head. "And what about you? How are you dealing with all of this, honey?"

"I'm okay," I say. "But I was so worried, you know? That I made her dig up all the old wounds again."

"I'm sure that's not how she feels," Mom says.

"You know when I met her the first time, I wasn't expecting to feel the way I did. There was so much heartache when she was talking about giving me up and how my father had just ghosted her like that."

"I know exactly what you mean," Mama says. "Mom and I have been talking about those months when Ayesha lived with us, and we remember how we used to say the same thing. She was so broken in a way, and we tried to help her however we could, but I always felt that her pain was just too much."

"When I met my father for the first time, I thought he'd be some sort of jerk, but he was so nice and then when he and Ayesha met, I could tell they still care for each other."

"Really?" Mom says. "So, he never got married or had a family?"

"No, I guess he focused all his energy on his business. At least I think he did, because he's pretty successful."

"Life can be strange sometimes," Mom says. "But, sweetie, I'm just so happy for you."

"I'm glad I came," I say. "At least now all of us got some closure. And I'm happy that they talked. I mean, I don't think that Ayesha's ever going to completely forgive him for how he handled things, but maybe now she can move forward."

"So, when can we see her?" Mom asks. "If it's okay with you, of course."

"I can call her tomorrow morning," I say. "She was saying she'd love to see you again one day when you visit . . . and now you're here, so it all worked out."

Moms are going to sleep in my room, and once I get them settled in, I can't help but think how weird it is for both my worlds to come together like this. But it's not a bad thing, because it finally feels like all the pieces of my life are falling into place.

CHAPTER THIRTY

Ayesha has invited Moms and me for afternoon tea. I'm a little bit nervous at how this will go because it's not exactly every day that this sort of thing happens. At least not in my life. Until now that is. The last few weeks have been a series of life-altering, emotionally packed revelations, and I'm not sure what to expect.

"Ayesha, it's good to see you," Mom says when Ayesha answers the door.

"Mel, Sam, I'm so happy that you came," Ayesha says, putting her arms around them one by one and then turning to me to kiss my cheek. "Mira, you look beautiful in that kurta."

Last week, she gifted me a gorgeous silk kurta in a peacock blue shot through with silver thread. It paired really well with my black jeans.

"Ayesha, we never thought we'd see you again," Mama says, tearing up, always the emotional one.

"I'm so sorry for the way I left," Ayesha says. "Especially after everything you both did for me." She has tears in her eyes too, and I have to admit I'm almost there as well.

"Please don't apologize," Mom says. "What you went through was harder than anything we can imagine, and we're just sorry we couldn't do more."

"I'll never be able to thank you enough," Ayesha says. "And after meeting Mira, I'm so happy that you came into my life when you did."

"Well, she's always been our pride and joy," Mom says. "She's been a wonderful daughter."

Now I'm the one crying, and then we're all hugging and sobbing. I'm just glad no one is around to film it.

"I have something to tell you," Ayesha says, extricating herself gently from the group hug. "I've told my family about everything."

"Wow," I say, for once at a loss for words. I know this cannot have been easy for her, so it's a huge deal.

"And how did they react?" Mom asks.

"Actually, quite unexpectedly," Ayesha replies. "They're heartbroken that I didn't tell them before."

"Are you kidding me?" I blurt out before I can stop myself. "I thought the whole reason you couldn't tell them was that they would disown you or something."

Moms give me a warning look. They know I sometimes forget myself and speak inappropriately. But right now, I'm a little pissed because it seems like Ayesha is the only one who was always trying not to hurt others, but no one seemed to ever do the same for her. It isn't right.

"They're old now, and they said seeing me living my life all alone made them sad." She rolls her eyes as she says that. "I'm quite happy with the life I've chosen, but you know how people are when you're still single and childless at the ripe old age of thirty-six."

Moms are nodding. "Trust me, we know," Mom says. "Before Mel and I got married, our parents were getting very worried too."

"So now they're okay with it?" I'm not sure I buy that. First, they make their daughter feel that she has to give up her child at eighteen, and now they're going to pretend to be sad that they missed out?

"Mira, you have to understand," Ayesha pleads with me. "I never gave them the chance. I just assumed they wouldn't accept it, and I made my decision based on that. I didn't have the courage to face them at the time. I was so scared."

"But I—"

"Mira," Mom says sternly. "I think Ayesha understands her family better than you, don't you?"

I can feel the blood rush to my cheeks, and Ayesha looks quite uncomfortable too.

"Ayesha, I'm so sorry," Mama says. "Sometimes our Mira can be a little too outspoken."

"It's okay . . . it's a difficult situation." Ayesha smiles awkwardly at me, and I don't know what to say.

"Mira, honey," Mom starts. "I know this has all been a lot for you," she says. "But that's no excuse for being rude."

"But it's not fair," I say. "She's been through so much because of them and—"

"Enough." Mama is angry, and I can tell she's trying hard not to yell at me in front of Ayesha.

"Please don't be angry with her," Ayesha says. She takes me by the hands and pulls me down next to her on the couch. "Look, Mira, I get that you're mad, and I know you don't think it's fair. But they're my family and they mean the world to me."

"But it's their fault that . . ." I don't finish my thought. My anger has dissipated abruptly upon hearing her talk about her family.

"Whatever happened, whatever decision I made all those years ago, that's on me. And now I have a chance to be a part of your life again, and I'm not going to waste it by holding on to the past."

She looks at me, and there's so much love in her eyes. And regret. I can feel it seeping into me, and I finally understand.

"I'm sorry." I look down at my hands in hers, and it's like I can see clearly for the first time in a long time. Family is messy, relationships are complicated, and there aren't always second chances.

"I just want them to know you," she says with a smile. "And my sisters too. You're going to love them."

"It can't have been easy for you to tell them after all these years," Mom says softly.

"It wasn't at first," Ayesha says. "But then it felt so good to finally be completely honest with them."

"It must be a relief that they were happy for you," Mama said.

"It is, but you know after all this time, I think I was ready for anything." She smiles at my moms. "It's so strange to think that if I'd had the courage to do this years ago, all of our lives would be completely different."

I'm pretty sure that Moms are thinking the exact same thing. I know I am.

"Would you like to meet my family?" Ayesha asks. "My parents would love to have you over for dinner tomorrow, if that's okay?"

"Of course," I say quickly. "I'd love to." I'm not 100 percent okay with the whole situation, but I'm not about to say that out loud.

"And you'll come too?" Ayesha looks at Moms.

"Oh, no, that's all right, we don't want to intrude," Mom says. "We'll keep ourselves busy, won't we, Mel?"

"I insist," Ayesha says. "And you won't be intruding. You're family too." Her eyes well up a little. "I don't know what I would have done if you hadn't been there for me back then," she adds softly.

"You gave us an amazing gift, Ayesha," Mama says.

"And look at what a beautiful daughter we all have," Mom adds.

Ayesha has tears running down her face again as she throws her arms around my moms. As I watch them share an embrace, I can't help thinking how lucky I am that I get to love these three incredible women.

● ● ●

As the car pulls up in the driveway with Ayesha in the front and me between my moms in the back seat, I can't help but worry about how this afternoon will go. I promised Moms I'd be on my best behavior, but at the same time, I'm nervous and worried about what Ayesha's parents will think of me.

The door opens while we're still walking up the steps, and a woman comes out. I barely have time to register anything about her when she practically lunges at me and pulls me into a tight hug, her shoulders heaving as she cries in my arms. This is not what I expected at all, and my eyes well up when she pulls back slightly to look at me and takes my face in her hands and kisses me on both my cheeks.

"Mira, a thousand thanks to Allah that I am alive to hold you in my arms," she says, smiling at me through her tears.

She pulls me into a hug again, and then I feel someone pulling at me from behind and I turn to see an old man, already crying, holding his arms out for me. He holds me close to his chest, mumbling words I don't really understand but that are full of love that I can feel. So much love, as if they're trying to make up for all the years we've lost with a single embrace. I look up to see Moms and Ayesha, all with tears running down their faces.

I have so many questions, but in this moment, I can honestly say that my heart has grown a thousandfold so that I can fill it with all the love from my family. Some I am bound to by blood, others by the purest of love, but all of them will be in my life from now on, and for that I am immeasurably grateful.

ACKNOWLEDGMENTS

It takes a village to write a book and there are many people to whom I am immensely grateful.

First and foremost my agent, Hillary Jacobson, who has been a constant source of encouragement and support through all the moments of panic and frustration but also for the many joyful times. I am filled with gratitude for my editors extraordinaire, David Levithan and Jeffrey West. Their guidance and words of encouragement throughout my writing journey have meant more than I can express. Thank you for always helping me shape my stories with so much love and respect; it means the world to me. A huge thank-you to Maeve Norton for the gorgeous book design and Muhammed Sajid for the stunning cover art. To my entire Scholastic family, Shannon Pender, Rachel Feld, Emily Heddelson, Lizette Serrano, Janell Harris, Jackie Hornberger, my amazing publicist, Elisabeth Ferrari, and everyone else who was involved in this book's journey, I am incredibly thankful for what you've done.

Thank you also to Nikole Kritikos and everyone else at Scholastic Canada.

To my friends and fellow writers: Mason Deaver, Nafiza Azad, Meredith Ireland, Rob Bittner, Julian Winters, Robin Stevenson—thank you for being there through all of this. It means everything. Thank you, too, to Jess Verdi for helping me better understand some of the nuances of adoption.

Finally, to my husband and daughters, without whom my light could never shine: Thank you for filling my world with more love and laughter than I can hold.

ABOUT THE AUTHOR

Sabina Khan writes about Muslim teens who straddle cultures. She was born in Germany, spent her teens in Bangladesh, and lived in Macao, Illinois, and Texas before settling down in British Columbia with her husband, two daughters, and the best puppy in the world. She is also the author of *The Love and Lies of Rukhsana Ali* and *Zara Hossain Is Here*. Visit her online at sabina-khan.com.

Don't miss